B as in BEAUTY

B as in BEAUTY

ALBERTO FERRERAS

GRAND CENTRAL
PUBLISHING

NEW YORK   BOSTON

PENA DE LOS AMORES
Words and Music by JOSE LUIS ALMADA
© 1981 INTERSONG USA
Translated lyrics Reprinted by Permission of ALFRED PUBLISHING CO., INC.
All Rights Reserved

Grand Central Publishing
Hachette Book Group
237 Park Avenue
New York, NY 10017

Visit our Web site at www.HachetteBookGroup.com.

Printed in the United States of America

First Edition: April 2009

10 9 8 7 6 5 4 3 2 1

Grand Central Publishing is a division of Hachette Book Group, Inc.
The Grand Central Publishing name and logo is a trademark of Hachette Book Group, Inc.

Library of Congress Cataloging-in-Publication Data

Ferreras, Alberto.
    B as in beauty / Alberto Ferreras.—1st ed.
      p. cm.
    ISBN 978-0-446-69789-7
    1. Young women—Fiction.   2. Overweight women—Fiction.   3. Advertising—Fiction.   4. Manhattan (New York, N.Y.)—Fiction.   5. Cuban Americans—Fiction. 6. Chick lit.   I. Title.
    PS3606.E739B37 2009
    813'.6—dc22
                        2008023672

Book design by Giorgetta Bell McRee

To Myrna
Olga
Juline
Teodora
Trina
Yolanda
Diana

And to all the wonderful women who
have taught me how to love myself.

"To think that this body that I hated so much could nurture another being..."
—OLGA FERRERAS-ANDERSON

B as in BEAUTY

CHAPTER 0

There are a few theories about my weight. One of them places the responsibility of my extra pounds on my reckless behavior: I eat too much, I don't exercise enough, I combine the wrong foods, I eat late at night, etc. The truth is that I watch carefully what I eat, I exercise every day, and I'd never eat carbohydrates past 7 p.m. So there goes that theory.

There's also the "I take after my aunt" theory—which implies that I'm fat like my aunt Chavela because we're genetically predisposed. The problem is that Chavela is my aunt by marriage, so we don't share a single gene. There goes another theory.

My second therapist told me that I "avoid intimacy with my weight," implying that I subconsciously got fat to avoid being touched. I know this theory is also bullshit, simply because I love being touched.

But my favorite explanation of why I'm fat is the most complicated and romantic of them all. I call it "the nanny theory," and it involves a crying mother, sharks, a military base, and sex out of wedlock.

Allow me to explain. My mother hired a nanny when I was just a baby. Our nanny was a teenage girl from a small town in Cuba. Her name was Inocencia, but we called her "Ino." She was young and naïve, she had never been in a big city like New York, and, like any other lonely teen, she was looking to fall in love.

And she fell in love. Yes, she fell in love with pastries.

My friend Wilfredo's aunt claimed that after menopause all her sensitivity left her genitals and went up to her mouth, making her replace sex with food. I can imagine that something similar happened to Ino, but during her adolescence.

I can almost see her. The year was 1975, she had just turned sixteen, and was bursting with the nervous energy of a high-school athlete about to compete in a cross-country marathon. The night was warm, but she was shivering as she gathered the courage to jump in the waters at Caimanera Beach, determined to swim through the shark-infested Guantánamo Bay. Was she alone? Was she with others on this suicidal attempt to reach the American base? I don't know, but I can imagine her saying goodbye to her teary-eyed mother. I can almost hear her mother warning her — not only against the hazards of her trip, but of an inevitable danger, those blond and blue-eyed men who would — no doubt — knock her up and abandon her with her baby once she reached the United States.

"¡Cuidado ¡con quedar preñada!" her mom probably said in a tone of voice that would haunt Ino forever.

What a great example of Cuban motherly logic: never mind the risk of drowning, getting shot by the Cuban military police, or being eaten by a "great white." The real danger here was that Ino could get pregnant out of wedlock once she reached American soil. I have to say that, even though I might be suffering the consequences of Ino's love affair with cinnamon rolls, I do understand where she was coming from. Under such intense conditions, Ino must have made a secret promise to the Virgin of Regla to never give up the flower of her virginity, and to remain celibate if she made it safe and sound to the United States.

My mother was the first one to hire Ino when she got to New York. She heard about her through what Cubans call Radio Bemba, a sort of Cuban-emigrant broadcasting service that consisted of a bunch of Cuban housewives calling each other every day to deliver news and gossip. Mom decided to hire Ino for two reasons: first, to help a fellow Cuban in need of a job; and, second, because she badly needed a full-time maid/nanny at home. My father's food-import business was going down. His partner had stolen the company's cash and moved to Florida, so Dad, on the verge of bankruptcy and too traumatized to trust anybody, asked Mom to run the business with him.

Mom, understanding Dad's desperate plea for support, was forced to work full-time in the Jersey City warehouse, keeping track of shipments of yucca and plantains, while she trusted the care of her home, her three prepubescent sons, and her baby girl to the sweet, young, innocent, virginal Ino.

Every week while employed by my mother, Ino would spend her complete salary on pastries. She would even bring some to our home. My mother, who is certainly not the Mae West type, was so shocked by her oral fixation that she encouraged her to slow down her sugar intake and go out on the weekend to someplace where she could meet boys. But Ino showed no interest in men, romance, or sex. Just dessert.

One day, Mom had a minute to spare and joined Ino and

me for my spoon-fed dinner. Mom decided to taste the oat-meal that Ino had cooked for me, but as soon as it touched her lips she had to spit it out.

"*¿Qué carajo le pusiste a la avena?*"

"*Un poquito de azúcar para que la niña la coma.*"

The oatmeal had so much sugar that it was virtually ined-ible. Ino confessed then that, given the natural reluctance to eat which most children show, she had been adding absurd quantities of sugar to all my meals, making me a tiny and plump sugar addict and probably screwing my metabolism for life. Mom never told me if this incident got Ino fired or not, but Ino left our lives very soon after that episode. I've noticed that Mom silently suffers every time I bring up Ino and "the nanny theory." Often I hope that my Cuban nanny ended up fat, knocked up, and abandoned by the same ruth-less young male that her mother warned her against.

Thanks to Ino, my first childhood memory is standing in front of a mirror and saying to my already overweight self, "I'm a three-year-old girl and I'm about ten pounds heavier than I should be." I'm twenty-eight years old now, and I've always been fat—by a few pounds or a lot of them, since it kind of fluctuates. And I can proudly say that I owe it all to the sweet, stupid, and innocent Ino.

I have never known what it is like not to be fat. I'm always trying to lose weight, or worried about getting even fatter than I already am. My size has varied considerably through the years—sometimes within weeks, depending on how absurd the diet of the moment was—but no matter what I do, the fat always comes back. Let's see: I've tried the Scars-dale, the Atkins—the first time around and the second time around—the anti-diet, homeopathic remedies, acupuncture. You name it and I've done it. If it works, it's only temporarily.

My mom took me to a dietician in the eighties who helped me lose weight incredibly fast with little effort on my part. It was the infamous Dr. Loomis. He was so popular that the long line of patients spilled into the hallway outside his office. But the line moved fast, because Dr. Loomis ran four examination rooms at the same time. He would spend an average of five seconds with each patient. In that short time he'd manage to weigh you, make you stand naked in front of a mirror, and insult you.

"Look at yourself," he would say, contorting his face as if he were just about to puke, "look at those rolls of fat. Aren't you ashamed of yourself?"

This is what he called "encouragement." Then he would give you a prescription for a powerful — and now illegal — drug whose long-term side effects will become evident one day. Unfortunately, permanent weight loss wasn't one of them. Eventually, Dr. Loomis was incarcerated for giving speed to his patients.

But enough with the whining, and let's deal with the reality: I'm fat. I have big boobs, a chunky butt, and thick legs. I will say, in my defense, that my waist is kind of small, so at least I have an hourglass figure. Unfortunately, hourglasses are not terribly popular nowadays.

The bottom line is that I'm fat. I'm a fat chick. We could come up with nicer ways to say it: plump, full-figured, overweight, chubby. But after all these years of fatness, I finally feel good about saying it the simple way: fat. Just fat. If you happen to be fat, I strongly recommend you to say it out loud at every opportunity you have. If "fat" is a word that defines you, you should embrace it, and never give other people the power to use it as an insult. And now that we're discussing linguistics, I have to bring up another concern: my name.

Latinos have an odd tradition of giving weird names to their kids. Sometimes we combine the parents' names. If they are, for instance, Carlos and Teresa, they could name the baby girl Caresa. Other times we pick a word in a foreign language and slap it on the newborn without thinking of the consequences.

There was a kid in school whose parents named him Magnificent. Yes, once I knew a Magnificent López. The only problem was that Magnificent was short and skinny, and he wore thick eyeglasses. To be brutally honest, he looked anything but magnificent, and his very name was a painful reminder of his shortcomings.

I have a similar problem. My name is Beauty.

Beauty María Zavala, to be precise.

I have three brothers who bear standard Latino names: Pedro, Francisco, and Eduardo. But in my case, my parents decided to take a poetic license, and as a tribute to the land that saved them from Fidel Castro, they decided to name me Beauty. I'm sure that at the time it sounded very cool to them, but you have no idea what a pain in the ass it is to drag this name along with all my extra pounds.

For obvious reasons, I ask people to just call me B.

I've gone through life pushing this extra weight — that I simply can't get rid of — and bearing a name that sounds like a bad joke. It's particularly annoying when I'm on the phone with my bank, or the credit-card company, and they ask me to spell my name. I can't blame them for being confused — let's face it, there are not too many Beautys out there. But what really bothers me is that every time I spell it out for them, I do it in the same stupid way:

"B as in 'boy,' E as in Edward..."

Why do I say "B as in 'boy'"? I'm not a boy. Why can't I

just say "B as in 'beauty'"? The answer is very simple: I have never felt pretty. I'm fat, and I've grown up in a world where fat is anything but beautiful.

At this point I have to take a moment to acknowledge that there are other things in life that are much worse than being fat. We can go through a whole list. I could be blind, deaf, paralyzed, starved, or brain-dead. The truth is that, in the category of curses, fat is nothing more than chump change.

I strongly believe that the worst curse you can suffer in life is to be unhappy. I can tell you of many rich, beautiful, young, healthy, and — of course — skinny people who have tried successfully and unsuccessfully to commit suicide out of pure, plain misery. I've been sad, angry, and mortified about my weight, but, thank God, never suicidal.

But I'm bringing up the happiness factor because I've realized that it's the one thing I could change. Let's face it, I might never be able to control my weight, but I've learned that I can choose to be happy. How did I learn?

You'll soon find out.

CHAPTER 1

I work in an ad agency in New York City. In case you don't know it, let me tell you that New York is a bad city to be fat in. Most people actually manage to stay thin, and I have no idea how.

If you go to any of the many fantastic restaurants in Manhattan, you'll run into slender men and women who don't seem affected by sugars, carbohydrates, or partially hydrogenated oils. I honestly wonder if they're all puking after every meal, or if in fact they truly have an industrial boiler installed where I have my sluggish metabolism. These people are so thin — they must burn everything they put in their mouths at the speed of light. Meanwhile, I store everything, in preparation — I guess — for a nuclear holocaust.

I see the skinny ones on the street wearing designer clothes, or in the gym fighting some extra milligram of fat that I couldn't see with a microscope even if I tried. They sit comfortably in the bus or on the subway, in seats that are specially designed for people of their size. They cross their legs in positions that I can only imagine. They wear jeans and leather pants, never having to worry about wearing off the fabric between their thighs. I know, I know, I'm coming across a little obsessed with the differences between them and me. I'm not always like this; I don't see myself as an outsider all the time. The feeling comes and goes with the seasons, or with the frustration caused by realizing that it's time to go up one dress size. But in spite of this rant, I'm not prejudiced against the skinny ones. Some of my best friends are very thin. As a matter of fact, my best friend, Lillian, is particularly slender.

Lillian and I met at the ad agency on my first day at work. That morning I was very nervous, and I didn't know anybody at the office. Lillian came up to my desk and did one of the nicest things you could do to a rookie like me: she introduced herself, and took me out to lunch. Even though we work for different departments—I'm a copywriter and she's an accountant—we have been inseparable ever since.

Lillian is Asian, tall, slender, with perfect boobs, a tight little ass, and—believe it or not—she is sweet, nice, and friendly. She can be a little self-centered, a tad narcissistic, and a teeny bit insensitive, but the truth is that I love her to death. Based on my experiences with my mother, I've come to believe that people who love you are bound to push your buttons, and sometimes Lillian really knows how to push mine.

In any case, my story begins—sorry, it hasn't started yet—on the morning of April 14, just a couple of years ago. I'm bad with dates, but events that happened on Christmas Day, New Year's Eve, or Valentine's Day are always easier to remember. This one happened on the day before taxes were due.

It was a nice spring morning. I was particularly proud of my hairdo that day. My hair is long and curly, and I usually wear it in a tight bun because I think that makes me look skinnier and professional. I wear glasses — I'm a bit near-sighted, and I should have contacts, but I've been so busy at work that I haven't had a second to go to the eye doctor and get a new prescription. I like my glasses, though, because they make me look professional, and I need to look professional as part of a long-delayed plan to get ahead at my job. There's this unwritten rule in corporate America that establishes that if you are not promoted every two years, you are considered filler. I was two years overdue for that promotion, and I was starting to worry that if I didn't see any movement soon, I might never be anything in life other than a senior copywriter.

Let me explain what I do at the ad agency. I take a bunch of marketing information and I turn it into a paragraph, a slogan, or a word. If they tell me, "We need to sell more peanuts to eighteen-year-olds," then I find the words that make peanuts irresistible to that demographic. Maybe you've heard of one of my masterpieces: "Gotta go nuts." Yep, I came up with that one, even though Bonnie, my boss, took the credit for it. But we'll get back to Bonnie in a minute.

I like to think of myself as a poet who pays the rent writing infomercials, food labels, and even catalogue captions. I'm aware that I'm not writing the great American novel here, but my job allows me to be fairly creative. I perform what I call "art on demand." I know we think that artists are not pressured by the needs of the market, but let me remind you that Leonardo da Vinci didn't paint the *Mona Lisa* because he wanted to. He did it because someone paid him to do it. Some rich guy in Florence probably told his wife, "Hey, honey, maybe we should get someone to paint your portrait. Let me call that Leonardo guy." That's how Leonardo paid his rent.

In this respect all artists — or at least most artists who make a living with their craft — whore themselves out. You give us cash and we sell our soul. What we should remember, though, is that we might be whores but we're still artists. And making art — or coming up with a slogan for a new brand of tampons, as I was doing at the time — is really hard when you're not being acknowledged.

In my agency, it didn't matter if you were dumb as a rock, and you got the promotion by sleeping with your boss. As long as you had your promotion every two years, you were well on your way to corporate success.

Sleeping with Bonnie was not an option, since she's a woman — and not a pretty one, if you ask me. So I decided to take the long road for that promotion: working hard.

I extra-busted my ass for years, trying to convince them that I deserved the title of creative director, but my efforts had not paid off. The funny part is that I already had the job — what I was missing was the title. I'd been doing two jobs for the last three years. When the last director left, they gave me her work responsibilities, but I continued doing mine as a senior copywriter. So I was supervising a whole team of copywriters — like me — but I also had to write the ads, just like they did.

When the other creatives wrote their copy, they gave it to me. I reviewed it, corrected it, approved it, and then I passed it on to Bonnie. But the absurd part of the whole arrangement was that when I wrote the copy for an ad, I, technically, had to submit it to myself first — for review, correction, and approval — before I showed it to Bonnie. Does that make any sense? I don't think so. But that's how big companies operate nowadays: they squeeze you for as many years as they can, "to see if you are prepared for that promotion," and then — once you've proved that you can do it — they go and hire someone else. The craziest part is that, since you are the one who knows how to do it, they then expect you to train your new boss. Pretty fucked up, huh?

But there was no point in entertaining those negative thoughts that morning, since I was convinced that that wasn't going to happen to me. I was determined to get that promotion, so for the last thirty-six months I had missed every meaningful family gathering — important birthdays, major surgeries, and Christian holidays (which is a mortal sin in Cuban families). I made my career my number-one priority. I was basically living in the office.

When they asked for a volunteer, I always raised my hand. When they asked for two ideas, I delivered twenty. I laughed out loud at my boss's bad jokes and asked about the health of dogs and cats that I didn't give a rat's ass about. I have felt guilty about taking vacation time, and I have actually canceled anticipated trips because Bonnie forgot that she approved my days off. I ate my lunch at my desk every day, carried a BlackBerry everywhere I went — including the bathroom — because it's a fact that Bonnie would call or e-mail me the moment I briefly removed my butt from my chair. Just to give you an idea of how committed I was to my job, let me tell you that my doctor and my dentist mailed me notes wondering if I was dead, because all my checkups were long overdue.

I became so dedicated that I was that person who went to work sick. If I was scolded for spreading the virus and I stayed home to recover, then I was scolded for "getting sick too often." I mastered the art of showing up sick at the office and breathing as little as possible, to keep my germs to myself.

Determined as I was to move up, I patiently listened to every stupid idea that came from Bonnie's mouth. I heard her dumbest comments with respect and reverence. I even allowed her to walk all over me — something she seemed to particularly enjoy — just to prove to her that I was there to support her and not to threaten her. I always made her look good, gave her credit when she didn't deserve it, and allowed her to present my work as if it were hers. I did it all to fulfill a simple dream: if I got the position as creative director, I could use that to get a decent job in a different company, and free myself from Bonnie.

To give myself courage through this ordeal, I created a mantra that I repeated to myself over and over, every time I clashed with her: "Hard work will set you free." After a year of saying that every day, I read somewhere that this same phrase was the slogan of the Nazi concentration camps, so I decided to switch to "one day at a time." I was a prisoner in Bonnie's camp, but it couldn't last forever.

How can I describe Bonnie? She's skinny, wiry, with black — dyed — hair, reddish skin, and no lips. Physically, she is the Joan Collins–at–sixty type. She's the kind of person who, if you are entering a building and you hold the door for her, will walk right through without saying thank you. She won't even look at you, because she believes that God created all human beings to serve her. As a matter of fact, I've never heard her utter the words "please" or "thank you." She's the kind of guest who would wear white to a wedding and chew gum in a funeral. She just couldn't care less. But enough of her for now. Let's continue.

That particular morning in April was lovely. Spring was in the air, and I remember rushing to work wearing my navy-blue suit. I had the exact same suit in four colors (when I find something that somehow fits me, I always buy a few of them, 'cause I never know when I'll find something that actually looks half decent on me again). Anyway, I was wearing the blue suit, and I noticed that it felt a little tight. I started wondering — in a vague attempt to cover up for the possibility that maybe I had gained some weight — if the dry cleaners had shrunk my clothes.

As I walked up Fifth Avenue toward Fifty-ninth Street, I tried to calculate how many calories I was burning with this short but brisk walk. The streets of midtown Manhattan can be a nightmare when you're a fat chick at rush hour. I wanted to run but I was in high heels. I could not wear sneakers to work, because a creative director would never fall to that temptation. Moving through the sea of people felt like speed-walking an obstacle course. To top it off, while I had to hurry to make it to work at a decent time, I couldn't walk too fast or I'd end up all sweaty.

I walked into my office building and smiled at the security guard, who — once again — ignored me. Let me just point out that smiling and flirting are two very different things, and flirting with this guy was not in my agenda because:

a) I don't particularly like him.

b) I've noticed that he's missing a few front teeth.

c) It's not like he even bothers to make eye contact with me, and eye contact is essential for flirting.

But, in any case, I smiled at him. I smiled at this idiot every morning, simply because it is my philosophy that if you see someone regularly it makes sense to at least acknowledge him with a smile. It's called "being polite." But the son of a bitch — who clearly doesn't have any social graces — just looked at the horizon as if the *Titanic* were passing by with Kate Winslet riding topless at the bow of it.

I took a deep breath, decided not to let him bother me, and rushed to the elevators. The doors to one were about to close, so I ran a few steps while yelling, "Hold it!"

Big mistake.

I found myself faced with a crowded elevator that barely had room for one more person, and definitely not a woman of my size. Since they held the elevator for me, I felt obliged to squeeze in. I landed next to a skinny old lady who smelled like an ashtray. As I sucked in my stomach in an effort to occupy less space, and held my breath to avoid the stench of cigarette butts, my worst nightmare occurred: the over-weight alarm went off.

I know it's silly to allow something like this to humiliate me, especially since it's not like I'm an elephant and the alarm sounds even when I ride alone. But while one side of my brain knew that the elevator was already packed, and — for all I knew — even a squirrel could have triggered the alarm, the other side of my brain reminded me of a big, fat fact: my weight.

"Somebody's gonna have to step out or we're not going anywhere," said the skinny old smoker, giving me a nasty look.

She was ugly, but she was right. I stepped out graciously, and turned around — embarrassed but smiling. For a brief second, I wondered if I smiled too much.

"Bon voyage!" I said to them as the elevator's doors closed. Nobody answered, and nobody smiled back. Okay, not a happy moment, but I'm a strong girl, and it takes way more than that to ruin my day.

Once I had stepped into the next available elevator and pushed the button, I closed my eyes and tried to invest the ten seconds that it takes to go up to the twentieth floor in visualizing something positive that could make me forget the elevator incident and restore my natural glow. I took a deep breath and reminded myself of how much I used to love coming to work, just a few years ago. The agency had beautiful offices on Fifty-ninth Street. With its floor-to-ceiling windows and its ultra-modern furniture, it looked like corporate heaven. Most of the space was open, with cute little cubicles spread out throughout the floor, but a few executives were given closed offices overlooking Central Park. That was my dream: having a big, windowed office overlooking the park. This dream kept me going despite the fact that working for Bonnie made my corporate heaven feel more like Alcatraz. As if I worked at a grisly jail that happened to be furnished by Knoll.

As I finally made it to the twentieth floor, I checked my watch and saw that I was half an hour late. I had worked past midnight the night before, so I hoped that there would be a little leniency regarding punctuality — or lack thereof — on Bonnie's part.

"Are you serious? Are you from L.A.? 'Cause I hear a Southern twang," I overheard as I walked by the reception desk. Deborah — our new receptionist — was being cornered by two jerks from Marketing. They were your typical young and bratty Ivy Leaguers, who are always preying on interns and executive assistants.

Deborah is the perfect example of the kind of woman I'd love to hate, but can't. She's skinny, blonde, petite, and sweet as hell. I almost feel guilty when I envy her.

"Hi, B!" she said.

"Hi, Debs!" I answered.

The marketing morons gave me an up-and-down look—no surprise—that expressed very little sympathy for "a woman of size," as I sometimes call myself. I smiled at them with no reciprocation on their part—of course—and that's when the next humiliation took place.

"Hey! You dropped your ID," one told me.

Yes, I had dropped my ID at their feet. For a second I thought they were actually going to pick it up for me, but of course they didn't. They looked at the card, they looked at me, and then they turned away, back to Deborah, to continue their mating rituals. Why waste any chivalry with a fat chick when sweet, skinny Deborah was sitting there, trapped behind her desk? So down I went to pick up my ID card.

First it was the ripping sound, then the relief of expanding flesh, then the cold air in my ass, and, finally, the shame. My pants split open right in front of them.

I couldn't see their expression, but I could picture their sneer very clearly. I came back up and pulled down the back of my jacket to cover the damage.

"B? Are you okay?" Deborah asked.

"Of course I'm okay," I lied.

"I have a sewing kit here somewhere..." Deborah offered while looking through her drawers.

"Don't worry! It's nothing!" I graciously declined, since I had my own supply at my desk. But then I made the mistake of trying to justify the accident to her, and to the morons: "I sent this suit to the cleaners and I think they must have washed it instead of dry-cleaning it, because..." Before I could finish the sentence, they turned back to Deborah. I took another deep breath and walked into the office. Luckily, my jacket partially covered the rip, so I walked slowly, taking short steps to try to make it less noticeable. But as soon as I got to my desk, ready to look for my sewing kit, Mary Pringle — Bonnie's secretary — popped her head above the partition of my cubicle.

"Hey, B! Bonnie wants to see you immediately."

By the tone of Mary's voice I knew that I was going to be yelled at. And I would have to endure it with my ass exposed — so to speak.

There are a few things that I resent about my college education. I hate the fact that some theoretical classes should have been practical, and some practical classes should have been theoretical. I'm also angry at the high cost of the tuition — and its ensuing student loan, which I'm still paying. But the one thing that pisses me off more than anything else is that nobody taught me how to survive the office politics of a corporation.

Let's face it, most people go to college so they can eventually find a decent corporate job that'll give them money, status, business-class seats on a plane, and a cute box of presentation cards engraved with an intimidating logo. Most lawyers, journalists, engineers, and accountants end up working for large companies where they become one more bolt — or one more screw — in a long conveyor belt. Our destiny is to endlessly climb the proverbial corporate ladder. But once I got my first corporate job, I realized that no one in college had taught me how to survive in a snake pit, and that — I hate to tell you — should have been my number-one skill.

In school, nobody explains to you that you'll automatically be blacklisted if you happen to exchange more than a "good morning" with the boss of your boss. If you're caught in the act, your manager will assume that you're befriending the bigger guy to step all over him and take his job. In school, nobody warns you that you should spend only half of your time working, and the other half telling everyone what you're doing; otherwise nobody will know what you've done, or — worse — somebody else will take credit for it.

Nobody told me that in a big company it's better to be feared than to be loved. Nobody taught me that people who invest their time in staking their territory do better than people who work their asses off. Yes, there are so many useful things that I could have learned in school that nobody taught me. If I went back to college I would demand courses like:

- How to work for a boss who doesn't know how to use a computer.
- How to work for an alcoholic boss who shows up at noon, changes everything you've written, and then, around 9 p.m., changes it back to the way it was originally.
- How to work with someone who's *not* your boss anymore but keeps bossing you around as if he still was.

And last, but not least:

- How to work for a plain bitch on wheels.

Naturally, this brings me back to none other than Bonnie.

Bonnie is what I call the classic corporate nightmare. She's in her late fifties, never married, uptight, controlling, and ambitious. She has a sweet tooth for bureaucracy, no talent whatsoever, and an incredible ability to navigate the corporate waters in order to gather power. Bonnie is evil, tyrannical, insecure, and envious. What's not to love?

Bonnie came from a VP position in another agency, where — I heard — she did a lousy job, and everybody hated her. My friend Irene always says, "Executives just keep falling upward, no matter what," meaning that, no matter how bad they screwed up in their last job, they'll go from vice-president here to senior vice-president there. That was Bonnie's case.

According to Lynn from Operations, Bonnie started as the assistant of some big-agency VP years ago, and since she had access to all his papers and e-mails, she blackmailed him for some sexual peccadillo, making him turn her into a director. Rumor has it that she always walked through the offices with a manila envelope that contained the evidence, and if her former boss didn't do what she wanted, she would pull the tip of the compromising documents out of the envelope, just to "motivate" him. That's how her career was jump-started.

So, the moment I got the message from Mary that Bonnie wanted to see me immediately, I picked up my five pounds of tampon-usage research—carefully organized in color-coordinated folders—and headed toward her windowed office with the faint hope that she would be impressed with my work. I had gathered every recent marketing study on the behavior of menstruating women for Bonnie. I know, it sounds far-fetched, but the agency was pursuing a big account with a British company that was trying to market a new brand of tampons called UK Charms. They wanted to position them as "the new cool tampons" for the youngest demographic, so, instead of the traditional discreet white packaging, they came in the brightest and loudest wrappers you can imagine. With their little red strings and their colorful applicators, the UK Charms looked a lot like firecrackers. I wouldn't be surprised if someone lighted one up by mistake on the Fourth of July.

As I rushed into Bonnie's office, ready to present myself as the dynamic senior copywriter that I am—a team player who's perfectly qualified for the available position of creative director—I tripped on Bonnie's fake Persian carpet, dropping the results of my research all over her floor.

Bonnie—who was having her usual poppy-seed-bagel-with-cream-cheese breakfast with Christine from Business Affairs—looked at me with open disdain. I felt her condescending eyes on the back of my head as I got down on my knees to pick up the papers while avoiding further ripping of my pants. There I was, literally on my knees with my butt exposed, in front of the woman I hated the most in the whole world. Could it get any worse? I stood up and faced her with my now messed-up stash of paperwork and notes.

"You're late again," she said.

"I stayed really late last night doing all this research..."

She looked at me as if staying at the office past midnight was nothing less than my daily duty. So I felt compelled to add a few more details—fictitious, of course.

"...and I had to stay home a little later because the water pipe of my upstairs neighbor broke, and it flooded my bathroom..."

She kept looking at me with a "So?" expression, so I kept lying.

"...and I had to stay to open the door for the super, because I couldn't leave the keys with the other neighbors. See, they went to Cancún for their anniversary..."

At this point, I had to acknowledge that my story had more holes than a block of Swiss cheese. Even I wasn't buying it. Bonnie cut me off.

"We start working at nine a.m. This is the second time you arrived late this month. This cannot happen again."

"It will not happen again," I said, repentant, as if I were

apologizing for murdering her nonexistent husband. Scrambling to find a way to interrupt the emotional flogging session, I tried to change subjects.

"I found very interesting stuff. If you give me another day to work on it, I could write some bullet points for the meeting..." I offered courteously, pointing at my paper mess.

"No. I want to see it myself," she cut me off.

"Would you like me to organize them a little, and maybe go through them with you so I can explain...?"

"I'm busy now. Just leave them over there."

Yeah, she was busy. She was busy gulping a poppy-seed bagel with scallion cream cheese. And the bitch doesn't even get fat. We should call her Bony instead of Bonnie, as a tribute to her flat and narrow ass. She made me stay past midnight the night before because it was "urgent," but now eating her bagel was more important than looking at my work. I pulled down the back of my blazer in a vague attempt to cover my generous and semi-naked butt, and silently left her office.

On the way back to my cubicle, I decided to stop at the kitchen to get a coffee. Of course, I ran into Dan Callahan. When it rains it pours. Here I have to make a sad parenthesis to explain who Dan Callahan is.

Dan is not physically disgusting, but he is way far from being good-looking. Half Irish—I don't know about the other half—with black, thinning hair, greasy complexion, virtually no upper lip, and a couple of inches shorter than me, he's not exactly what I would call a knight in shining armor. He's like a cross between Jack Black and Rick Moranis. And he's the last guy who asked me out on a date.

It happened about three weeks earlier. Was I interested in him? Not really, but—hell—when you don't have a lot to choose from, you just go for anything. In any case, Dan asked me out probably thinking that I would be an easy lay, and — why deny it — at that time I was. After months and months of not having one man approach me with a romantic interest, I would have dated Quasimodo.

Unfortunately, the night of our date Dan got so drunk that when we finally got to my apartment he vomited all over my — real — Persian carpet.

You would think that, after such a first date, I would never talk to the guy again. But I'm a very understanding person. I give everybody the benefit of the doubt.

Who knows? I thought to myself. Maybe he drank on an empty stomach. Maybe he is hypersensitive to alcohol. Maybe he liked me so much that he had an extra drink to gather the courage to make the first move.

So, when I saw him shit-faced and half covered in vomit, I did what any decent woman would do: I cleaned him up, took him downstairs, and hailed a cab for him. I called him for the next two days, trying to find out how he was doing, but the bastard didn't even have the courtesy to return my phone calls. As a matter of fact, I suspected that he had been avoiding me in the office for the last three weeks.

Back to the kitchen. I could have kept walking and ignored him for the rest of my life, but something — I don't know what — made me step into the pantry to say hi. Actually, it doesn't really matter why I said hi — the point is that I did it. Dan was talking to Mark Davenport, a new account executive from England, who had made Dan his office buddy. Mark gave him a funny look and left as soon as he saw me stepping into the kitchen. I suppose that my reputation preceded me.

"Hi, Dan!" I said.

He stiffened up when he heard my voice.

"Hey, B!"

He barely made eye contact with me, maybe hoping I wouldn't stay. But I like a challenge: if he was going to ditch me, he better do it in person. With Mark Davenport gone, it was easier to corner him, so I blocked the exit. Dan started fumbling with the sugar and the coffee. Faking the laborious attitude of an alchemist, he started adding a little bit more sugar, a touch of milk, and then a little bit more coffee again, as if getting that coffee right was vital to the preservation of the human race.

"I called you a couple of times on your cell, but I couldn't get through," I said.

"Oh... yeah, my battery died..."

Oh sure! His battery was dead for three weeks. The nerve.

"Well, I just wanted to make sure that you arrived home okay," I said. "The other night, you were a little..." There was no need to say "drunk," we both knew it. "... but I had a great time," I finished, with my voice going up an octave.

"Cool," he said. "Cool."

God forbid he should say, "Thanks, B, I had a great time too." At this point I just wanted to torture him, so I brought back some of our fondest memories.

"I was able to clean up the..." There was no need to say "vomit," we both knew it. "You can hardly see the stain," I added.

"Cool," he said, one more time. "Well... listen, I gotta run, so... I'll catch up with you... I don't know, at some point, okay?"

Yeah, at some point. In my next reincarnation, maybe. He walked out, but I didn't say goodbye to him. I had said enough.

Anyway, here's the part about myself that baffles me: Dan is not good-looking, he treated me like crap, he ruined my rug, which I literally carried on my shoulder all the way from Istanbul. But in spite of all that, when he rejected me, it hurt. It hurt like a punch in the gut. So I bit my lower lip, served myself a cup of coffee, tried not to cry — which was exactly what I felt like doing — and went back to my desk to deal with my ripped pants.

I picked needle and thread from my second drawer, where I keep my office survival kit (Band-Aids, nail polish, tampons, etc.), and walked into the empty bathroom. I locked myself up in one of the stalls and proceeded with the complicated task of removing my pants in the confined space. I sat on the toilet, propped my legs against the door, and started sewing.

A few seconds later, I heard two women walking in: Bonnie and Christine. Every morning after breakfast they came to remove traces of cream cheese and poppy seeds from their teeth and to retouch their makeup. As I sat there quietly sewing, virtually invisible with my feet up against the wall, I couldn't help eavesdropping.

"Did you see that memo from Operations?" asked Christine.

"I don't even open their e-mails anymore. What a bunch of assholes," Bonnie replied.

The restroom probably wasn't the best place to discuss business, but since they couldn't see me, they likely thought that there was nothing to worry about.

"So who's getting the director's job?" asked Christine, referring to the creative-director position I was applying for. "Have you talked to Kevin about it?" she added. Kevin, or, as he's often called, the Chicago Boss, is the president and founder of the agency.

"It's between Laura, and Ed Griffith. I still have to meet with Kevin, but just as a courtesy, because he's going to do whatever I say," was Bonnie's reply.

Great. I was out of the race. And her strong candidates were Laura, who comes from Account Management — no creative background whatsoever — and Ed Griffith, who has worked in every agency in the city, but never longer than six months, because he gets fired every time. Awesome choices. Naturally, the breaking news bothered me, but I had no time to grieve, because, before I could give another stitch to my pants, I heard something even more disturbing.

"How about B? She's a bit of a workhorse, isn't she?" said Christine.

Wow! Christine taking my side? Praising my work? Acknowledging my efforts? She made me feel a little guilty for all the times I'd referred to her as "the bitch's bitch." But Bonnie helped me snap out of my guilt.

"B? No way! That position is too visible, too 'hands-on' with the client. She doesn't have the skills, and doesn't have the look either. She's too fat! I can't send someone like B to have lunch with a client. She'll spoil his appetite!"

Then they laughed. They fucking laughed.

"I mean, it's okay to have B locked in the dungeon doing her work, but . . . B? Director? I'm sorry, but I just don't see her in a window office."

There went my dream of having an office that overlooks Central Park — along with any hope to move up in this company. I was so devastated that I felt physically weak, so I gripped the toilet-paper holder for support, accidentally dropping a spare roll that the cleaning lady always leaves in the stall. I saw Bonnie's shadow move, as she looked for potential eavesdroppers. I guess she checked for legs under the partitions, but since mine were propped against the door she couldn't see anything — thank God.

"We should keep it down," said Christine.

"Nah! Who cares? What are they going to do if they hear me? Fire me?"

And they laughed again.

Convinced that none of their indiscretions were falling on unwanted ears, they made a few more nasty remarks about other employees until Bonnie finally said, "Okay, showtime!" — hinting to Christine that it was time to go back to work and continue faking it.

Bitches.

They left the bathroom, but I stayed there for what felt like an eternity. I was weeping and sewing, sewing and weeping. *She's too fat! I can't send someone like B to have lunch with a client. She'll spoil his appetite!* I kept repeating Bonnie's words in my mind, and my tears kept flowing, burning my face on their path. Tears of joy are refreshing, but tears of pain and anger are different: they're bitter, and feverish. They burn like acid on your cheeks.

"Okay, bitch," I said to myself, as if I were talking to Bonnie, "as soon as I'm done crying my eyes out, you'll see who I really am." I just said this to say something, because at the time I had no idea how I could get back at her without just shooting her in the head with a rifle and spending the rest of my life in jail. It sounded tempting, but — who am I kidding? — I can't even kill a fly without feeling guilty.

I dragged myself back to my desk before people started thinking that I had drowned in the toilet. That's when Lillian, my beloved and loyal Lillian, decided to come in and tell me everything about her extended weekend.

Talk about being in the wrong place at the wrong time.

CHAPTER 2

"Wanna see some pictures of the Hamptons?" Lillian asked me at the worst possible moment.

Okay, at this point I have to make a parenthesis.

When Lillian came by my desk, my eyes were still red from crying, my hands were still shaking, and my makeup was a mess. But Lillian didn't notice a thing. She wanted to show me the pictures of her weekend and tell me her adventures in the Hamptons — so even if I was covered in blood, with a steak knife sticking out of my back, she would have pursued her agenda without wondering if I was in the mood to hear her story or not. That's Lillian. She's got a good heart — that's why we're friends — but when she's in her self-centered mode, the world can be coming to an end, and her main concern will be "What will I wear when the world ends?" Nice and generous and lovely as she is, she's the kind of person who would say shit like "They have no bread? Well, then, maybe they should eat cake!" She is clueless. She is beautiful, generous, and well intentioned, but totally clueless on the struggles of other people's lives.

It is in moments like these that I wish I were an alcoholic, not because I'd like to drink myself to oblivion, but because if I were an alcoholic I could go to AA meetings, and I would have a sponsor who could help me deal with the hardships of my life. I learned about the joys of Alcoholics Anonymous with an ex-boyfriend who used to go to meetings every single day. I'll protect his anonymity — very important — by just calling him "my AA-ex."

My AA-ex was a sweet guy who'd been to hell and back because of his drinking, but he was now committed to staying sober for the rest of his life. Thanks to AA, not only had he stopped drinking, but he also became a more mature and serene person.

One of the most helpful things about the program was that every time something made him feel like drinking again, he would call his sponsor, which was another guy in the program, and his sponsor would talk him out of it. He tried rehab, psychotherapy, and medications, but the only thing that kept him sober was going to meetings every day.

I wished I could have that. Some kind of support group that could pick me up when I'm down, and infuse me with strength when I'm weak. I wished I had a sponsor that I could call when I felt hopeless and ready to give up. But the closest thing I had to a sponsor was Lillian — a friend who had good intentions but an extremely short attention span.

How could I tell her that I was trying to be rational and professional and do my job like I do every day, while my anger, self-hatred, and the feeling of being used were driving me insane? How could she talk me into acting as an adult when I just wanted to kick and scream like a child?

That very moment, I was suffering what I've come to identify as the "charioteer syndrome." To explain this I might have to go back to ancient Greece, or at least to my high-school years, when I studied ancient Greece, so bear with me for a second.

When I was in high school, I had an art-history teacher called Grazia. She was Italian, but she married an American soldier and moved to the States. She looked very exotic to me: skinny as a rail, with a fantastic big Italian nose and jet-black hair. She knew so much about the Greeks, the Egyptians, the Renaissance, and the Impressionists—and she talked so comfortably about all of them—that I was convinced that the golden bracelets she wore had been extracted from Nefertiti's grave. I learned more from Grazia than from all my other teachers, or even from the books I read in college. This woman was a genius, and she managed not only to know, but also to explain things in a way that made learning enjoyable and fascinating. If all my other teachers had been like her, I could probably put a rocket on Jupiter.

One of the things that she explained to me, which I will never forget, was how the ancient Greeks conceptualized life. The Greeks saw one's life as a chariot pulled by two horses: one horse represented "reason," and the other one "passion." According to the Greeks, if you allowed either horse to pull too hard, your chariot would flip over and you would die. That's why everything had to be kept on balance: a little of this and a little of that.

It's easy to see how the "passion" horse can screw you over. Just think of the stories in the newspapers: wives who kill their husbands, husbands who kill their wives, politicians who ruin their reputations for a torrid love affair, celebrities who kick paparazzi in the face when their picture has been taken outside a strip joint. In each and every case there was a passion horse that pulled way too hard, causing people to flip and suffer the consequences.

What we don't see right away is how the reason horse can screw us as well, but there are plenty of good examples. The ruthless business decisions that destroy people's lives are often excused as rational. The most obvious example is the typical executive who, instead of spending the money in a pricey system of refuse processing, prefers to save a few bucks by dumping his toxic waste in a river. If you happen to be swimming that day — well, good luck.

I see people on TV all the time explaining the most inhumane behavior with a bunch of dollar figures. We pile up money as if we were going to be able to take it with us to the grave. Just like the Egyptian pharaohs, we want to stuff our mausoleums with gold, jewels, and honors that are not going to come with us to the other side.

I felt that in my office we had allowed the reason horse to pull too hard; the atmosphere of fear and overdiligence was ruining our lives. We spent too much time at work, forgetting the passion horse — love, relationships, and family. Talking, laughing, feeling loved and appreciated became just an afterthought, something we did only when we had a little time to spare.

Louis — an old friend of mine — is the perfect example of someone who suffered the effects of an overactive "reason horse." Louis was a white boy who worked on Wall Street, and he was dating a sweet Puerto Rican girl who worked at the Gap. Louis, who already had an awesome job and a fantastic apartment, cold-bloodedly decided that he deserved a better girlfriend, someone who could help him reach up to the next social and professional level. The Puerto Rican girl simply wasn't enough for him. Without any explanations he dumped her, and decided to continue with his skyrocketing career to money, status, and success.

Then, a couple of weeks later, Louis realized a small detail: he loved his Puerto Rican Gap-working girlfriend. He realized that he truly, deeply loved her, but he didn't see it until he lost her.

Poor Louis spent hours and hours hanging out in front of her little apartment in Spanish Harlem, buzzing, begging, and bringing flowers, letters, and diamond rings to her. But it was too late: she never opened the door for him again.

Louis went crazy trying to get her back. He couldn't concentrate anymore, so he lost his job, started going to therapy, took antidepressants, and finally got all spiritual. He was the last guy I ever thought I would hear quoting Buddha and Paulo Coelho in the same sentence, but that's what losing the love of his life turned him into. The last time I saw Louis, he was talking about previous reincarnations, meditating on the "om," and moving to Santa Fe to become a yoga instructor.

This is what happens when the reason horse pulls too hard. Reason can screw you just as hard as passion can.

Sometimes I wonder if Latinos let the passion horse pull too hard but others do the same with the reason horse. As a Cuban American, I'm somewhere in the middle, and I feel the clear and constant pressure of keeping both my horses in line.

My reason horse makes me feel smart and in control, but also empty and dead. My passion horse makes me feel volcanic and powerful, but childish and vulnerable at the same time. However, more often than not—maybe because my Cuban blood runs deep, my passion horse is the one who gets out of hand. When that happens, I cry, yell, kick, and scream.

That particularly awful morning — as every single event seemed to push each and every one of my most reactive buttons — holding both horses on an even leash was a challenging task. It was something that could be achieved only by some Greek action hero of ancient times, and not a simple chubby girl like me. My passion horse was telling me to grab my handbag, yell a couple of expletives at Bonnie, and slam her door behind me as I left that office forever. My reason horse was telling me to keep it cool and not do anything that I could regret tomorrow. This horsy dialogue was driving me nuts.

That morning, I wished I had an AA sponsor. Someone with more experience at being "me" who could tell me, "Easy, big girl, don't go crazy, don't let all this crap bring you down. Don't unleash the horses."

Unfortunately, I wasn't an alcoholic, and I didn't have a sponsor. All I had to rely on was Lillian, my best friend in the whole world. Someone who works a few desks away from me, but sometimes makes me feel like she lives in a distant galaxy. With her tight and slim body, and the permanent court of hunky guys taking her out and sending her flowers at the office, how could she understand what I was going through?

So, now that I've said that, we can go back to the story.

Where were we?

Oh yes, the Hamptons.

"Wanna see some pictures of the Hamptons?" Lillian asked me at the worst possible moment.

In case you don't know, the Hamptons is the most beautiful and obnoxious place on earth. A couple of hours away from New York City, on the coast of Long Island, it's a collection of little towns by the sea, crowded with elegant mansions, English gardens, overpriced antique shops, and arrogant people rolling around in expensive cars and wearing faded jeans. It's a place frequented by people with money or people who like to pretend that they have money. If you live in New York and you don't go to the Hamptons on the weekend, you are nobody. People don't go there to enjoy themselves, they go there to tell other people that they went there, and that is neither my thing nor my scene. I've been out there a few times, and the crowd was so pretentious and unwelcoming that I won't miss it a bit if I never go back.

So back to Lillian... Without waiting for my response to her question, she started laying out her weekend memories in front of me, and though I could have said no, chances were she wasn't listening.

"Just look at this house," she wowed. "And the owner is crazy about me."

"Lil...I'm not sure if I'm in the mood for this right now," I said, trying to stop her. It didn't work.

"This is the guy—the lawyer who sent me the flowers—he's not so cute, but he's got this house—not a share—and a Beemer—wow! But then his friend, who's super-cute, shows up. Now, here's the problem: he's a paralegal..."

Lillian placed an imaginary "L" on her forehead, in case I didn't know that she might date lawyers but *never* "para-losers."

"...But then their boss shows up—now, this one is *beyond* loaded, okay? So the boss starts chasing me around, and asking me things, and being all flirty...but the thing is that I know that he's married to this *fat thing*—so I'm all like 'Mister, you have to step back...'"

Oh, Lillian! You had to bring up the fat factor, didn't you?

I wish I'd had enough strength at the time to laugh at it or send her to hell. But after the events of the morning, there was only one thing I could do, so I went ahead and did it. I started weeping.

The weeping seemed to capture her attention—she only responds to crisis mode. Since the office is pretty much a big open space, and my wailing would immediately attract unwanted attention, in a matter of seconds Lillian managed to find my sunglasses, covered my mascara-stained eyes with them, and gently but assertively—with the elegant determination of a geisha—dragged me by the arm out of the office. Lillian clearly wanted to keep me from making a scene in front of my co-workers.

"Don't say a word. Wait until we're outside," she hushed, as we walked toward the exit.

She took me downstairs to the smokers' corner to ask me what the hell was going on. I was brief: the pants, the marketing morons, Dan Callahan, and—of course—Bonnie.

"B, you cannot take this personally."

"How can I *not* take this personally?" I blurted out. "Let's ignore all the shit that happened to me this morning. You would think that I could say, 'Fuck all this, I'm going to devote myself to my career.' But it turns out that even though I work my ass off, my fucking boss thinks I'm such a dog that I should be locked in a dungeon!!!"

"B, honey, it's not all about looks. You have to understand that beauty . . ."

I lost it then and there, and yelled at her, "Do not tell me that beauty is in the eye of the beholder!"

"Actually, I was going to say, 'Beauty is on the inside.'"

"Well, don't say that either!" I shouted.

My position is that if you're going to console me you

should be creative and not throw a couple of clichés to see if they stick. I'm fat, but I'm sophisticated. Lillian stopped for a second to rethink her words.

"Look, B, you're smart, and sweet, and talented, and responsible...and...and...yes, you are beautiful too." Naturally "'beautiful'" was the last compliment on her stupid laundry list. I almost smacked her, but she continued: "You have a weight problem, but you can't let that stop you!"

"Lil," I said, "my weight is not stopping me. They are stopping me! So if I don't turn into a skinny anorexic thing, then that's it? I'm never gonna find a boyfriend, I'm never gonna have a family, and—obviously—I'm never gonna have a window office either?"

Let's face it, my logic was sad but hard to refute, and poor Lillian couldn't come up with anything that could comfort me. The best she could say was "You just have to get serious about losing weight. Make it a health priority!"

Let me make something clear: the last thing that a fat girl needs to hear is that she "needs to get serious about losing weight." Trust me, she knows it. Take this from someone who was dieting before she could talk. And if you add sexual frustration to the weight problem, then you really have a deadly cocktail in your hands.

So I tried to explain my point to Lillian without scratching her eyes out. I started by posing a rhetorical question: "Do you know when was the last time I got laid? I can't even remember! It must have been—when?—a year ago? Yeah, it must have been a year ago, because I was doing my taxes..."

I had to stop my train of thought, because it suddenly hit me that it was April 14—again—and I had not done my taxes yet. Oh boy, what a day. I was angry, frustrated, and now in a panic.

"Relax," she said, "just go to your accountant tomorrow morning and you'll be done in no time. But today we're going to make a plan so you can reinvent yourself."

The thing about Lillian is that sometimes she doesn't come through, but when she finally does, she hits you right where it really hurts. "And the first thing you have to do" — she made a dramatic pause before shooting me in the head with the truth — "is drop that bitchy self-deprecating attitude, because, to be honest with you, it's not very attractive."

In other words: I'm fat *and* whiny.

I hated her. I hated her so much for saying that that I instantly knew she was absolutely right. She was so right that I had to laugh. I laughed so hard that the smokers next to us, who had seen me crying hysterically a second before, now thought I was bipolar. Lillian hugged me, and it felt good and sincere. Even though her comforting techniques are not very good, her intentions certainly are. That's why she is my best friend.

"I know you're going through a bad moment, but there's gotta be a reason for this. There's gotta be something you need to learn. Trust me, nothing happens by accident. God has a plan."

"I'm not religious," I said, shaking my head.

"I'm not religious either! This is not a religious thing, it's a spiritual thing," she said.

"Well, I'm not spiritual either," I replied, just to contradict her and piss her off.

"Oh! Fuck you, then!" she fired back, knowing that I was just messing with her.

I called her a bitch, she called me a fat ass, and we both felt as good as new.

"Let's go for a drink tonight," she insisted.

"I have to do my taxes."

"You have until tomorrow. Come on! Tuesdays are the new Thursdays!"

Someone said that madness is repeating the same mistake over and over while expecting a different result. I knew that if I went out with Lillian every man in the bar would hit on her and nobody would even notice me. But at this point I wanted to make Lillian feel good about having tried to make me feel good. I'm such a people pleaser. But I'd be lying if I said that that was my only motivation; the truth is, I had nothing better to do that night, so I hopped along.

Big mistake.

CHAPTER 3

*I*f you are a true New Yorker, you might already know the secret rules of Manhattan's nightlife, but in case you are not, let me take a couple of lines to explain how the bar scene operates in the Big Apple.

Turns out that — as Lillian pointed out to me — Tuesdays have become the new Thursdays.

A few years ago, going out on a Thursday night was a true adventure. Only the freaks, the fashionistas, or the addicts ruled Thursday nights. They would go to a bar after work, someone there would invite them to a party, the party would suck, and somebody else would invite them to another party, and then they'd fly off to yet another one. Finally, after crashing Thursday-night gallery openings, charity events, clubs, after hours, etc., you could find them in Chinatown at 4 a.m., having salt-baked shrimps for breakfast, surrounded by a string of strangers that they picked up along the way.

These night creatures would show up at work the next

morning with dark sunglasses covering their eyes, and praying for Friday to fly by, so they could go home to take a nap.

In essence, Thursdays were the night when people went out in order to avoid the Friday and Saturday crowds. New Yorkers—who are not into waiting in line to go to clubs, or even to go to heaven—needed a night to have the city for themselves, and for a long time that night happened to be Thursday.

The problem is that Thursdays became too popular. So suddenly—as if an invisible force made the whole city agree on the same subject—Tuesdays became the new Thursdays.

As a result, no respectable party happens on a day other than Tuesday. And if you're planning to go to a swanky bar, don't even dare show up if it isn't Tuesday. Tuesday is now *the* night to go out. The night for people who either don't have to wake up early the next morning, or like to pretend that they don't. Typically, it's the latter.

Now, this is the fascinating part. Since Tuesdays became Thursdays, all the other days of the week have gotten screwed up:

Wednesdays have become the new Fridays. The bars are way too crowded, and too many out-of-towners cruise the streets in their SUVs.

Thursdays have become the new Saturdays. Therefore, Thursday is a night to catch a foreign film or an art show, but nothing more complicated than that. There's no way anything exclusive or interesting happens on a Thursday anymore.

Fridays are without a doubt the new Sundays: a night for staying home and watching TV. You'd rather die a slow death than wait in line with a bunch of tourists to get into a club on a Friday night.

Saturdays, obviously, have the quiet appeal of the old Mondays. Saturday is the preferred night for Manhattanites to do laundry, clean out the closets, or visit friends in the suburbs.

Sundays are starting to look a lot like the old Tuesdays. Since Sunday is kind of an off-night, it's cool to go out in search of adventures.

Finally, we have Mondays, but I haven't figured out what their new status is yet. I'll try to keep you posted on that.

To be honest, a long time ago I stopped caring about all these stupid rules, but understanding the nuances is vital to this part of my story. Lillian's insistence on going out that night had a lot to do with the fact that it was a Tuesday. She chose the right night and the right bar: we arrived at Baboon when the happy-hour crowd was already settled and half happy.

Baboon is one of the cool bars in the Meat Packing District — an industrial area on the Lower West Side of Manhattan where all the meat distributors had their freezers until gentrification turned it into a trendy neighborhood.

When I was growing up in Upper Manhattan, the Meat Packing District was not a place to hang out in. By day, you could smell the stench of bovine blood and carcasses emanating from the buildings. By night, the sidewalks were splattered with prostitutes and slow-moving cars that only stopped to negotiate rates for after-dark services. In other words, there was meat packing by day and meat packing by night. No neighborhood has ever had a more appropriately explicit name.

But times have changed, and the old meat lockers have been renovated and turned into fancy bars and restaurants for the Wall Street types and their chasers. The carcasses and prostitutes have been replaced by hunky brokers with big cigars, and skinny girls with little black dresses and stiletto heels, who constantly stumble and fall on the cobblestoned streets, breaking their heels in the best cases, and their necks in the worst. There's so much arrogance and bullshitting going on in this area now, they should change its name to the Shit Packing District. Everybody seems to be full of it.

As we approached the bar, I realized just how much I've learned by hanging out with Lillian. Lesson number one: always let Lillian walk first into a crowded bar. Why? Because she'll open the way for me.

It's fascinating to see how men react to an Asian beauty. They move out of the way...stare...howl...It's frankly pathetic. If women reacted toward men the way men react toward women, the world would probably come to a screeching halt. I'm convinced that, given the same pressure and attention that pretty girls get, men would suffer a vicious attack of performance anxiety and never have another erection again. But Lillian loves the attention, and I basically get some of it by association. For the record, it takes a lot of strength to be friends with Lillian. I honestly don't think she thrives on having me around just to be neglected. I simply think that she doesn't get it. I'm telling you, when she's on "self-centered-mode" she can't see past her perky boobs.

This scene that revolves around Lillian when we're together makes me feel like I'm a supporting character in my own life. I know it's ridiculous, but when I hang out with her, I've noticed that I start behaving like a sidekick. It's as if she's Calista Flockhart and I'm Camryn Manheim. I might have a few good scenes, but I'm just her supporting actress. It has always bothered me, but I've never known how to stop it.

We walked into Baboon through the crowd of Wall Street primates and tried to park ourselves near the bar. Immediately some guy offered Lillian his seat. With a big smile she demanded the one next to hers, and the other guy gave me the adjoining stool. I perched myself up there and observed how they circled her and started the mating rituals. The bar was loud and it was hard to follow their conversation, so I chose to study the crowd instead, while having one, then two, then three appletinis — courtesy of the apes.

"Thank you!" I said three times. They wouldn't even "you're welcome" me back.

Suddenly a big smile across the room caught my eye. I'd never seen that guy before, but he was openly smiling at me. Very discreetly, I looked over my shoulder to make sure that he wasn't smiling at someone behind me. Once I confirmed that I was the object of his attention, I smiled back. Then the Smiley Guy proposed a long-distance toast that was interrupted by one of Lillian's monkeys, who bumped me in a desperate attempt to position himself closer to her. I rolled up my eyes, and the Smiley Guy laughed out loud. I was starting to have fun with him when Lillian announced that she was going outside with her apes to look at the car they had parked in front of the bar.

"Peter says that it's a Porsche, but Roger says that it's a Mustang," Lillian said, laughing with her court of idiots.

I suspected that the whole argument was just an act to pull Lillian out of the bar and impress her with the actual eighty-thousand-dollar Porsche 911 Turbo that I saw parked on the street when we walked in. As Lillian turned toward the door and stepped away from her drink, she noticed the Smiley Guy looking at me. She arched an eyebrow and whispered in my ear, "Save my seat for him." Good thinking, Lillian.

As they left, I waved the Smiley Guy in, and he moved next to me. Physically he wasn't anything to write home about, but he had the wholesome looks of a good boy from the Midwest. He was wearing low-rise jeans, a cute T-shirt, and a very light and smooth leather jacket.

"Hi! I'm Stuart!" he said to me.

"Hi, I'm B."

"Bea? B-E-A?"

"No, just the letter B, as in . . . 'Bolivia,' " I said, correcting my vice of always saying "B as in 'boy.' "

"What happened with your friends?" he asked.

"Oh, they went outside to look at someone's car."

"Are they coming back?"

"I hope not!" I said, and we both laughed.

We laughed and then laughed again, looking into each other's eyes. I don't know if you've ever done that, but it's super-sexy.

"What's your friend's name?"

"Lillian."

"Is she a good friend?"

"She's the best!"

"Cool!"

As the Smiley Guy and I talked some more and smiled some more, I started seeing it all: our wedding, our tight little New York apartment that would inevitably be small but filled with love, our first baby, the good times and the bad times. I pictured a whole life of victories and obstacles, domestic joys and dramas that we survived with each other's loving support. In a fraction of a second, I learned to love and forgive his imperfections, and I felt blessed because he learned to love mine too. And it all started in a bar, smiling at each other across a crowded room, as he chose me in a sea of skinnier women. I pictured myself with grandchildren on my knees, telling them in detail the love story of their grandparents. I saw myself dying in peace, knowing that my life ended up like the Hallmark Hall of Fame movie that I wanted it to be.

Just when I thought that nothing could burst my bubble, he broke my concentration.

"Your friend is hot. Can you introduce me to her?"

Okay. This was a low blow. A really low blow. I take responsibility for my overly active imagination. I can't blame him for not partaking in the Claritin-commercial future that I pictured for us. I even understand that he liked Lillian more than me—what's not to like, right? But to flirt with me to try to get to her was just wrong. It's something I wouldn't do to anybody. Something that made me really, *really* angry. And I'm not nice when I'm angry.

With the same speed with which I'd pictured our life together, and with an anger fueled by appletinis, I came up with the perfect revenge:

"Oops!" I dropped my bag and—predictably—he volunteered to pick it up.

"Let me get that for you."

As he bent over, I noticed his low-rise jeans and emptied my drink down the crack of his ass. As expected, he jumped up screaming a very loud "What the fuck...?" I apologized profusely, and blamed the accident on the faceless crowd.

"I'm so sorry! Somebody pushed me," I said innocently, while pointing at the group of people standing behind us.

"I'm going to the bathroom," he said, without acknowledging my apology. "Watch my jacket," he added, referring to the beige lambskin bomber jacket hanging from the back of his stool.

He left for the bathroom, and I headed for the door—my bag in one hand and his leather jacket in the other one. Outside, I threw the jacket in a dumpster and walked away. As I headed for the corner to stop a cab, I heard Lillian's laughter from across the street. She couldn't see me, and I didn't stop to say goodbye. I knew that if she noticed how upset I was, she would insist on leaving with me, and I didn't want to ruin her night. It wasn't her fault.

Was I proud of what I did? Not at all. As I stepped on the cobblestoned street to get in the cab, I broke one of my heels.

"Damn...!"

Revenge has never worked for me, and I wondered if I was being instantly punished by Karma. True, the Smiley Guy did something wrong, insensitive, and foolish. He deserved a lesson, but was it worth it to teach him that lesson, at the expense of feeling like a bitter bitch afterward? No. Not at all.

As I rode silently in a taxi with my swollen feet, a sore ankle, and an angry frown that would surely cause me to age prematurely, I realized that I was hitting rock bottom. But the good part of going all the way down to the bottom is that there's nowhere to go but up. So, before we continue, let me take a second to apologize publicly to the Smiley Guy for dumping his jacket in the trash. Hey, Smiley, I'm sorry. Yes, you are an idiot, but I wasn't better than you, so please accept my sincere apologies.

Okay, now that I've made amends, let's go on, because now is when the story gets good.

Real good.

CHAPTER 4

My friend Jorge had an Argentinian bakery in the West Village. He sold the best croissants in town—at least ten pounds of my weight can certify that. I'd walk out of my building every morning at eight-thirty to go to work, stopping only to grab my coffee—with skim milk, no sugar—and a butter croissant from Jorge's. Since he had to wake up at four in the morning to bake the goods, his wife, Fabiana, would come later and run the shop in the afternoon. I would chat with the husband in the morning and with the wife in the evening.

"*¡Querido!*" I would greet Jorge, which is a very Argentinian way to address your friends.

"*¡Hola preciosa!*" Jorge would answer me back, with a big smile. I loved it when he called me precious.

In the couple of seconds that it took him to serve my coffee and pack my croissant in a brown paper bag, I would update him on my career, my love life, and my plans for the weekend.

"¿Y este fin de semana que hacés? ¿Con cual novio te vas de paseo?"
He would ask me which of my many boyfriends was going to
take me out that weekend—as If I had any. But I never took
these comments as an offense, first because I knew that his
intentions were good, and second because he spoke with this
delicious Argentinian accent that some people find annoying
but I honestly think is adorable. Jorge would celebrate when
I was up, cheer me up when I was down, and feed me well in
between peaks. He was like a second mother to me.

In the afternoon, I would stop by just to chat with Fabiana.

"¡Che querida!" she would greet me, lifting her eyes from
her *¡Hola!* magazine, a celebrity tabloid that she was addicted
to. Fabiana was in her mid-forties and very well preserved.
She was blonde and petite, but she had a huge bosom and
she knew how to use it. She wore tight sweaters in the winter
and tight T-shirts in the summer. She'd do anything to bring
attention to her fabulous knockers.

"Tell me everything. Who are you sleeping with?" she
always asked.

Every time Fabiana and I talked, things would get down
and dirty very fast. She often stepped outside to have a cigarette and talk about anything intimate, from yeast infections
to sex toys. She was funny and open, and had a way of discussing sex that made you feel comfortable talking about it,
and willing to share your own adventures.

"There's this German guy who comes here. He is so damn
hot. You have to fuck him for me, and then tell me absolutely
everything."

"Fabiana, please!" I would say, amused and scandalized.

"¡Nena! You're single! Live your life!"

She always encouraged me to do what she wanted to do
but wasn't supposed to. Now, of course, these conversations

never took place within earshot of Jorge. Jorge was terribly jealous and hated when Fabiana flirted with other men. I don't know if she actually slept with any of the guys that she had an eye on, but you would always see men stopping by the coffee shop with flowers and gifts for her. I have never met a bigger flirt than Fabiana in my entire life.

But Jorge wasn't stupid, and he knew what was going on; very often they would have nasty fights, and they would go for days without talking to each other.

One morning, I walked into the shop to find Jorge with black circles around his eyes and a somber expression. I looked at the tray of croissants and noticed that the usually fluffy and flaky butter wonders looked like fried sparrows. It was so obvious that they were not the croissants that he had gotten us addicted to that I had to ask him if the oven was broken or if something was wrong.

"It's because of Fabiana," he said, breaking his usual privacy. "Every morning I prepare the croissants following step-by-step the exact same recipe. But if she gets me angry they just don't grow. No matter what I do, they just won't grow."

From that moment on — and based on the look of the croissants — every customer knew if Jorge and Fabiana had had a fight the night before. An organized group of concerned patrons almost encouraged Fabiana to make peace with him — first because we cared for them, but mainly because we couldn't live without Jorge's baked marvels. This whole drama was ruining breakfast for everybody.

But, putting my carb addiction aside, this experience with Jorge's baked goods was quite a revelation. If disappointment can wither a croissant, imagine what it can do to a human heart.

That Wednesday morning, I was feeling a lot like Jorge. I

had the chemical hangover of the appletinis mixed with the emotional hangover of the exchange with Smiley. In addition to that, I felt completely unmotivated at the office. My drive and determination to do a good job had disappeared, thanks to Bonnie's comments in the bathroom. It's a good thing I'm a copywriter and not a rocket scientist, 'cause otherwise my rocket would have ended up on the wrong planet.

I came to work with all my miseries swirling inside my head, and that made it virtually impossible to work on the British tampon's slogan. I had an impressive amount of information on the customs of American menstruating women sitting on my desk, but I didn't have a brain to process it.

To make matters worse, I knew that even if I came up with a good idea, I would just get more misery and more humiliation from Bonnie. My professional relationship with her always followed five easy and dysfunctional steps:

First, I would come up with a brilliant idea.

Second, I would give it to Bonnie, who would change it, ruin it, and pitch it all twisted to the Chicago Boss.

Third, the Chicago Boss would invariably say, "Interesting . . . ," but he would turn it around and, because great minds think alike, would rewrite it back to the way I originally wrote it. Then he'd send it back to Bonnie.

Fourth, Bonnie would jump up and down, clapping her hands like a wrinkled teenager in love, telling him that he was a genius.

Finally, Bonnie would give me back the notes, telling me that the Chicago Boss brought the whole concept to a higher level. Higher level, my ass. Since I never had the chance to pitch my ideas directly to the Chicago Boss, he never knew how talented I was. And that was exactly what Bonnie was trying to achieve. She wanted me in the dungeon.

So, that fine morning, the workhorse that Christine referred to in the bathroom was staring blankly at the wall. I just couldn't get myself to write one word for those tampons. Period.

I strongly believe that there are a lot of stupid people running corporate America, people who think that if they treat you like crap you are going to work harder. Maybe it works like that with donkeys—and even that would surprise me—but I guarantee you it doesn't work with human beings. When you feel exploited at work, you simply turn into a clock watcher. You sit there letting time go by, and two weeks later you pick up your check and you mutter, "Fuck you all," as you walk away from the payroll window.

It's a situation where nobody wins. The company becomes less productive, and the employees don't feel any sense of accomplishment. I believe that most people actually enjoy working, because there's a pleasure in doing things and doing them right. But all this joy that comes from a job well done goes to hell when you feel used and abused by your boss.

In my case, the sensation of being used was making me so furious that I would catch myself compulsively sharpening pencils—as if I were planning to impale an army of vampires—while concocting crazy and irrational revenge plots against Bonnie.

"What if," I would catch myself saying, "I rub poison ivy all over her phone . . . or I break a few toothpicks into the keyhole of her Mercedes Benz?"

Yeah, revenge thoughts were the only thing that could alleviate the pain of replaying Bonnie's comments over and over in my head: *I can't send someone like B to have lunch with a client. She'll spoil his appetite! It's okay to have B locked in the dungeon doing her work, but . . . B? Director? I'm sorry, but I just don't see her in a window office.* Oh Lord, I so hated her.

After a rather painful yet uneventful morning, I took my lunch hour to do my taxes. Actually, I went to one of these places where they prepare them for you.

The place was packed with those who, like me, had waited until the last minute. They had installed a few temporary desks with additional clerks, and I ended up with a Russian lady who seemed very efficient.

"Are you Beauty Maria?" she asked looking at my tax forms.

"Yes."

"Lovely name. So you are single? No kids?"

"Yes," I sighed.

"Why?"

I shrugged but I didn't answer a word. I hated when people asked me that. I knew why I was single—or I thought I knew it at the time—but there was no reason to discuss my self-deprecating thoughts with a stranger.

The Russian lady asked me a couple more questions and hammered the keys of her computer as if she were playing a piano concert.

She was quite an interesting character. She was much older and more elegant than any of the other clerks, who looked like college students holding on to a temp job while waiting for something better to come their way. The strange thing is that, even though she was obviously older than the others, it was impossible to guess how old she was. I've noticed that Russian and Hungarian women have the most amazing skin, and maybe that's why so many of them run spas or give facials in New York. She wasn't necessarily fat, but she had that roundness that European matrons acquire in their sixties. Not only did this particular Russian lady have perfect white skin, but also her hands were carefully manicured in the French style, her reddish hair was nicely groomed in some sort of modern "beehive," and her makeup was simply flawless, if perhaps a little overdone for such a pedestrian environment. Her wardrobe was equally intriguing. She wasn't wearing anything flashy, just a simple white silk shirt with wide lapels, and a gray flannel jacket that seemed tailored to complement her shirt perfectly. The whole ensemble looked quite elegant. On top of that, she had a simple white-gold necklace with a lengthy canary-diamond pendant that playfully trickled down her generous cleavage. This woman had a *je ne sais quoi* that you just don't see every day. She managed to be motherly and sexy at the same time, and even in the simple action of typing my tax return she projected a self-confidence that I found irresistible. More than pretty, she was an imposing figure who looked out of place in the context of such a generic office.

Suddenly she gave me a quick look over her reading glasses. I felt guilty, realizing that maybe I had stared at her too much, so I politely smiled and looked away. But from that moment on, she kept giving me those quick looks, as if she was sizing me up for something. I felt embarrassed and decided to avoid her eyes, but her looks continued until she finally said the fatal words in her thick Russian accent.

"Honey, how can you live in New York with such a crappy income?"

"I get by," I replied.

But then, to my surprise, she added, "You are a beautiful woman. You could make a fortune."

I looked at her in disbelief. Did she just say what I thought she just said? Was this a lesbian advance, or an invitation to commit a federal offense? What was this woman up to? As if she had read my mind, she again looked at me over her reading glasses and repeated her words, adding one more vital piece of information to clarify herself.

"Honey, you are a very beautiful woman. You could make a fortune. There are men who would pay you very well. *I know men* who would pay you very well."

I couldn't reply. I didn't even understand what she was trying to tell me.

She went back to the computer and finished my document. I sat there speechless, trying to process her last words while she printed my tax papers.

"Make one check for the feds and one for the state," she said as she handed me my documents. I was ready to leave when she stopped me, and repeated for the third time:

"You are a *very* beautiful woman, and *I know men who would pay you.* Call me."

I have a rule: When I encounter crazy people, I don't contradict them. I just say, "Yes, sure," and try to walk away as fast as I can. So after her last statement I said, "Yes, sure, I'll call you," and I reached out for one of the business cards in the stack she had on her desk. She stopped me.

"No, not that card. Take this one."

She opened up her Chanel bag — a *real* Chanel bag — pulled out a gold-and-ostrich-skin card case, and gave me a very elegant business card made with the most exquisitely watermarked paper I've ever touched. The card read "Madame Natasha Sokolov." Her cell-phone number was written on it.

"Natasha?" I asked.

"Call me Madame," she replied.

Wow. That was pretty direct. As I walked away, I looked over my shoulder and noticed that she was staring at me with a Mona Lisa smile. I got a little bit scared, but I had never been so intrigued in my whole life. This woman's words certainly managed to get me out of my head for a few minutes.

I rushed back to the office. My lunch break was over, and since I'd spent it at the tax office, I picked up a stale turkey sandwich on whole-wheat bread—no mayo—to eat at my desk. I wrote my tax checks, walked into another painful meeting with Bonnie and the account executive in charge of UK Charms, and soon forgot everything about the woman who did my taxes. There were so many things to do at the office, and so many personal reasons to beat myself up, that I had no time to entertain insane proposals from mysterious Russian ladies.

That night, like every night, I went to the gym for my workout. I'm one of those heavy girls who actually enjoy exercise, but I hate going to the gym—if that makes any sense. I hate it because it feels like a punishment for the unforgivable crime of being fat. If I could feel that I'm going there to enjoy myself, to have fun while I get in shape, then I would see it differently. But all I see at the gym are angry people. People who don't say, "Hi, how are you?" They just run in and out of the spin class, as if exercising were one more burden in their lives, and any second they waste being social is going to screw their goal and throw off their heart-rate monitors.

When I was about eight years old, I fell in love with ballet, and took classes for a few years. Ballet is hard work, but every once in a while when doing a *grand jeté,* or a *pas de bourrée* across the floor, I had the thrilling sensation that I was one with the music, and all the hard work at the bar would be justified by that fleeting but delicious sensation. I stopped my ballet classes when one day I saw a picture of my whole class. I looked so chunky in comparison with my classmates that I never went back.

I'd love to dance ballet again, but I had been telling myself that first I had to lose some weight. That's why I chose this gym uptown: it's right across the street from Cha-Cha, a dance studio that I stare at through the windows and use as my inspiration to fight the fat. As I run, bored out of my head, mile after mile on the treadmill, I look through the windows to the ballet class across the street, and live vicariously through their pirouettes.

That night, though, the vision of the studio wasn't an inspiration, it was a painful reminder of how far I was from the things that I loved and from the person I wanted to be.

I strongly believe in the power of the human mind. I'm convinced that if you walk down the street saying to yourself, "I'm invisible…I'm invisible…I'm invisible," people won't see you. They might even bump into you. So, if you walk down the street thinking, "I'm a big fat slob…I'm a big fat slob," that's exactly how people will perceive you. I must have been thinking that, because as I walked out of the gym a homeless guy who always hangs out at the corner of Seventy-second and Broadway yelled at me, "Hey, fat ass! Gimme a dollar!" It was one more drop in a glass that had overflowed a long time ago. Needless to say, I didn't give that stinking bastard a dime, but I took advantage of his comment to torture myself all the way home to the West Village.

While dragging my sorry feet around the city, I went through the long list of my miseries, and finally concluded that nothing exciting was happening in my life. I was fat and I didn't know how to lose weight; I had an evil bitch for a boss and I didn't know how to defend myself; I had no boyfriend and I had no idea how to find and reel one in. "Yep,

I'm pretty pathetic," I thought to myself as I walked home, counting the cement slabs on the sidewalk.

There's a dusty deli around the corner from my apartment that hasn't changed in years. My friend Craig calls it the Salmonella Deli, because its meager shelves have held the exact same products ever since I moved into the neighborhood.

The only things I buy there are nonperishable goods, like toilet paper or dishwashing soap. The Salmonella Deli is always open, but it's always empty. As I walked by, I wondered if my life was just like the Salmonella Deli: open, but empty, with a few untouched goods collecting dust on the shelves, destined to remain the same way forever and ever.

I climbed the three flights up to my apartment, and slammed the door behind me.

I checked my answering machine — no messages — and I felt like the most unwanted monster on the face of the earth. I bit my lower lip and sat alone on my couch, ready to throw myself a big-ass pity party.

But just when I was about to strap on my pity-party hat, a strange thing happened. My bag, which I had left on the couch just as I always do, tipped over by itself — yes, by itself — as if an invisible hand had pushed it on the side, and one single item fell out of it. A business card made of the most exquisite watermarked paper I have ever touched. It read: Madame Natasha Sokolov.

I picked up the phone and called her.

CHAPTER 5

The trip all the way down to Coney Island from Manhattan can be a pain in the ass, but it's always rewarding, because, after spending almost an hour in the dark tunnels of the subway, the train comes out into a parallel universe. The subway runs aboveground in some parts of Brooklyn, so even before you get out of the train you can get a glimpse of what you are going to find in this area.

Coney Island still had some of the old buildings and rides that were world-renowned in the twenties, but now were run-down in an oddly wonderful and magical way. It was like going to the ruins of Disneyland. I couldn't help imagining the era, the people, and the smells of that time. It was a lot like going to a ghost town, in that you knew that something happened there but you have to guess what it was. On top of that, you had the Russian neighborhood of Brighton Beach, with rows of stores that didn't even bother to advertise their merchandise in English. Entire Russian families were hanging out on the boardwalk, or — because their homes lacked porches—on the sidewalk in front of their houses. I've never been to Cuba myself, but when I hear my mother talk about La Habana in the fifties, I imagine that it must have been a lot like this, the men playing dominoes by their stoops and the women gossiping and looking at the people walking by.

That Saturday morning I got off the subway at the Brighton Beach station and rushed down Surf Avenue to meet Madame. I walked by a group of old Russian men who had turned the sidewalk into a traveling casino. Comfortably seated around a folding table with assorted dining-room chairs, they played cards while chain-smoking. As I passed by their table, I heard them saying something in Russian that—obviously—I couldn't understand, but I sensed that it had to do with me. I crossed to the other side of the street, and then I heard them laughing. Not knowing what they were saying made me feel paranoid, so I sped up until I couldn't hear them anymore.

Following Madame's instructions, I walked past the old Nathan's with its famous hot dogs, and the Cyclone, the ancient wooden roller coaster. I've heard that roller-coaster lovers think that the Cyclone is the best ride in the world, but it scares the hell out of me. It squeaks and screeches on every dip and turn, as if it's about to fall apart.

"You gotta be crazy to get on that thing," I said to myself as I finally made a right into an alley that led to the boardwalk. Just as Madame described it, I found a Russian diner that had large trays of knishes in the window.

I stood outside for a minute and started to hyperventilate. I had been preparing myself very carefully for this meeting. "This is going to be just an informative interview to quench my curiosity," I told myself. I wasn't planning to let this woman lure me into something I didn't want to do. But

I desperately wanted to know in more detail what she meant when she said that men would pay for me. What kind of men were these? What would they want me to do? How much money would they pay? Actually, money was the last thing on my mind, but that someone would actually pay for my company sounded like a bad joke to me.

Maybe the whole thing was a deadly trap. I fantasized that Madame was going to sell me to a horde of Russian mobsters that would lock me up in the basement of a creepy Long Island whorehouse, forcing me to scrub dirty floors while the skinny girls pleasured nasty senior citizens.

As irrational as these fears were, I confess that I was truly scared. I had brought my tiny can of Mace with me — just in case — and I left a note in my apartment explaining where I was going, and who I was going to meet, in case I disappeared. I figured that eventually Lillian would come to my apartment with her copies of my keys, discover the letter, and call the police. With some luck the cops would find me — or whatever was left of me.

I walked into the diner and found Madame sitting comfortably at the counter, having a knish. She looked as regal as she had in the tax-preparation office. She was wearing another fine white silk blouse, an olive-green pencil skirt with a high cut on the back that playfully showed her calves when she walked, and, to top it off, a light wool coat that was perfect for the crispy April wind.

Call me crazy, but the lack of hordes of Russian mobsters willing to abduct me somehow disappointed me.

"I was starting to think that you had been abducted or something," she said with her Russian accent. Was her concern a coincidence, or was she reading my thoughts?

"I'm so sorry for being late..."

"I'm just teasing you, honey."

She had a funny way of saying "honey." She would pronounce the "h" in a hard and throaty way, the same way
Spaniards pronounce the "j." She also turned her "w"s into
"v"s, so every time I talked to her I had the impression that I
was talking to a Russian Cold War spy.

"Joney, vy don't vee get a couple of potato knishes and
then vee go for a stroll on the boardvalk?"

"I'm trying to stay away from carbs," I replied politely,
mentally calculating, then cringing from, the barrage of calories I supposed were contained in those Russian delicacies.

"Nonsense!" she said. "These are the best knishes in New
York! Good food doesn't make you fat, it makes you beautiful." She ordered me to eat one, as she handed it to me on a
paper napkin.

"Okay, I'll just try a little piece," I replied.

"And what are you going to do with the rest? Feed it to
the pigeons? Come on!"

"I'm down to one piece of bread a day," I said, thinking of
Jorge's croissants. "I really can't . . ."

"Joney," she said, pushing her throaty "h," "we could be
dead tomorrow. Eat the knish. Live for today."

I couldn't say that she was manipulative, but she certainly
knew how to present a hard-to-defeat argument, so I grabbed
my knish, and after one bite I realized that she was right: it
was delicious. I tried to eat it without guilt as we made our
way out of the diner and strolled down the boardwalk.

"What a beautiful day," she said, taking a deep breath.
"It's one of those days when you feel that the world is yours
to take, right?"

I had never felt that the world was mine to take, but I
nodded as if I understood the sensation that she described.

Knowing that I was lying, she looked at me with her Mona Lisa smile and went straight to the point: "So we have to make this fast, because I have a business to run. First, let me ask you something, honey. Are you by any chance a law-enforcement agent?"

"Me? No!"

"I thought not. I can smell them a mile away, but I had to ask anyway."

Okay, I'm not that naïve. I watch HBO. This is your classic crime-safety question. Law-enforcement agents can't lie, so if a drug dealer or a prostitute asks that question, the agent has to answer with the truth. That's how they avoid getting arrested.

The fact that she asked me that freaked me out in a major way; and yet it made our meeting much more appealing. *Wow! She was real! A real pimp!* I don't think I had ever met anyone who could be accused of a felony, so being in her presence was like hanging out with the star of a movie, or with a character from a TV show. As these ideas were rushing through my head, she came up with a line that totally threw me off.

"So tell me, how can I help you?"

"How can *you* help *me*?"

"Sure. You are the one who called me."

This woman was smart. In one sentence she turned the tables around. All along I was thinking that she wanted something from me. But, as she pointed out, I was the one who wanted something from her. I'd requested the meeting — she just made a remark and gave me her card. But I was well prepared mentally, so I didn't fall into the trap right away. I acted like a seasoned real-state buyer and requested more information.

"Well, I was very intrigued by what you told me."

"What? That you are a beautiful woman?" she said, looking at me straight in the eye. There was something about the way she said it that freaked me out. She noticed my reaction and laughed out loud.

"Don't worry, honey, I'm not a lesbian—not that there's anything wrong with being one."

Then she softened her tone, and with the trustworthy warmth of a loving grandmother she said, "Why are you so *intrigued* by my compliments?"

"Well, it's just that I don't hear them very often..." I choked up as I said this.

She realized that what I was saying was extremely painful to me, so, very softly, she took me by the arm and, leaning gently on me, as if she were telling me where a treasure was hidden, she whispered, "You don't hear them very often because you're hanging out with the wrong crowd. If you are interested, I can introduce you to men who will shower you with compliments. Men who would very much enjoy your company."

Here we go again with the emotional roller coaster. I went from trusting this woman to wanting to run away from her as fast as I could. I stopped in my tracks and looked at her.

"What exactly are you talking about?"

She pulled me by the arm again and, without giving any importance to the tone of alarm in my voice, said, "Let's go to a place where we can talk."

Okay...if you don't believe what happened next, I can't blame you, but I swear on my ancestors in Cuba, Africa, Spain, and Ireland—yes I have a bit of Irish in me—that the following events actually happened.

Madame took me to the Cyclone. Since the old roller coaster was made out of wood, it was loud as hell, and every time the cars took a turn, or a dip, it rattled as if the whole thing was about to fall apart. This was the spot that Madame was referring to as "a place where we can talk." I guess you could talk at the Cyclone, but who the hell could hear you? It's like trying to have a conversation inside of a maraca. And, to my surprise, that was exactly the point.

We stood on the platform waiting for the cars to stop and unload a pack of screaming teenagers, but I noticed that at least four of the cars remained occupied by rather old, rather serious, rather mobster-looking fellows. The car adjacent to ours was occupied by two Italian guys in their late sixties. They didn't move out of their seats, they just pulled a long string of tickets and gave a couple more to the attendant.

"Ciao, Rocco," Madame said to one of them.

"Ciao, Madame," the man replied, taking off his hat for a second. "Signorina..." he said to me, bowing respectfully. I smiled and nodded.

"Who are these guys?" I asked Madame as we sat in the roller-coaster wagon and strapped ourselves to our seats.

"A lot of people come here to discuss business," Madame simply replied.

To discuss business? The noise in there was enough to defy any FBI microphone, so you can only imagine the type of business that they were discussing. Those guys could be disclosing the location of Jimmy Hoffa, or even the Lindbergh baby, and not even God could hear them.

The roller coaster started moving, and as soon as the rattling noise began, the mobsters behind us continued with their calmed conversation. Madame smiled at me and continued with ours.

"First of all, let me explain that I have been arrested, but never convicted, because what I do is not illegal."

A chill went down my spine.

"So if this is not illegal why do we have to talk in a roller coaster?" I said.

"Better safe than sorry."

Who could argue with that logic? Madame continued, "This is the deal. I run a very special agency. I connect my customers with women like you. Women who can provide *comfort* to them."

"Are you running an escort service?" I asked point-blank.

"No," she answered without flinching. "My customers don't buy sex, which as you know is illegal. They are men who have a lot of money, and they're willing to pay top dollars for...certain services."

I have to pause right here to analyze that last exchange. In two sentences, Madame disclosed that:

a) She had been arrested.

b) She ran something that sounded a lot like an escort service.

c) Her clients were so kinky that they didn't even buy sexual favors. They paid for something way more expensive than sex.

As I was pondering all these thoughts, the roller-coaster car started slowly climbing up the first hill of the ride, loaded with the Italian mobsters and the two of us.

"So what type of 'services' would I have to provide to your customers?" I asked, arching an eyebrow.

"Comfort, you just have to provide comfort to them."

"And how is that comfort being provided?" I asked, trying to corner her.

"Oh! Comfort can be provided in so many ways! It depends on the customer. Some need a hug, some need a little slap on the butt. Some like to be heard, some like to be ignored. The bottom line is that these are men who appreciate voluptuous women, and they would pay a lot of money to worship a body like yours," she answered.

"Wait a minute!" I said, "Worship a body like mine? I'm sorry, but that sounds a lot like sex to me. What do you mean, worship a body like mine?"

"I meant exactly what I said: they'll pay to worship a body like yours. That makes them feel good."

At that precise moment, the roller coaster took a sharp dive and I screamed, but I couldn't tell you if it was the dive or her statement that made me shriek.

As the car started climbing the next hill, I managed to ask another question.

"So what will they do to me?"

"Oh, you can make them so happy with so little! These are guys who'd feel honored if you let them give you a massage, or . . . I don't know . . . even smell your feet."

"Smell my feet?" I uttered in complete disbelief.

"Are you interested or not?" snapped Madame impatiently.

The car dived again, I screamed again, and I threw my hands over my mouth. I had to stop talking for fear of puking out the potato knish, which was starting to rise in my digestive tract. I wanted to get the hell out of there, excusing myself with a line like "Okay, this has been fun, but it's time to get going," but on a roller coaster, once you're on, you have to stay for the whole ride. I was on for a ride with Madame too, and I could already tell that jumping off was not an option anymore.

I was feeling dizzy when we left the Cyclone. We walked in silence. Madame was letting me take it all in.

I looked at the ocean. The seagulls were flying low, and some were eating breadcrumbs that a child was throwing on the boardwalk. A young couple in Rollerblades swirled around us, and then skated away, laughing and holding hands. Seeing them was inspiring and depressing at the same time. I felt that I had a question stuck in my throat, but I didn't have the courage to speak.

I finally broke the silence with, predictably, my biggest concern.

"Okay, the part that I don't understand is why anybody would worship my body. Do you realize that I can hardly remember the last time I got laid?"

Talk about timing—as we walked by, an old man sitting on the boardwalk said something to me in Russian that made Madame laugh out loud.

"What did he say?"

"It's a catcall. He said that he would eat you with all your clothes on, even if he had to spend a month pooping rags."

"Eeeeeew!" I said

"What's your problem?" she said, offended. "It's a compliment! I find it flattering."

"Not from him!"

"From *anybody*."

"But he's a dirty old man."

"Why is he dirty? Because he is speaking out his mind?"

"That *eating*-and-*pooping* thing is disgusting," I replied.

"It's a metaphor. He's just telling you that you are a sexy woman."

"But he must be a hundred years old!"

"He is someone who finds you attractive," Madame said as if she had never said anything more serious in her life. "Be humble, and be grateful to anyone who pays you a compliment." Her tone was so ominous that for a second I thought she was quoting the Old Testament.

The strange part is that she was somehow right. Here I was — whining about being rejected — and then, when some guy paid attention to me, I felt entitled to dismiss him. I realized that I was wrong, but I still tried to defend myself by beating on a dead horse: my self-esteem.

"I guess I'm not used to hearing too many compliments."

She looked me in the eye and added, "I'm sure you get many compliments. You just don't know how to listen."

I guess if I hear compliments in Russian, chances are I won't understand them, but I knew that she was referring to something else. Could this Russian Madame who was trying to lure me into her comfort-providing agency be right about this? Did I not know how to hear compliments?

She realized that she was making a dent in my will, so, while I asked myself these and another thousand questions, she went for the kill.

"Look," she said, "I have no time for this, I have a business to run. So why don't we do this: One of my girls canceled an appointment tonight. It's an old customer that I know very well. Why don't you take over? See if you like it, and if this is for you or not."

I stopped and thought about it for a second.

"What do I have to do?" I asked.

"Very little. Just hang out with him for an hour."

"No sex?"

"No sex."

"You swear?"

"You will never, ever, under any circumstances, be asked, made, or paid to have sex. This is not about sex, trust me."

"You swear?" I asked again.

"On Stalin's grave."

"Wasn't Stalin a son of a bitch?"

Madame laughed so hard that I thought she was going to choke and die. I guess she didn't realize I knew who the Russian dictator was. Not to fit the stereotype or anything, but sometimes the fat chicks actually read a bit more than the cheerleaders. In any case, the fact that I caught her swearing in vain made no difference. I was in for the ride, and that night I was heading for my first date as a professional comfort provider.

"Do you want to know how much you are going to make?" she asked.

I thought for a second.

"No," I replied.

"I knew it," she said, smiling. "And that's exactly why I chose you."

I couldn't understand what she meant by that, but her statement gave me goose bumps.

"So what do I wear?" was all I could ask.

"Something sexy . . . and comfortable," she replied.

CHAPTER 6

I don't know if this is a Catholic thing, or a Latin thing, or a my-family thing, but I have major issues when it comes to sex. I was raised to think that good women couldn't enjoy sex. For my mother, any woman who enjoyed sex was little short of being a whore, so I carry that irrational notion with me, like an ugly tattoo that I can't laser off.

The problem is that, in spite of my moral baggage, I'm still a girl of the twenty-first century, so I've tried to be as sexually active as any of my friends. The difference is that unlike my friends, I've been tormented with guilt every time I had sex.

I lost my virginity voluntarily when I was seventeen. I was the last of my circle of girlfriends to remain a virgin, so I went for it, basically, because I had the chance and I didn't want be left behind by my cronies.

Losing my virginity wasn't a terribly exciting event. It happened in Miami with a summer boyfriend called Darren, whom I met through one of my cousins.

The truth is that I wasn't in love with Darren, I just wanted to be done with the whole virginity thing and move forward, so I orchestrated the evening with that goal in mind. I wish I could talk about the fear, or the pain, or the violins I heard, but unfortunately none of that really happened. It was all so unmemorable that I can't really tell you much about it. What I do remember is that it was followed by a terrible remorse, which only subsided after I had discussed every single anticlimactic detail with my cousins.

When I went to college, I learned to talk about sex with my girlfriends in the same terms that men talk about it in: direct, unapologetic, and even a bit crude. We told each other stories of good dates and bad dates. We complained about men who moved too fast, but we also bitched about those who moved too slowly. We talked about getting horny — and even desperate — when a long time went by without getting laid, and, just like my friends, I had sex every once in a while "just to have it," knowing beforehand that it would be a completely meaningless and empty experience.

But, unlike most of my friends, every time I had casual sex, I felt guilty as shit. Sometimes I would even develop this stupid attachment to the guy I had sex with, as if he were the man of my life. "Don't confuse Mr. Right with Mr. Right Now," my cousin Mariauxy always told me. But I kept falling in my own trap, over and over.

How could I act like a woman of my times and still feel like a woman of my mother's times? I have no idea, but this duality between what I learned and what I did drove me nuts. It's as if I was a virgin and a slut at the same time. How could I be so liberated on the one hand, and so prudish on the other? I suspect that it had a lot to do with my introduction to sex. Looking back, I can say that the experience was

50 percent funny and 50 percent traumatic, and it begins back in the days of elementary school.

I had a friend in second grade called Monique. She was the cutest, most innocent, angelic-looking blonde girl I'd ever encountered. I believe her parents were Belgian and Mexican, which added to her exotic allure. But behind Monique's angelic face there was a filthy agitator in disguise.

Monique knew everything there was to know about sex. Apparently, this three-foot-tall *Little House on the Prairie* blonde had an older cousin, and that cousin had an older cousin who explained to them everything one needed to know about the ancient art of human reproduction. I must have been only eight when Monique told Gina—my other best friend—and me tons of technical information that to this day I'm still trying to cross-reference. We would spend every single recess sitting in a corner of the playground while Monique demonstrated *Kama Sutra* positions with our Barbie dolls.

Every day she would bring up one more dirty and fascinating piece of information that we obviously kept to ourselves. That was actually the best part: the fact that we kept it all secret. This made me feel that I had a life outside home, that I knew things that no one in my family would even suspect.

The sex updates continued for a whole school year, but then it was all put on the back burner when we went away for our summer break, because when knowledge is not supported by hormonal activity, little matters what you know. Of course, when hormonal activity is not supported by knowledge, you somehow manage to figure it out anyway.

But we were eight going on nine, and when September came in and I went back to school to start third grade, someone threw a wrench in my tiny psyche.

We were standing in line outside, on our way to enter the school building, when Alix, another blonde, decided to share the sex facts that she knew. I was never a big fan of Alix, so I wasn't really paying attention to her, but my ears perked up when she said something about sex and babies.

"What does sex have to do with babies?" I asked her.

That's when, with one line, Alix disclosed the painful truth. "Babies come from sex, you silly! Where did you think they came from? Paris?"

Turns out that Monique had explained to me all the mysteries of sex, but she forgot one simple fact: babies were the direct result of sex.

Oh-my-total-God.

I wanted to faint, vomit, and run all at the same time. It's a good thing I didn't do any of those things, because I've seen people running, puking, and falling on their asses in a puddle of their own sick, and it's not pretty.

Anyway, what threw me off so bad about Alix's revelation was the realization that the secret, dirty things that Monique had explained to me in detail had been practiced at least four times by my parents.

Yep, there was no mistake about it: my parents must have been engaged in active intercourse to conceive my brothers and me. Worse, they were probably naked. Did they actually enjoy it? "Oh Lord!" I silently prayed as my little eight-year-old self tried to digest this information.

The more I thought about it, the sicker I got. I simply couldn't see my parents associated with the same depraved guilt that made me enjoy Monique's forbidden stories. I came home that day and I couldn't even look my mother in the face.

If a responsible adult had explained things to me early

on, I would have known about it when Monique first arrived with her subversive ideas, and I could have said, "Old news, bitch!" If sex had been presented to me in a more natural way, I would have saved myself some serious trauma, and probably thousands of dollars in psychotherapy.

But my mother never talked to me about sex. However, when I had my first period, she automatically started throwing at me lines like "You better not show up pregnant" or "If you get knocked up, it will kill your father."

I should have told her, "Mom! Aren't you supposed to explain to me how to get pregnant, so I know what to avoid?" But my mother is not a sex talker, and the only evidence we have that she is a sex doer is that she gave birth to four kids.

Mom often referred to women who showed any sexual interest as *putas,* whores. For some reason it sounds even worse in Spanish. *Puta* — isn't that an ugly word? Every time Mom talked about *putas* they were juxtaposed with good mothers, making me assume that a good woman could never enjoy sex.

"That woman upstairs," Mom would say, referring to our divorced neighbor, "she goes out with her 'boyfriends,' all made up, with that mink coat, and she leaves her kids at home...Ugh! She should be ashamed of herself." I didn't know much about our upstairs neighbor, but the simple fact that she showed any romantic interest outside her motherly duties was enough to gross my mom out. Who knows? Maybe she was an exemplary mother, but by Mom's standards she was automatically placed in the whore bin. And for me — as a child — the boyfriends, the makeup, and the mink coat all became symbols of whoredom.

As years went by, I realized how unfair society was to women, how it gave men license to be sexual and forward, and how it forced women to be shy and virginal. Eventually, I questioned and dismissed Mom's arguments, but only intellectually. In my heart, I still carried the fear of that word: *puta*.

Sor Juana Inés de la Cruz—the Mexican nun who in the seventeenth century wrote the most subversive feminist poetry—has a great poem about prostitution:

> *Who is guiltier?*
> *The one who sins for the pay?*
> *Or the one who pays for the sin?*

A few months after my first night as a comfort provider, I gave Mom a book of Sor Juana's poems. She took a long time reading it, and never made a comment about it, until one day while she was compulsively cleaning the kitchen cabinets.

"That book that you gave me . . ."

"Which one?" I asked, pretending I didn't know which one she was referring to.

"The one by the nun."

"What about it?" I asked, mortally afraid of hearing her take on it.

"It's a good book," Mom said. "She was smart."

She didn't say one more word, and I didn't ask her anything else. There was a quiet understanding between us that has kept us together from that moment on.

But I'm getting ahead of myself. That night—my first night working for Madame—none of this had happened yet. So, while I was getting ready for my appointment, I was deeply tormented by my mother's ideas, while I somehow felt empowered by Sor Juana's words.

Who is guiltier?
The one who sins for the pay?
Or the one who pays for the sin?

I didn't care about the pay, but I still wondered: Was I whore? Was this a sin?

It was certainly a big mind-fuck. That much I can tell you.

CHAPTER 7

I won't lie to you. That first night I was shitting in my pants. I had a shot of anisette liquor — an old Cuban remedy to cure hiccups — to appease the butterflies in my stomach. Then I had another shot, and then another one. At the end, I was still nervous but also slightly buzzing.

I couldn't even tell you how long it took me to get dressed, because I basically pulled out everything I had in the closet, searching for the right outfit. In this anorexic society, shopping for clothes is nothing less than torture for the fatties.

When skinny people buy clothes, they look in the mirror to see how they look; when the heavy ones shop, we only look at the size that's written on the label. It doesn't matter how good or bad I look in a dress, what really matters to me is the label on the back. Is it a twelve? A fourteen? A sixteen? That's what hurts me or rejoices me.

As a consequence, I shop for practical purposes. I don't look for clothes for work, or leisure, or an elegant soirée. My goal is simply to cover my body with the garment that has the most generous label. In other words: if in reality I'm a sixteen but the label says twelve and the dress fits anyway, I buy several of those in different colors.

I understand that the garment industry is well aware of the psychological effect of their labels, and they're mislabeling everything they do to hook the fatties. I know that it's a marketing scam, but it works on me. It makes me think I'm thinner, and that makes me — sadly — happy.

I usually go for blazers, and tunics, always conservative, always vertical lines, lots of blacks, and grays, and dark blues. That's the New York palette, but it's also a fat thing. We all know that dark colors make you look skinnier.

Anyway, there I was, looking at this closet full of black and blue fake size-twelves, but with not one sexy thing to wear.

"What the hell do you wear on your first night as a whore?" I caught myself saying — half joking, half serious — as I grew more and more impatient with my wardrobe. After much browsing, I ended up picking something black — duh! — a little skirt ensemble that comes with a short jacket, and a red silk blouse that's a bit too much to wear to the office, but not terribly trashy either.

Pearls? No pearls? I settled for a gold chain with a crystal pendant that was supposed to keep evil away. My aunt Carmita gave it to me when I turned fifteen and everyone thought I could get pregnant at the drop of a hat.

For me, turning fifteen wasn't the thrill that you would expect in a Cuban American girl. Instead of throwing a big *quinceañera* party, we went to church and then a Cuban restaurant for a big meal — as if we didn't eat Cuban food every day of the year. My father, who was a very conservative guy, gave me a choice: either they would throw me a party, or they would give me the money for my college tuition. I was

smart enough to choose college, which turned out to be a
relief for my parents, first because it demonstrated that I was
an intelligent and mature girl, and second because the last
thing they wanted was to celebrate my quince with a bunch
of teenage boys who — given the excuse of a waltz — could
rub themselves up against me.

As I recalled these "fond" memories, I stood in front of my
bedroom mirror and pulled my hair up in a tight bun, chose
a pair of small gold hoops, threw my cell, my Mace, and my
lipstick in my bag, and headed out of my apartment, carefully leaving the proverbial note for Lillian and the police on
the coffee table: "Lillian, if you are reading this, it's because
I have disappeared. Please tell the cops to track down Natasha Sokolov..." In a nutshell, I wrote the equivalent of "The
Russian Madame made me do it," but as I was writing it I
realized that the note wasn't fair. I was an adult, and whatever
I decided to do that night — out of curiosity, desperation, or
stupidity — was very much my responsibility. This thought
made me feel empowered. I was in charge of my destiny, and
that felt good. If I had the balls to descend into hell, I should
have them also to fight my way out of it.

I stepped out of my building and found a black and elegant limo waiting for me. It had a sign with the letter "B"
posted on the window. As soon as I approached it, the driver
rushed out of the car to open the door for me.

"Good evening, Miss B. My name is Alberto, and I will
be your driver," he said respectfully.

"Nice to meet you, Alberto."

I immediately realized that Alberto was Latino and
probably in his early forties. He was dark-skinned, tall, and
well built. He looked like one of those Dominican baseball
players that sports fans worship. He was nice and proper — not

chummy, like some of us can be when we run into another Latino. As a matter of fact, he was so serious that I wondered if he knew what I was doing and maybe disapproved of it. Damn the guilt! I was too scared to talk, so I kept quiet. I simultaneously wanted to do this and not to do it. The antagonizing voices in my head were enough distraction to keep me company as we traveled from my apartment in the West Village to the Upper West Side.

"I will be waiting for you downstairs to bring you back home after you are done," Alberto told me briefly, making eye contact with me through the rearview mirror.

"How long do you think this will take?" I asked, trying to get more information than the cryptic Madame had given me.

"I'll be waiting for you no matter how long it takes," he responded.

His answer made me feel good and protected, but it didn't disclose one bit of information on what I was about to encounter. So far, all I knew was that my customer had money, because Madame had said "top dollar" in our conversation, but when the limo pulled over at the fanciest building on Central Park West, this confirmed that my customer had to be loaded.

Only extremely rich people could live in a place like this, I thought to myself. *People who take about eighty years to amass their fortune. This guy has to be eighty years old at least. He's probably as old as the guy who complimented me on the boardwalk.* But it didn't matter how old he was; I was already there, and I was going to go for it, so there was no point in speculating.

The doorman opened the door of the car for me.

"Good evening, madam. Mr. Rauscher is waiting for you."

I rose out of the car with wobbly steps, but as soon as I

started crossing the lobby escorted by the doorman, I felt the blood rushing back into my limbs. Yeah, I was scared, but I could pull this off.

What I didn't know at the time was that in extremely fancy New York buildings the doorman escorts you all the way up to the floor you are going to, and indicates the door you will knock on. They don't even bother putting numbers on the doors. If you don't know where you're going, you shouldn't be roaming down the hallways to begin with.

Anyway, he pointed to the door at the end of the corridor, and I stepped out of the elevator, admiring the decor: the lamps, the carpets, the flowers. There were better furnishings in the hallway of this damn building than in the living room of any house I had ever been to. I swear that you could smell the stench of money just by standing in the hall. As I passed a Venetian mirror, I decided to stop to check myself out and reapply my lipstick, with trembling hands.

I looked in the mirror, and suddenly I wanted to cry. I've heard that women with anorexia can be walking skeletons but when they look in the mirror they can't see themselves, they just see fat. I was having a similar problem. When I looked in the mirror I didn't see myself, I just saw a collection of flaws. In my mind, the example of beauty was someone like Nicole Kidman, and I was far — way far — from that. I didn't have her height, I didn't have her figure, or her bone structure, and no matter what I did, I'd never have it.

"I will never be like Nicole Kidman...I will never be like Nicole Kidman..." I said out loud while I stood there. And then an incredible shift of gears took place, and I started laughing.

"Why the fuck do I have to look like Nicole Kidman?" I said to myself, and I decided to give myself an improvised makeover.

With the attitude of a gay and ruthless interior decorator determined to refurbish a cheesy apartment, I observed myself in the mirror. "What the hell is that, reflected in front of me?" Here I was selling myself for the first time, and I just looked like a frumpy executive assistant (nothing wrong with being an executive assistant, by the way; I've been a secretary myself several times). I looked old, matronly, and boring.

Something had to be done, so I opened my blouse one button, then two buttons, then three buttons, and then I went back to one, but I pushed my boobs up so high that I could almost rest my chin on them.

"Good," I said.

I took off my jacket—turned out it looked better hanging over my right shoulder than on me—I rolled up the sleeves of my shirt—which I think gave me a little bit of a Sharon Stone vibe—and then I started working on my hair. I undid my tight bun—ugh, no good, my hair ended up all over. I tried to go back to the bun, but it was already too late. Cuban hair—or at least my Cuban hair—has a mind of its own, and once you unleash it, it takes hours to tame it again. What could I do? I guess I could get it wet and go for the "just out of the shower" look. I found a flower vase next to the mirror. Grabbing the vase, I thought about using the water to dampen my hair. But as soon as I poured some water on my hand, I realized the water stank—duh! After drying my hands with the velvet drapes, I remembered—duh again—I had hair gel in my bag. I applied the gel profusely, got my wet-curls look, and then looked in the mirror again.

Better. Not "Wow!" but definitely better. When my hair is wild, it is very wild. After a childhood of learning to tame it toward a sleek look, I felt that letting my curls go wild was letting myself go wild as well. Tonight I was pretending to be a whore, so I had to play the part. The problem is that with my hair down—and curled in all its glory—the little gold hoops that I was wearing got completely lost in the jungle. I needed to spice that up somehow. That's when I noticed the chandelier. A beautiful crystal chandelier was hanging from the ceiling. Should I? Shouldn't I?

"It's for a good cause," I told myself. I pulled up a chair, climbed on it, and reached out for two strings of crystals. There were so many of them in that lamp that nobody would notice the missing beads. They would match my virginity pendant nicely. After one last look in the mirror, I took off my glasses, pulled up my skirt a bit more, and finally walked toward Mr. Rauscher's door.

I was ready. And as I stood in front of the door with my curls, my cleavage, my crystal earrings, and my jacket hanging—very casually—over my shoulder, I rang the doorbell. I waited for my first customer with my knees shaking, my heart pounding, my mind racing, and the profound knowledge that this was the beginning of something and the end of something else. But the beginning and the end of what?

CHAPTER 8

The door opened and — predictably — a butler was on the other side. We've all seen butlers in movies, but I had never seen one in real life. He had a butler's face that perfectly matched his butler's uniform. I couldn't imagine that this guy ever considered doing anything in his life other than being a butler or playing one on TV.

"Hello," I said with the deepest and sexiest voice I could fake.

"Welcome, madam. Please follow me."

And he talked like a butler too. Cool. Very proper, very courteous, but detached at the same time.

"My name is B. What is your name?" I said, trying to become his friend.

"My name is Bradley, madam."

"How long have you worked here, Bradley?"

"Eleven years, madam."

"So Mr. Rauscher must be a nice guy," I said, hoping to get a scoop on the eighty-year-old pervert I was about to encounter. Maybe Bradley would turn around and, risking his job, advise me to run for my life. But, no, Bradley remained proper, courteous and detached.

"Mr. Rauscher is no less than a gentleman."

Okay, no point in trying to squeeze blood out of this rock. Suddenly I got distracted by the decor of the sumptuous apartment, and everything I learned in my art-history classes came to mind. First I noticed the centerpiece of the vestibule. Proudly displayed on a pedestal was a prehistoric sculpture that looked a lot like the *Venus of Willendorf.* That Venus looks a bit like a raw piece of rock, but when you look at it carefully, you start noticing human features—mainly enormous breasts and a huge ass. It happens to be an ancient representation of a rather fat woman. "A goddess of fertility," my teacher Grazia explained to me in art class.

I next noticed the walls, which were covered with huge Botero and Rubens—or at least Rubenesque—paintings. I would have checked the signature on the canvas, but I wasn't wearing my glasses, so I could barely see my hand in front of my face.

I followed Bradley, hallway after hallway, to the room where I was supposed to meet my customer. *My customer.* Just thinking it freaked me out, but the whole adventure had a twisted allure to it. So I kept walking right behind Bradley, flanked by these oversized images of voluptuous women being abducted by strong warriors. It certainly takes a nice set of muscles to abduct me, that much I can tell you.

"Nice pad!" I said and Bradley finally cracked a smile, making me feel as if I had conquered the tip of Mount Everest.

"Mr. Rauscher will be with you in a moment," he said as he opened the door of the library for me and immediately disappeared. I was relieved to see that I was not being taken to a bedroom. Maybe Madame was right, and sex wasn't going to be part of the agenda. But, then, what the hell did this senior citizen want from me?

Incapable of sitting still and with nothing else to do, I started looking at the artwork in the library. The walls were covered with mahogany bookcases filled with leather-clad volumes, but he had left a little space here and there to display a collection of ancient illustrations from the *Kama Sutra*. I believe that most people think that in ancient times sex was always very boring, very reproductive, certainly nothing kinky. Well, if you take one look at this stuff, you'll change your mind. Mr. Rauscher's illustrations looked like sex at Le Cirque d'Soleil. I mean, those were positions I couldn't do even if I wanted to. So Mr. Rauscher was a dirty old man after all: one with a lot of money who — judging by his art collection — probably was on the mailing list of Sotheby's.

The sound of the door opening caught me by surprise and almost made me jump to the ceiling.

"I'm sorry for making you wait," he said with his cavernous voice and his thick German accent.

I turned around and finally met face to face with my client. He was younger than I'd thought, and not bad-looking at all: tall, blue-eyed, square-jawed, mid-fifties, very well preserved, and with salt-and-pepper hair. He was wearing a shirt, slacks, and an elegant navy blue velvet robe on top of it. If he were one of the paintings on his own wall, his title might be *Millionaire at Home*. Saying that he looked Aryan would be an understatement; Mr. Rauscher looked like the hot Nazi officer from a spy movie, the one you feel guilty about lusting after because he is so evil. He walked up to me and extended his hand.

"Hello, I'm Ludwig."

"I'm B," I replied, shaking his hand, and trying to control my shaky knees.

"Would you like something to drink, B?"

I wanted a Diet Coke, but I realized that it didn't sound very sexy, so I went for what I knew.

"You don't happen to have anisette, do you?"

"On the rocks?" he asked promptly.

"Sure," I said.

Mr. Rauscher opened a secret door in the wood paneling, revealing a hidden and very well stocked bar. Once again, my hands got cold, my mouth got dry, and I felt like running away. Mr. Rauscher handed me the drink, and his phone rang almost immediately.

"Excuse me, please," he said courteously.

He picked up the phone, listened for a second, replied something in German, and then hung up.

"Forgive me, but there is a matter that requires my immediate attention," he said, and, promising that he would be back shortly, he left me alone in the room, and on the verge of a panic attack.

After he left, I had a moment to regroup. Slut-me, virgin-me, cautious-me, paranoid-me, wild-me, and raised-by-Catholic-Cuban-parents-me—we all had a little powwow inside my head that I'll try to reproduce.

"You better get your ass out of here immediately!"

"But you're here already, the guy is loaded and not bad-looking at all. Why can't you stick around and see what happens?"

"What? Even more reason to get out of here now: you'll let your guard down because he's handsome, and before you know it he'll slash your throat and throw your body into the river."

"A rich guy like this won't drag a corpse to the riverside!"

"Of course, he'll send the butler. Have you considered that he might have put something in your drink already?"

"Relax! You're a big girl. You know how to defend yourself!"

"I'm sure you can defend yourself, but since when did you turn into a whore?"

Believe it or not, that last remark was the one that put the fire under my ass and made me decide to abort the operation and get the hell out of there as soon as possible. But I couldn't just get up and leave. I had to wait for him and — at least — apologize. To make a silent statement, I buttoned up my shirt, pulled down my skirt, and then started working on a little speech. I would say something like "Ludwig, I don't know how to say this, I don't want to disappoint you or hurt your feelings, but I just can't go through with this. I understand that you have expectations, desires, manly needs, but I've never done anything like this in my life, and I don't think I can go through with it." I know, my rehearsed spiel sounded way too corny, but I was in a panic, okay?

How would he react? Would he turn violent? Would he force me into something? He was a pretty strong guy, and I could tell that he went to the gym a lot. Maybe he was like one of the gladiators in his paintings: he could lift a girl of my size, flip her around, and rape her if he set his mind to it. And he was German — and we all know the kind of reputation that Hollywood has built for the Germans because of World War II.

In the middle of all these considerations, the door swung open and Bradley walked in with an envelope.

"Mr. Rauscher wanted me to give you this."

I took the envelope with trembling hands and found a stack of hundred-dollar bills inside.

"There's a little extra for your trouble, and if you could follow me to the exit," Bradley added.

Totally confused, I started following Bradley toward the exit. I managed to pose a question as we walked back through Mr. Rauscher's fat museum.

"Wait a minute, Bradley, is he not coming back?"

"That's correct, madam. He wants to thank you for your time and let you know that your services are no longer needed."

"So we're not gonna..." I didn't know how to complete the sentence, since Madame never really clued me in on what Mr. Rauscher wanted.

"No, madam, you're not," Bradley stated.

That's when it finally hit me: Mr. Rauscher was kicking me out. He met me, didn't like me, and decided to pay me and send me home. I wasn't even worth his time. Needless to say, I was beyond pissed.

I jumped ahead of Bradley, blocked the exit, and confronted him face to face.

"Wait a fucking minute, Bradford!"

"Bradley, madam."

I knew that I said his name wrong. I did it on purpose. I wanted him to get angry — as angry as I was. If I was going to be rejected, I wanted to hear the reason.

"I want to know exactly why Mr. Rauscher is suddenly *not* interested."

"I'm afraid that I'm not allowed to discuss that, madam," he answered.

I had nothing to lose, so I shot, point-blank.

"Is it because of my weight?"

"I'm really not allowed..."

"I am not leaving until I get a straight answer from you or from that German jerk!"

"Madam, I must insist..."

"Is it because of my weight?" I yelled.

"Madam..." he said, trying for the last time not to yell back. I pushed him even harder.

"Is it because of my weight?" I shouted.

Clearly fed up by the scene, Bradley took a deep breath, looked me in the eye, and finally answered. "Yes, it's because of your weight, madam."

Funny how people can be. Here I was, yelling, hollering, demanding an answer—by force almost—and then, when the answer came, the answer that I was expecting, the answer that had tormented me all my adult life, it still hurt me. It hurt like a slap on the face. Emotionally, I dropped to the floor.

Embarrassed, humiliated, and defeated, I looked down to the ground, turned around, and slowly dragged my feet out of the apartment. Once outside, with tears in my eyes, I looked back at Bradley and with a tiny thread of voice I managed to ask him, "Am I *that* fat?"

I asked so softly that I'm surprised he even heard me.

Bradley, who was probably more than sick of me by now, simply replied, "Madam, you're not fat enough," and slammed the door in my face.

You might be laughing. Good for you. But guess what, though? I wasn't. I was even more furious. The nerve! To tell me, someone who has dragged her body around for so many years, that I wasn't *fat enough* was like telling the Elephant Man that he was fired from the sideshow because he wasn't ugly enough.

I had no dignity left, so I started banging on the door.

"What do you mean, I'm not fat enough? Bradley! Bradley! I'll show that son of a bitch what fat looks like, goddamnit! Bradley!!!"

Bradley must have called Security, because almost immediately the elevator opened and the doorman held the door, indicating that it was time for me to leave. Defeated, I walked away from Mr. Rauscher's apartment. As I got to the elevator, my cell phone rang. It was Madame.

"Madame?"

"How was it?" she asked.

"Horrible!" I whimpered.

"Did he pay you?"

"Yes, he paid, but who cares? According to him, I'm not fat enough! Can you believe that?"

The doorman pretended not to be paying attention, but I totally knew that he was following every word of our conversation, so — putting Madame on hold — I decided to focus-group with him.

"How much do you think I weigh?" I asked him.

"I couldn't tell, miss."

"Oh, come on, give it a shot."

"Hmm. One hundred and twenty?"

Talk about being polite. In any other circumstance I would have been flattered, but now I was just annoyed.

"Give me a fucking break!" I screamed. If you know me, you would know that I don't throw the f-word around too easily, but clearly this issue was pushing my buttons.

"Come on!" I insisted. "Try a little harder."

"I'm really bad at this," he said.

"Let's put it this way, if you saw me in the corner, you'd say 'that fat chick in the corner,' right?"

"Er . . . well . . . I don't know . . . Yeah, most likely."

"Thank you very much." That was exactly what I needed to hear at that moment. By then we were already stepping out of the building and approaching the car. I was still on the phone with Madame.

"See? Even the doorman can tell that I'm fat! What the hell is wrong with this moron?"

Madame, with a peace that almost bothered me, kept trying to calm me down by educating me in the tricks of the trade.

"B, this is your first and most important lesson: the customer is always right."

"What do you mean?" I replied.

"You got paid, right?"

"Right..."

"So whatever he wants to do or not is his business, not yours."

"But, Madame, you're not listening to me! He thinks that I am—"

"B," she said very seriously, "this is your second and equally important lesson: what other people think of you is none of your business."

"But—"

"B, stop it! Think!" she said, and she was so serious that I actually stopped yapping for a second. "He paid you for your time. It's not about what you want, it's about what he wants."

As I was trying to process the logic of her argument, we arrived at the limo. The doorman opened the car, I stepped in, and almost had a heart attack when I found Madame comfortably sitting in the backseat, with her cell phone in hand.

"What are you doing here?" I asked.

"I wasn't going to send you alone on your first job!" she said as if she had been sitting outside kindergarten on my first day of school. Crazy as it was, I felt a certain tenderness that made me collapse in her arms crying.

"My first job? Clearly I'm not even 'fat enough' to do this," I sobbed.

She held me in her arms and softly whispered in my ear, "Honey, that crazy bastard does the same thing to every girl I've sent."

"He's done this before?" I asked.

"Over and over."

"What?" I yelled, pushing her away. "And you sent me to this asshole just to be rejected?"

I got out of the car in one swift motion—thank God it was waiting for the red light to change. This revelation was just way too much for one night. Not for anything I closed the deal with this woman in a roller coaster. It was going to be an emotional one for me.

"B, come on!" she said as the car followed me down the street.

"How could you?" I cried.

I had left Mr. Rauscher's money on the seat of the car, so Madame pulled it out and started counting it. The nerve!

"B, don't be silly! It's easy money! Look!" she said, dangling the stack of bills in my direction.

"Don't you understand that I don't care about the money? I feel like shit!"

"I'll never send you again to someone like him. I promise. I just needed to see if you could take it."

"Oh! You wanted to see if I could take rejection. I guess, being the whale that I am, I should be used to it, right?"

That's when she went from sweet to sarcastic. She had a way of switching back and forth that always threw me off.

"Oh, boo-hoo!" she said, mocking me. "Poor little me!"

"Yeah, poor little me!" I snapped back.

"Honey, there are no victims, only volunteers."

I could have punched her. She made me think of my mother at her worst.

"Look," she said, switching from sarcastic to impatient. "I don't have time for this, I have a business to run. If you want to feel like a victim, go home, cry on your pillow, and stop wasting my time. But if you want to learn something from this experience, get back in the car, and let's talk like civilized people."

Her words made me feel like a screaming baby having a temper tantrum. I felt weak and silly and immature — but I continued walking as if I were Joan of Arc on my way to the bonfire. However, she had made a dent in my will, and she probably noticed it, because she softened her touch.

"B, you know that he's a moron! Are you feeling bad because a moron doesn't like you?"

"Yes! I feel bad because a moron doesn't like me!"

"Why?"

I stopped walking. I needed to think; even though I seem to have an answer for everything, I didn't have an answer for this.

The limo stopped next to me, and Madame, still sitting by the window, waited patiently, knowing that I had finally reached a dead end.

I took a deep breath, and — still frowning — I stepped back into the limo. Madame smiled and handed back to me a stack of bills, which I took reluctantly.

"Congratulations," she said.

"For taking the money?" I asked.

"No. For growing up."

Was I growing up? I had no idea. I just needed a bit of time to understand what this crazy Russian Madame was telling me. If she was trying to screw with my pattern of thinking, she was off to a damn good start.

CHAPTER 9

*A*ll my Latino friends in school had what, to me, seemed like a determining influence in their lives: an *abuela*. They all had a granny that lived at home with the family. For everybody else, it might be acceptable to send Granny to a nursing home, but for Latinos, sending *la abuela* to an institution is unthinkable. If there's money, she gets her own house or apartment next door. If there's no money, she will live in the same home with the family, and it's very likely that she'll share a bedroom with the youngest kid. That's how it works, and nobody can question that. Some of my friends had *both* grannies living with them, for better or for worse.

Unfortunately, I grew up missing the granny link. My granny Brígida died when my father was only fifteen, so she wasn't around when I was growing up. My granny Celia refused to leave Cuba. She hated Castro, but she just couldn't move to another country with a different language at seventy. On top of that, leaving Cuba meant leaving her eight sons and thirty-two grandsons behind, and that was something her poor heart just couldn't take. So, basically, I grew up grandmotherless.

My mom, like most moms nowadays, had to go to work, so I ended up in the hands of idiotic nannies like Ino, and a long list of other caretakers for whom I have little sympathy. Now that Mom is semi-retired and I see her being a granny with my nephews, I realize how special the bond that a grandmother establishes with her grandsons is. It can be a bit irritating when I see that Mom didn't let us get away with half the crap she condones in her grandsons, but I understand that maybe this is the right balance of life. Parents are supposed to be strict, and grandparents overindulgent. But since I had no granny, I ended up only with the strict side of the equation. And since the amount of time that my mom could dedicate to me was limited by her responsibilities in the family business and fulfilling her family's basic needs, I ended up with a mom who only paid attention to me when I needed to be yelled at.

Everything has been understood and processed in psychotherapy: my mom did what she had to do, considering her circumstances. I forgot and forgave all these growing pains a long time ago. But here's my problem: I never had an older woman who sat down calmly with me to explain the mysteries of life, and I'm not just referring to sex or menstruation. I mean deeper and subtler tips on how to grow up to be a woman, things that you can only learn with a patient coach.

I'm telling you all this because that night, after I got back in the limo with Madame, made peace with her, and understood that she had every right to test my emotional capacity to perform the job that she was recruiting me for, she invited me to go to her apartment. And that brought up all those nonexistent memories of my absent grandmothers.

Madame's loft was part of an old factory in the Long Island City section of Queens. It was a huge space, with skylights, French windows, tons of antiques, and colorful carpets and pillows.

Have you ever seen *Citizen Kane*? I bring it up because Madame's apartment looked a bit like the Xanadu palace of Charles Foster Kane: exotic and overdone, with every possible antique from every possible corner of the world. Delft porcelain from the Netherlands, a silver samovar from St. Petersburg, ivory carvings from China, ceremonial masks from Africa. Every single element in that room had a story to tell.

Among the many objects that she had lying around was a clothing rack full of elaborate evening gowns. While I looked around, fascinated by the Renaissance paintings and the marble sculptures, Madame went through the clothing rack fast, picking large and elegant dresses that she threw on the couch behind her.

"Take these dresses. I have the feeling that you don't have anything decent in your closet. Tomorrow, call Gerik," she said, referring to the Russian optometrist of her choice. "He'll give you a good price on your contacts. Tell him I sent you. Your eyes are beautiful. You have to show them. If you get colored contacts, just do hazelnut, or honey—don't do blue or green. Those look too fake."

"I've had contacts in the past, but I've been so crazy busy at work that I haven't had time to get a new prescription," I apologized.

"Well, get them now. Don't give up your looks for your job," she advised.

At that point I found a photograph of Madame in what I assumed was her twenties.

"Wow! Is this you?" I asked.

She was breathtaking. She reminded me of a young Ann-Margret, with a fabulous figure and long red hair.

"Yes," she said without paying much attention. "I was thinner then, but at my age a woman has to trade her face for her ass."

"What?" I had never heard that before.

"Honey," she explained, "past a certain age, the skinnier you are, the older you'll look. Your figure might be slim, but you'll look wrinkled and emaciated. If you keep some weight on—she winked at me—"your ass will be bigger, but your face will stay tight and soft."

I'd never thought about that. Maybe that's why Madame—who was well into her sixties—had the youthful glow of a matron of the Pyrenees, with virtually no wrinkles, and pores so tight you couldn't see them with a microscope if you tried.

As I was entertaining those thoughts, I found a bunch of diplomas hanging on the wall.

"Do you have a Ph.D. in psychology?" I asked, surprised.

"I have three of them."

"You have three doctorates in psychology? How come?"

"I like people," she replied, without giving any importance to her academic accomplishments.

"Then why don't you just work as a therapist?" I asked.

"Well, I like people . . . but I like money too." She smiled.

"So why do you prepare taxes, then? That can't pay well. Do you do it just to recruit girls?" I asked with a drop of sarcasm.

She laughed. "I only do it once a year, in April. I'm good with numbers, it keeps my mind active, and I enjoy meeting new people. I don't like watching movies; I prefer watching people. Reality is much more interesting than fiction."

As she invited me to sit next to her on her big, comfortable couch packed with silky pillows, she pulled out a little red cell phone.

"This is going to be your work cell phone," she said. "Don't give this number to anybody. Only I will call you on this line. I'll call you every day at noon to give you your instructions, and if you ever need to reach me, just press one. Alberto will be your driver and bodyguard. If you ever have a problem with a customer, press two, and he'll come in to help you out. If you get paid in cash, you will deposit twenty percent of the payment — including the tip — into my account," she said as she gave me a piece of paper with a number written on it. "Then you'll call me, and you'll tell me the amount and the number of the transaction. Yes?"

"Yes," I replied. "But, you swear that I will *not* be expected to have sex with anyone, right?"

"Honey, there are better things than sex."

"What do you mean by that?" I said, confused.

"Honey . . . sex is totally overrated. And most people only have bad sex anyway."

"I've never had bad sex," I defended myself.

Madame looked me in the eye.

"Honey, if you think you've never had bad sex, chances are you've never had good sex either."

And with that line she shut me up.

"Let me explain," she continued. "My clients are not into sex per se. They have fetishes. It changes from customer to customer but, essentially, they are buying your trust. Understand?"

"No."

"Okay, let me put it this way," she said, taking a deep breath, "do you like when people make fun of you?"

"No."

"Well, my customers don't like it either. So it doesn't matter how silly or weird their requests are—do not ever make fun of them. They are putting themselves in a very vulnerable position, and they pay well to make sure that they can trust you, and that it all remains confidential. If they ask for something you don't want to do, just say no, but *don't judge them*. Understand?"

I nodded, but I still didn't understand—I was so naïve. Madame continued while casually retouching her lipstick.

"Now . . . can you take a little constructive criticism?" she said.

"Sure, I guess," and once again I was surprised to see how afraid I was of *any* criticism.

"You dress to hide. From now on, you have to dress to show."

"Show what?"

"Your assets. You can borrow these dresses until you find your style, but I want to see cleavage and I want to see ass. I want you to wear jewelry that trickles between your breasts. You have a gorgeous bust, so always bring attention to it."

"Gee . . . thanks," I said, realizing that I had been hiding my breasts all my life.

"But most of all," she continued, "I want to see you comfortable in your skin, because nothing is sexier than a woman who's comfortable with her body. Cotton might be the fabric of life, but—trust me—spandex is the fabric of love. Now: your posture . . ."

"What about my posture?" I asked.

"You slouch."

"I do?" Honest to God, I didn't know it—but I stiffened up immediately.

"Now you look like a soldier," she said, and I collapsed in my bones, slouching again. Madame lifted her head up as if she were giving a master class at Harvard, and explained, "The posture comes from within: when you love yourself, you offer yourself. The head is high, so that you can look at everyone straight in the eye. The expression is confident. The lips are soft, ready to be kissed. Your bosom rests in bloom under your chin, your shoulders are relaxed, so your arms are open and free to embrace the man that madly desires you. And never, *never* forget" — she looked at me in the eye when she said this — "that *you are* beautiful."

My reaction to her statement was completely physical. I squirmed, and sank in the couch.

"Well, that's the problem," I said.

"What?"

"I don't feel beautiful."

Vaguely annoyed by my whiny attitude, she just looked at me — mercilessly — and said, "Well, honey, you're going to have to fake it until you make it. Yes?"

"Yes," I said, as if I were signing up to cross the North Pole on my knees.

"Honey, the obstacle is in your mind. It's not what you have, it's how you feel about it."

I wished I could believe her. But as she kept giving me all the advice that I imagined my grandmothers would have given me, had they been around, I fell in love with her.

"Those shoes are too high and too small for your feet. The angle of the heel is too steep. Have you noticed that you walk with difficulty? It looks like you're about to fall on your face — and that is *not* sexy. You must wear comfortable shoes. What size are you?"

"Seven and a half, eight."

"Try these," she said as she handed me a pair of platform shoes. "They're high, but the angle is not so sharp. What do you use in the shower?"

"Antibacterial soap and a rag."

She picked up a cosmetic bag and handed it to me.

"You will be worshipped from head to toe," she said, "so I want you to be nice and soft. This is what you're going to do until your skin gets up to speed..."

She adopted a familiar pose that looked like a lesson in martial arts: with both arms extended and her palms exposed, she started alternating circular motions with her hands.

"I want you to...exfoliate...moisturize...exfoliate...moisturize..."

"It's like *The Karate Kid*!" I laughed. "Wax on, wax off—right?"

"Exactly, just like *The Karate Kid*."

I was laughing, but she wasn't laughing with me.

"I'm serious. You have to learn to nurture your skin," she continued. "I also want you to use a firming cream, and every time you pamper yourself I want you to do it with love. Enjoy your body the same way others will enjoy it. *It makes a difference.*"

Damn, the wisdom coming out of this woman's mouth! It felt like the Holy Scriptures taken from the pages of *Cosmopolitan*. Part of me thought that it was all so silly, and the other part of me was deeply grateful for having her address all these things with me. I wanted to hug her. I felt like I was borrowing her strength. But she needed to hit me one more time.

"And you wear too much makeup. Makeup is to enhance, not to cover. If you cover your face, you are covering your natural glow, and those colors you use don't look good on you. They look artificial."

"What kind of makeup should I use then?"

"I prefer Susie May."

"Susie May?" I said, surprised that she wasn't suggesting some exotic and absurdly expensive brand. "They don't even sell it in stores! You have to find a soccer mom who sells it! Shouldn't I use something a little more—?" I started saying but she cut me off.

"I prefer Susie May," she declared to end the discussion.

Overwhelmed by my own ignorance, I dared to joke, "Should I go on a talk show and get a makeover or something?"

Finally, Madame laughed.

"Honey, the only makeover that really works," she said while tapping her index finger against my forehead, "happens right here. Mind over matter."

I know, Madame's advice sounded a lot like "Dear Abby," but this woman was actually teaching me a course in quantum physics. Needless to say, that night I went to my apartment and I soaked and scrubbed and moisturized my whole body, and—for the first time in my life—I touched and caressed my skin with love and admiration.

And it felt great.

CHAPTER 10

I have a constant battle with time. I have too much or too little of it. I can't seem to measure it objectively. Sometimes it feels that a weekend flies by, and sometimes Saturday and Sunday can feel like a lifetime. This particular weekend with Madame felt like a month spent away from home, and coming back to the office on Monday was particularly sad. I dragged myself in to work, as if I had just arrived from a holiday in the Bahamas, resenting the very thought of sitting by my desk—never mind dealing with Bonnie.

I decided to lie low and just hang on to my weekend in my mind. I kept myself semi-busy doing some old paperwork, while keeping an obsessive eye on the red cell phone that I got from Madame. I went on the Web, looking for a Susie Day representative in my neighborhood, and it turned out that Mary Pringle, Bonnie's assistant, was one of them.

Until that day, I knew very little about Mary Pringle. The one thing I knew was that she had the kind of patience that belonged in a nursing home, and that's why she kept a job that no other secretary in the world would take. She was the last person that you would think was selling Susie Day products in the office. She wasn't social like Lillian, or exuberant like Madame. Mary was black, petite, quiet, and very low-key. She dressed impeccably, but maybe a little too conservatively for someone in her twenties.

"Hey, Mary! So — do you still sell Susie Day makeup?" I asked her as I approached her cubicle.

From the way Mary reacted, you would think I asked her if she was selling crack.

"Hush!" she said, lowering her voice and her head, as if it were harder to hear her when she was hunching over. "Do you want to have a coffee?" she whispered.

"Sure," I whispered back, "but what's the problem?"

"Shhhh!" she shut me up while pointing toward Bonnie's den.

She didn't need to explain anything else. I knew exactly what was going on, but it would always be fun to hear the gruesome details directly from Mary.

"She has a two-hour meeting," Mary whispered, referring to Bonnie. "Wait for my instructions."

So I went back to my desk, and five minutes later she walked by and very discreetly dropped me a note asking me to meet her in the coffee shop across the street in half an hour.

"¡Gracias por venir!" Mary greeted me when I walked into the shop.

"I didn't know you spoke Spanish," I said, truly surprised. "¿De dónde eres?" I asked her, wondering what her Latin roots were.

"Mi familia es de Panamá, but I was born in Brooklyn," she answered in perfect Spanglish.

It's amazing how wrong I can be about certain people. I always had the impression that Mary was very serious and uptight, but the truth is that, with all the rushing around that was going on in the office, I never took the time to sit down and talk to her. I spent years sharing the same office space with this woman, and I had no idea who she was as a person. I didn't even know how beautiful her smile was until I found her sitting at the coffee shop with all her catalogues and samples on display.

"When Bonnie realized that I was selling makeup at the office, she made a huge deal about it and almost got me fired," she explained.

This was so typically Bonnie. It was as if having an assistant make some extra cash selling makeup could threaten the very fiber of the organization, and the future of the advertising community.

"Every so often she sends her friends to ask me if I'm selling, just to check on me and see if I'm still doing it at the office. She didn't send you, did she?"

"Mary," I said, trying to put it nicely, "I'm not her friend."

"Thank God, B, because if I told you the things she says behind your back . . . I mean, she hates everybody, but you — I think she's afraid of you."

Afraid of me? I never thought that Bonnie could be afraid of anybody.

"I do have an idea of how she feels about me," I said.

"But it's not fair. You are too talented. She's holding you back, and she's doing it on purpose."

"I just don't know how to fight her back," I replied.

"Don't worry," she said, holding my hand, "we'll come up with something, but in the meantime . . . let me show you what I've got. How did you get interested in Susie May?"

Obviously, I couldn't answer that truthfully, so I came up with something on the fly. "My godmother told me about it."

"Your fairy godmother?" She laughed.

"Yes." I smiled. "My fairy godmother."

Mary started presenting her products, and as we browsed through her catalogues, I started paying attention to her face. That's when I realized that she knew how to work wonders with makeup. She applied it so well that you could swear she was wearing nothing. I suddenly felt like I was in the presence of a Rembrandt, or a Vermeer. Her face was so well crafted that you couldn't even imagine the amount of work and thinking that lay behind it. Mary had turned her face into her own work of art.

"Can I tell you what I would do to your face?" she asked, trying to control her excitement.

"Of course!" I said. With the enthusiasm of a chef working for the first time in a brand-new kitchen, she jumped off her seat, cleaned up my face with a handy wipe, and started applying shades and lip liner in all the right places.

"The lip liner and the lipstick should be different, but not noticeably different, see?" she said, putting a little mirror in front of my face. I saw it, and I had to agree.

She instructed me on the elusive art of mixing different hues of eye shadow, preparing the skin for foundation, and the advantages of using translucent powder—instead of colored—for someone with my complexion.

I noticed that she was thrilled that I wanted to listen to her, and that's when I realized that you could only work for someone like Bonnie if you kept quiet, so Mary had been pretending all these years that she didn't have anything to say. Given the freedom to talk, she would come alive in a way that I had never imagined.

Her demonstration was so impressive that the two Mexican ladies who work behind the counter of the coffee shop placed makeup orders at the same time I did. Mary was ecstatic.

Back in the office — about an hour later — I got a visit from Lillian at my desk.

"Hey, B!"

It was close to noon, and I was so focused on the red cell phone that she caught me off guard, making me jump to the ceiling.

"You scared the hell out of me!" I said.

Lillian immediately noticed my new cell phone.

"I love your phone! Is it new? Does it have a camera? Does it play videos?"

Since Lillian doesn't know the meaning of the word "boundaries," she helped herself to it. But it's never too late to learn, so, marking my territory, I snatched it right back from her.

"Give me that!"

"What's wrong with you?" she said, more surprised than offended.

"I'm waiting for a phone call."

"Okay, okay, no need to get all bitchy. Do you want to come to a fund-raiser tonight?"

"I have plans for tonight," I said.

"Tonight? On a Monday?"

"Well, aren't you the one who says that Mondays are the new Tuesdays?"

"No, they're not. Mondays are still Mondays, but all the cool charity events are on Monday night."

"Well, sorry, but I'm busy tonight."

"Busy doing what?"

"Busy doing . . . busy things." I know, it was a lame answer, but I had not prepared myself for Lillian and her pushy ways. She looked at me, suspecting foul play.

"Do you have a date?"

"Maybe."

"You do?" she asked, her voice going up an octave, as if she had never been so surprised in her life.

"What the hell is so strange about me having a date?" I said, arching my left eyebrow so high that my face hurt.

"Nothing, I'm just . . . I don't know . . . I haven't heard you mention anybody. Who's the guy?"

"It's . . . it's a blind date."

"Who set you up?"

"One of my cousins."

"One of your cousins in Miami?"

"No, another cousin."

"All your other cousins are in Cuba."

"It's a second cousin."

She stopped for a second and looked at me, trying to figure out what I was up to.

"Do you want me to go with you for moral support?"

Before I could say, "Are you out of your freaking mind?," the cell phone rang, and I was saved by the bell.

"I gotta take this call, but thanks for the offer," I said, covering the mouthpiece.

But before I could start talking to Madame, I realized that Lillian was still there, fixed to the floor, ready to listen to my whole conversation.

"Thanks again, Lillian. You can go now." I shooed her away. She finally left—half pissed, I could tell, but at least she left.

My mom always says, *"Donde hay confianza da asco,"* which

means, "Too much friendliness is just gross." Apparently, it's a quote from my *abuela* Celia, who until the day she died bragged about not having one friend in the world and not needing one. She was betrayed by her neighbors in the early years of the Cuban Revolution and never trusted another stranger again. Her philosophy of life was kind of radical, but it came to mind as Lillian walked away. Maybe Lillian knew too much about me. Maybe I needed to separate a little bit from her and live my adventure with Madame on my own.

As soon as Lillian was out of sight, I returned to my phone call. Before I could say hi, Madame had delivered her instructions:

"Alberto will pick you up at seven, and he'll take you to the Lancashire Hotel, where you will meet Lord Carlton Arnfield. You won't have any trouble with him; he's a complete gentleman. He'll pay you in British pounds, and you don't need to count them."

"Got you," I said, intrigued that I was going to meet a British noble.

"Oh!" she added. "One very important thing. Do *not* wash your feet."

"What?" I looked down at my feet — still trapped in the heels that Madame had advised me never to use again. Okay, my feet were not in terrible shape, but after a long day at work, the perspective of going on a date — let's call it a date for now — without refreshing them sounded preposterous. Not to mention somewhat gross.

So I went home that night and took a bath, but kept my feet out of the water. You should have seen me. Half submerged in water, holding my feet up in the air. It was like taking a Pilates class in a bathtub. It was a good thing that no one was watching me, because it was truly embarrassing, but I was determined to follow Madame's instructions to a T.

I needed music to get me in the mood, so I chose a Nikka Costa song called "Everybody Got Their Something" and I played it over and over while I was going through my beauty ritual. I picked one of Madame's gowns — it was a spectacular form-fitting caftan in black raw silk, with silver embroidery — and I posed in front of the mirror, getting used to my new posture. I went through the laundry list in my mind: the head high, the expression confident, the lips soft, the bosom resting under the chin, the shoulders relaxed. This was very interesting, because I realized that your mood affects your posture, but your posture also affects your mood. The moment you stand up straight, and you own the space above and around you, you feel like a different person. As I walked out of the apartment, I felt how the skirt of Madame's dress flowed softly behind my thighs. Was it the dress that made me feel beautiful? Or was it the way I was walking, tall and proud of my body?

Downstairs, Alberto was punctual and waiting for me. I didn't have my contact lenses yet, but I figured I'd take off my glasses as soon as I got to Lord Arnfield's suite at the Lancashire.

I entered the car, and my heart started pounding.

CHAPTER 11

As far as I know, there are two types of limos in New York City: the fancy limos, and the college-kid-on-prom-night limos. The college-kid-on-prom-night types are tacky and gross. They are huge and white, with televisions, disco lights, a bar full of cheap liquor, and the stench of vomit. The fancy ones are black and sober, and they smell like vintage leather, the way you would expect an expensive lawyer's office to smell. Needless to say, Alberto's limo was the fancy type.

That night, I was so afraid of what I might find in my second work-date that I couldn't start a conversation with Alberto—I just kept sighing over and over in the backseat. He probably noticed my anxiety, and at some point, as we were waiting at a red light, he asked, "Is everything okay, Miss B?"

I exhaled deeply and whispered, "Yes."

"If you have any problems, you just push the number-two key on your phone and I'll be upstairs in a second."

"Thanks, Alberto," I said, looking at him in the rearview

mirror. We smiled at each other, and then I took another deep breath and told myself, "Relax, B, relax."

Finally, we arrived at the Lancashire. I wondered if I was going to be seen as a hooker by the hotel staff. Would they stop me and kick me out? How the hell could I explain to them what I was about to do if I wasn't sure about it myself?

Alberto diligently opened the door for me, but I took a couple of seconds before stepping out of the car, just to get my mind out of the gutter. Following my own philosophy, I realized that thinking "I'm a hooker...I'm a hooker...I'm a hooker..." would make people spot me as one. I needed to repeat some other kind of mantra. First I thought about using "I'm invisible," but it didn't feel right, so just as an experiment I tried "I'm stunning."

I walked into the lobby repeating to myself "I'm stunning...I'm stunning," and I actually felt kind of stunning. I don't know if it was the dress that Madame had lent me, or my recently acquired posture, but each and every employee at the hotel greeted me as if I were some movie star who was staying in the Presidential Suite. My fear of being identified as an escort and being kicked out vanished as soon as I got into the elevator. I went straight to Lord Arnfield's door — unannounced — since I knew he was expecting me. I knocked and he opened.

Ludwig Rauscher may have ended up being younger than I thought, but Lord Arnfield ended up being older than I could ever imagine. Way older. He must have been eighty-five at least. He was wearing a tuxedo, and he had that aristocratic demeanor of people who seem to have been born wearing one.

"Welcome!" he said with a decrepit smile.

As soon as I stepped in, he gave me a tight roll of British

pounds, which I carefully placed between my breasts. *If he tries to reach for my boobs,* I thought to myself, *I'll pull out his hand and throw the money at him in one motion, and I'll get the hell out of here before he can say "I beg your pardon."*

No need to worry. Maybe I had "a gorgeous bust," as Madame told me, but Lord Arnfield wasn't interested in it at all. He seemed to have eyes only for my lower parts. Lower, as in below the ankles.

"Please, take a seat," Lord Arnfield invited me.

While I sat down on the couch, he turned on an expensive sound system that started playing a Marlene Dietrich song, "Falling in Love Again."

"Are you comfortable?" he asked.

"Sure," I said.

"I think you would be more comfortable if I removed your shoes."

Under any other circumstances I would have said, "No, 'cause my feet stink," but, invoking Madame's instructions (don't make fun of the customers), I said "sure," and he proceeded to kneel in front of me and delicately remove my shoes.

"Oh! Your feet must hurt after such a long day!"

"Sure!" I said for lack of a better answer.

"Maybe I should give you a foot massage."

"Sure!" I repeated for the third time.

He started stroking my feet gently and slowly. For the remainder of the song, he touched them and examined them as if they had come from outer space. It was a mix of sensuality with scientific curiosity. Marlene's song ended, and he must have programmed the stereo in "shuffle," because the next song was from a very different album. It was the eighties hit by Vanity 6: "Nasty Girl." And, naturally, that's when things got nasty.

With the faster beat, his movements increased in speed and intensity; now he was lifting my feet and sniffing them all around. He put his nose right between my toes and took deep whiffs that made him spasm. His tender touch was tickling me, so I started giggling, and he seemed to like that, because he started huffing and puffing. The more I giggled, the more he huffed, and the more he huffed, the more I feared that he would have a heart attack and die with his nose between my toes.

I was starting to freak out — first, because I wouldn't know what to tell the cops if Lord Arnfield died on me, but mainly because, though I didn't find him particularly attractive, this whole thing was somehow turning me on. I closed my eyes, but it was worse. If I didn't see him, it was even more of a turn-on. Then I opened my eyes and realized that the turn-on wasn't him as a person: it was the enjoyment he was getting out of me. To think that someone could have such a fantastic time with the most unclean and unsexy part of my body was the most powerful aphrodisiac I had ever encountered. Did I want to jump in bed with this guy? Certainly not; but the fact that he was enjoying my body in such an unexpected way was making my heart race. I decided to close my eyes, get lost in the music, and fantasize that I was in a shoe store being run by Chippendales.

Out of nowhere, Lord Arnfield pulled out a box from an expensive men's store, and, opening it, he revealed a whole collection of brand-new men's socks.

Yes, you heard me well: men's socks. Not silk stockings, not bobby socks, not fancy pantyhose from Christian Dior; he pulled out black and brown cotton and polyester socks, the type that businessmen wear to work.

He started trying them on me, and with every new pair

of socks that he placed on my feet, a longer and more intense spasm arched his body. His breathing got heavier and heavier, and in the middle of trying a pair of white cotton tennis socks, he convulsed and collapsed at my feet.

Before I could call 911 — and, trust me, I was ready to do that — he got up, with a smile, and, covering his groin with the lid of the box, he showed me the way out.

"Oh dear," he asked me before I left, "you wouldn't happen to have a pair of old sneakers that you were planning to throw out, would you?"

"As a matter of fact, I do," I said, thinking of an old pair of gym shoes in my closet that were barely held together by a thread.

"I would be most interested in purchasing them from you."

"Don't worry, you don't have to pay me for that," I replied.

"I insist; maybe I could send my driver to pick them up."

"Don't worry, I'll send mine," I said, thinking of Alberto. "Maybe you can tip him or something."

"I most certainly will. Thank you," he said as he closed the door behind me.

"Sure," I said. What else could I say?

I walked down the hallway like a zombie. I didn't feel dirty. I didn't feel guilty. I just felt terribly confused. Just like the Madame said, it wasn't sex per se, but clearly there was some kind of sexual undertone to this whole thing.

"Are you okay, Miss B?" Alberto asked.

A part of me was deeply embarrassed about what had happened upstairs, but the other part of me was dying to talk about it. I leaned over the partition of the limo and laid it all out.

"Alberto . . . do you know this guy I was with?"

"Who? Lord Arnfield?"

"Yes."

"Oh . . . !" Alberto said with a smile. "Yes, I've heard about him."

"Okay, what the hell was that?" I asked, still baffled.

"Miss B, I'm sorry, but Madame doesn't like me to talk about the customers."

"I'm just . . . I . . . I don't understand this foot thing. Could you believe that he wants to buy my old sneakers? Oh, by the way, could you bring them back to him? I'll give you twenty dollars, and I'm sure he'll tip you well too."

"Don't worry, it's my job. I'll bring them to him, and then I'll bring you the money," Alberto replied.

"No, I'm not taking any money! I'm just gonna give them to him. I'm not going to charge him for a pair of sneakers that are falling apart — that's crazy!" I said.

Alberto gave me a good look through the rearview mirror and wholeheartedly said, "You must have a good heart, Miss B, because you are the first girl that doesn't walk out of that apartment wondering how to squeeze more money out of that old guy."

"The guy just paid me a roll of pounds to give me a foot massage. It's the least I can do. Isn't it ironic? This guy is a rich British aristocrat, but he would be much happier working in a shoe store."

I could tell that Alberto was dying to talk, in spite of Madame's instructions. He thought about it for a second, and finally shrugged: "Some people have so much money they don't know what to do with it. In Santo Domingo you don't see these things. If you want to have a good time you go dancing, you have a few drinks, you hang out with your friends. I had never met anyone in Santo Domingo who likes to chew on dirty sneakers. But I have to respect that, you know? I don't like to trash people, because I don't like it when people trash me. This guy doesn't hurt anybody, he pays well—to each his own."

"You are right. To each his own," I repeated after him.

When we finally got to my apartment, Alberto parked the car and followed me upstairs to pick up my sneakers. After he left, I decided to take a full bath—this time with my feet in the tub. I scrubbed them and cleaned them with an affection that I had never felt for any part of my body before. I contemplated my toes for a long time, wondering what it was that this British noble found so fascinating about them. Minutes later, lying in the tub, I must confess that I touched myself. But here's the interesting part: for the first time in my life, my fantasy wasn't a man. This time I just thought of myself. I was my own thrill. I know, it sounds crazy, but my turn-on was to know how much of a turn-on I was for Lord Arnfield. I was glad to have given him my sneakers for free. He had given me a greater gift.

That night I slept like a baby. I didn't realize until the next morning—when I went to the bank to deposit the money—that Lord Arnfield had paid me close to twenty-five hundred dollars, just for the privilege of giving me the best foot massage of my life.

Pretty crazy, huh?

CHAPTER 12

The following morning flew by. I don't remember much of what I did at work, but I remember that at lunchtime I got a pedicure and I spent the rest of the afternoon staring at my feet. Bonnie called me about eight times, asking for eight different things that were already sitting on her desk. I think she expected me to get up and find them for her, but in every instance I simply told her where I'd left it and went back to my feet. Christine walked by my cubicle and was surprised by my level of introspection. Maybe the fat workhorse was slowing down. I'm not the kind of person who likes to take advantage of a staff job to spend the day looking at my toes, but all I had to do was conjure up the memory of Bonnie making fun of me in the bathroom to justify a few hours of leisure in the workplace. Screw her.

Madame called me a little later than expected with new instructions and a new customer. "Alberto will pick you up at nine p.m. to bring you to Mr. Akhtar's warehouse. Don't eat anything two hours before the appointment, and don't wear any makeup."

"Why?"

"You'll see."

"What is he into?" I asked with a guilty fear that was starting to become as addictive as heroin.

"Honey, he'll let you know. All you have to do is reciprocate. Yes?"

"Reciprocate? You said no sex!"

"Oh, stop being paranoid!" she said. Then she claimed that she was busy—that she had a business to run—and left me wondering for the next eight hours. What could this man be into that would make it mandatory to refrain from eating or putting on makeup?

That night, Alberto took me to an industrial area of Brooklyn. These were the kind of streets where you wouldn't want to wander alone after 5 p.m. There was not a house, a deli, or a gas station in sight—probably not one for several blocks. It was like the classical spot where, halfway into a movie, a mobster gets whacked. I was a little concerned, but Alberto calmed me down. As always, he would wait for me until the job was done.

"So what is this guy into?" I asked Alberto, hiding my fear with a fake tone of worldliness.

"I don't know. I've never seen him, and the girls never talk about him afterward."

Involuntarily I let out a huge sigh that probably clued Alberto as to how nervous I was. He tried something to relax me.

"Do you like music?" he asked.

"Of course!"

"What would you like to hear? Do you like *bachata*?"

If you're Dominican you're born to love *bachata,* a very sweet and romantic type of tropical ballad. My friend Zulay calls it "Dominican deli music," because every time you walk into a Dominican grocery store in New York you can hear the characteristic high-pitched plucking of the strings of the *guitarra bachatera.*

So, while Alberto hummed along to Monchy y Alexandra, his favorite *bachata* duo, I closed my eyes in the backseat and tried to relax.

He parked in front of a warehouse and pointed to a small door next to a loading dock. I walked up to it and banged on the door a couple of times before Mr. Akhtar—an Indian man in his mid-fifties, with thick glasses, a big mustache, and a bad comb-over—opened.

"Hi, I'm B."

"Hello," he said, looking at the floor, with a barely audible whisper.

That was the first and last word I heard from this guy. Without looking me in the eyes, he made a simple hand gesture to invite me in.

I stepped into a large factory where there were rows and rows of sewing machines, and hundreds of beaded gowns covered in plastic bags and ready to be shipped. The mousy Mr. Akhtar probably ran or owned the sweatshop. My friend Hugo, who works in fashion, explained to me once that designers produce only one dress, a prototype. They send that prototype to places like Mr. Akhtar's to get it reproduced.

I followed Mr. Akhtar to a corner of the shop, and he removed a dusty drape that I thought was covering a piece of industrial equipment but, surprisingly, revealed a fabulous antique three-way mirror. It was an original Art Nouveau piece with beveled glass and a deliciously complicated frame made of gilded carved wood. While I was admiring the mirror, he left for a minute and came back with a chair and a toolbox. He gestured to invite me to sit down, and he opened the toolbox, which turned out to be a professional makeup kit.

He proceeded to apply makeup to my face with masterful strokes. He knew what he was doing, and I'm sure he had done it before, possibly even professionally. He worked fast, and at some point it felt like more than applying makeup—he was sketching something on my face. Since he was standing between me and the mirror, I couldn't really see what he was doing; all I knew was that, based on the way he was working the mascara, he had probably given me a couple of additional inches of eyelashes.

When he was done, he put a fairly elaborate wig of black hair on me, and then he gave me a hand mirror so I could admire the outcome.

The makeup looked a bit theatrical for my taste, but not bad at all. He had applied thick eyeliner, and dark lipstick liberally, and created very sharp contrasts of light and dark shades, giving my face angles that were not really there. I was amazed to see how you can develop a finer nose or higher cheekbones with just a well-applied touch of powder. He turned my eyes into a masterpiece of their own: they looked huge, expressive, and quite dramatic.

He left again and came back with a clothing rack on wheels. Very respectfully, he helped me undress. I wasn't terribly comfortable—as a matter of fact, I was feeling quite anxious and embarrassed—standing next to him in my underwear, but he didn't even look at me. He was busy preparing the clothes and the shoes I was going to wear. He unveiled a fabulous red taffeta gown with crystal beading. It was the most sumptuous dress I have ever seen — the kind of garment that you need help to put on. But before he tried it on me, he pulled out a magnificent girdle. No, it was much more than a girdle; it was a sculpture. He put it on me, and, pulling the ribbons from behind — thank God I was on an empty stomach — he minimized my waist, and pushed up my boobs to almost illegal heights. The girdle was enough to make me feel like Miss Universe, but when he zipped up the dress, I was speechless: I looked like an overweight Barbie doll. He pulled out accessories, and jewels — even a tiara. I saw myself in the mirror and couldn't believe what this guy had done for me.

He had turned me into a Cuban bombshell. I looked large, voluptuous, imposing. There was a lot of me, but at the same time, everything that I saw in the mirror seemed right and appropriate. No skinny girl could ever look like this. Yes, maybe a slim girl could be a knockout in a mini-skirt and a tank top, but I looked as if I owned the world in that dress. I thought of Madame's words as I saw myself in the mirror:

The lips are soft, ready to be kissed. Your bosom rests in bloom under your chin, your shoulders are relaxed, so your arms are open and free to embrace the man that madly desires you...

As if going through a checklist, I breathed love and accep-tance into each and every one of the body parts that she men-tioned: the lips, the bosom, the chin, the shoulders...

And never, never *forget that* you are *beautiful,* she had said. And beautiful I felt, then and there.

As I stood in that corner of the warehouse, mesmerized, looking at my own image in the mirror, suddenly I found Mr. Akhtar standing next to me. But he wasn't looking at the

work of art he had put together. He was looking at the floor.
I looked at the floor too, to see if there was something he was
searching for. Turned out that he was staring at his own feet,
maybe because he was wearing the same red stiletto heels
that I had on. That's when Madame's instructions came to
mind: reciprocate.

I sat him down on the chair, and did my best to reproduce
the makeup that he had put on me. It was tricky, because I
had to keep stopping to check my own face in the mirror to
figure out what he had done, and then guess how he did it.
What brush did he use for my temples, the "mink blusher"
or the "tender smudge"? It was impossible to figure it out,
so, instead of freaking out, I decided to go with the flow and
improvise.

Truth be told, I didn't do a great job. And to make matters worse, I had to work around his walrus mustache and his
eyeglasses. But he seemed to be enjoying the process. I just
relaxed and tried to act professional, though he was starting
to look more like a clown than like a beauty queen.

There was a second wig, a second girdle, a second gown,
and a second set of everything I had on. So I helped him to
undress, and then I pulled the ribbons of his girdle, and helped
him into his red taffeta gown. I gave him the same attention
he had given me, from the shoes to the crowning tiara.

We stood in front of the mirror for a few minutes, looking
like twin queens. His glasses and mustache clashed with the
outfit, but I wasn't going to bring that up. To each his own.
Immediately, and in complete silence, he helped me out of the
clothes, waited as I put my own things back on, gave me a roll
of hundred-dollar bills, and escorted me back to the door. He
never said a word, but I could swear that I have never seen anyone so thankful in my life.

When Alberto saw me stepping out of the warehouse, he immediately got out of the car and opened the door for me.

"How was that?"

"Fine," I said, still confused and exhilarated by the whole experience.

"Here's some cleansing cream and handy wipes," he told me as he handed me a cosmetics case from the trunk.

I sat in the back, and Alberto drove slowly and carefully, while I started removing my makeup.

"He's a quiet one, isn't he?" he asked me.

"Very quiet," I said, and though I felt tempted to tell Alberto all the strange details of the visit to Mr. Akhtar's warehouse, I couldn't get myself to do it. I felt that someone had trusted me with a deep and painful secret. It's true, Mr. Akhtar looked funny and a bit ridiculous with his gown, his makeup, and his mustache, but I just couldn't go out and laugh about it. There was something deep and desperate about him.

"There's a lot of lonely people out there. It breaks my heart," Alberto said, voicing my thoughts.

As we crossed the Brooklyn Bridge, and I saw the bright city lights twinkling on the horizon, I thought of Mr. Akhtar with sadness and compassion. I'm always whining: I hate my job, I can't lose weight, I can't find a boyfriend. But as big as the obstacles may look to me, I know deep in my soul that somehow I can overcome them. I don't know how and I don't know when I'll jump these hurdles, but I have the hope that I can do it. But Mr. Akhtar is not the same. He may not be able to overcome his obstacles. He makes the most beautiful gowns in the world—but he may never be allowed to wear them. He may never know what is like to walk into a ballroom wearing one of his dresses, and flip a long headful of hair over his shoulder, without hearing laughter and mockery around him. Then I thought of every time I had cursed my pantyhose, or applied lipstick without giving much attention to it, ignoring the sad fate of those who have to hide and live in shame in order to do it.

The fact that someone would appreciate so much what I took for granted — that somebody would pay me two thousand dollars to experience what it is like to be a girl — was incredibly moving.

That night, I again slept like a log, but in the morning I woke up to a small domestic nightmare. I had nothing to wear. Absolutely nothing. It's not like I forgot to bring my clothes to the Laundromat, it's just that, after looking at myself dressed up as a Bollywood movie star, I couldn't make myself wear the bland pantsuits that I'd been wearing to work. I tried to combine and recombine jackets and skirts, but everything felt so "ugh" that I decided to take a detour on my way to work to get a new outfit.

I browsed through racks and racks of clothes, until I finally picked a chiffon blouse, a sunburst skirt, a long cashmere shawl, and a pair of gorgeous sandals with a short and comfy heel. Naturally, I couldn't wear those clothes with my old frumpy underwear, so I also had to buy new lingerie. From my brassiere to my shoes, I chose sexy, flattering, and revealing clothes, and I walked out of the store feeling like a new woman.

I wanted to wear something feminine, something ethereal, something that would flow like a cloud of silk every time the spring breeze blew around me. That morning, it made sense to let the natural curls of my hair go wild too. Before I left the store, I sat in the ladies' room and applied my makeup, trying to incorporate the principles and techniques that I'd learned from Mary Pringle and Mr. Akhtar.

As I thoroughly enjoyed the process of putting on my makeup, I thought of Mr. Akhtar again. It's funny how someone else's drama made me appreciate the small and wonderful things in my life. Now, every time I dress up, or put on makeup, I think of Mr. Akhtar and I'm a little kinder to myself, and I find an enjoyment in being a woman that I never had before.

I walked up Fifth Avenue wearing my new clothes, and I was surprised to realize that they had an impact on how I walked, and how I felt about myself. Every time the wind blew through my hair, I felt baptized by nature. I saw myself walking down the street firmly, but allowing my hips to swing comfortably with every step. The tight, short steps that I was used to taking, the compulsive need to crush my elbows and occupy less space as an apology for my large body, completely disappeared. I felt the expansion in my bones and muscles, and I felt that my roundness was blessed. Yep, I'm talking as if I was high on mushrooms, but it wasn't drugs. This trip was real. I had taken off to an unknown destination.

As I walked into my office building, the same faces that usually looked away and didn't acknowledged my smiles were suddenly following me as I crossed the floor. Even the toothless security guard responded with a broad smile when he saw me. It's almost as if he had never noticed me before. A part of me wanted to ignore him the same way he had ignored me so many times in the past, but why do to others what I didn't like done to me? Why ruin this moment of joy with silly thoughts of revenge and resentment, which always seem to backfire? I smiled at him—politely—and continued walking toward the elevators.

I arrived at my cubicle at noon, but I calmly turned on my

computer. I was in no hurry to enslave myself that morning.
As I started reviewing my e-mails, Mary Pringle stopped by.

"B?"

I looked up in time to see her eyes jumping out of her
sockets.

"B?" she asked again in shock.

"Yes?" I replied.

She walked closer to me and delicately held my face up with
her left hand, while analyzing and deconstructing my makeup.

"This is Cafe Au Lait, Violent Violet, and Toasted Hazelnut,
right?" she said, referring to my masterful combination of eye
shadows.

"It's not Toasted Hazelnut, it's Death By Chocolate," I replied.

"Egyptian Gold eyeliner?"

"Yep, Egyptian Gold eyeliner."

"Wow, I'm impressed," she acknowledged.

"You gave me good advice," I answered back.

She smiled, clearly grateful for the acknowledgment, and
then, in an apologetic tone, she delivered her instructions.

"I'm sorry, but Bonnie wants to see you *right now.*"

I took a deep breath, but this time I got up and walked
over to the bitch's den without an ounce of fear in my body.
As usual, Christine was there too, disgesting breakfast and
gossiping away.

"Good morning," I said with a big smile.

Bonnie and Christine looked up and almost choked. I
could be wrong about this, but it wasn't just my new outfit
or my hair or my makeup. Bonnie knew that something had
changed; though — in her best evil style — she immediately
turned her face into the dry, cold rock that it has always been,
and fired a round of ammunition.

"You're late again."

"Yes," I said with a smile.

"And?" she said, expecting to see me beg forgiveness.

"And what? I'm arriving late because very often I work late, and it's funny that you bring it up, because it never seems to bother you when I work late."

I had never seen the hyena speechless until this very moment. I threw her off. She couldn't come up with anything better than the oldest cliché: "Let's hope it doesn't happen again."

"Let's hope you don't ask me to work late again," I said, and walked out.

I have always heard with skepticism the stories of people who change overnight. This type of born-again attitude that I'm describing in myself has always been cause for mistrust, or at least an arched eyebrow. *A woman goes out on a couple of paid dates, and suddenly she finds the self-esteem that she never had. Yeah, right!* That's exactly what I would say if I were hearing this story instead of telling it. But I was taking a calculated risk. My new job was giving me money, recognition, and thrills that I wasn't getting at the office. I wasn't going to throw away the baby with the bathwater, but I certainly felt a financial security that would allow me to flex some muscle with the harpy. If Bonnie tried to fire me, it would take her at least six months—and that's if I *didn't* fight back. I could make her life miserable if I put my mind to it.

On the other hand, I did love my job, and as much as I knew that Bonnie would never acknowledge my talent, a small part of me still wondered if the talent was actually there to be acknowledged. I needed to bring it up to a higher level, but the corporate ladder was strict in that respect. I could never pitch my ideas directly to the Chicago Boss, or the client; my ideas would always go through Bonnie, and if she chose to keep them in the folder, forget it.

I know that Latinos have a reputation for being passionate and volatile. I hate to confirm stereotypes, but — at least
when it comes to my family — it is absolutely true. At home
we would rather be aggressive than passive-aggressive. I know
that others feel more comfortable fighting their battles with
that indifferent attitude that my aunt Carmita described with
one sentence: *"ellos ni huelen, ni hieden"* (they neither sniff nor
stink). They act as if nothing affects them. Whatever happens
inside, they keep it to themselves. But in my family we don't
just show our emotions, we blare them. Our fights are short
but intense. We have big blowouts and fast reconciliations. If
you're angry, it's clear and direct. I know it's more intimidating to deal with a Cuban spitfire than with an icy Massachu-
setts maiden, but at the end of the day, with the Cuban you
know exactly where you stand. That's how I see it.

Having been raised in New York City, I have learned to
play both sides of this game. I can be a hurricane or an ice
cube, depending on the circumstances. But playing it passive-
aggressive with Bonnie would never grant me the victory.
She was the queen of that genre. She probably invented it
herself. So reaching out for my Cuban arsenal of weapons was
only logical.

That's why, earlier that morning, after buying my new
"armor" at the boutique, I also stopped by Radio Shack and
got a secret weapon: a pocket tape recorder. So, after I left
Bonnie huffing and puffing in her office, I perched myself
feet-up in the bathroom stall again — but this time with my
pocket recorder in hand. Calmly, I filed my nails until I heard
Bonnie and Christine come into the bathroom, as always, to
examine their fangs in the mirror. Then I pressed RECORD,
as I overheard once again the nasty tirade that Bonnie was
dedicating to me.

"Well, the truth is that very often she does work late," said Christine.

"I don't care. I'm not putting up with this crap. Who does she think she is? That because she got a makeover she's going to walk around with that attitude? As soon as we're done with the UK Charms presentation, I'm getting rid of her."

"What are you going to tell her?"

"That she's too fat to work here," said Bonnie, sounding more like a high-school girl than the regional VP of an advertising agency.

"You can't say that!" replied Christine, laughing.

"Oh, I'll set her up. I've done this before. How do you think I got rid of Miller and Jessica? Nobody, I repeat, nobody fucks with me."

El que ríe el ultimo, ríe mejor, we say in Spanish. He who laughs last, laughs the hardest. And now that I'm sharing clichés, let me throw one more at you: it ain't over until the fat lady sings. And guess what? I was just warming up to sing a very high note.

I waited until I heard Bonnie and Christine leaving the restroom; then I stepped out of the stall. But before I could conceal the recorder, none other than Mary Pringle walked in, and caught me red-handed. She looked at me, she looked at the recorder, and, based on her expression, I immediately knew that she understood exactly what I was up to. A seasoned saleswoman like her is always aware of her surroundings.

She smiled, and winked at me. "I have a tape recorder just like that one. They work great."

I smiled back, and nothing had to be explained.

I went back to my desk to lock the recorder in a drawer, and the rest of the day flew by like a breeze.

It must have been almost one p.m. when I picked up a few reports and walked over to the copy machine, where I found none other than Dan Callahan chatting with Mark Davenport. He looked at me with his mouth semi-open, as if I were the centerfold of *Sports Illustrated*. I smiled innocently.

"Hey, Dan."

"Hey, B!"

Men are so obvious. Now that I didn't care about him, suddenly he was making goo-goo eyes at me, hoping that I'd fall in his trap again.

I moved closer to him, while he leaned proudly on the copy machine as if he were the only man on earth capable of achieving an erection. At perfume-smelling distance I whispered, "Can I ask you for a favor?"

Leaning even closer to me, he whispered back, "Anything."

"Can you move over so I can make some copies?"

Gotcha, you moron! I thought to myself. I didn't want to abuse my recently acquired powers, but he was asking for it. He moved away slowly and arrogantly, giving me a sexy look in the process. The nerve.

"Thanks," I said, and smiled.

As I was happily starting to make my copies, my red cell phone rang. I pulled it out of my brassiere, observing Dan's stupid expression. He was clearly impressed by my new phone, and by my new cleavage too. Coyly, I turned away from him to take the call. That was enough to make him understand that I was done talking to him. He left the copy room, and from the corner of my eye I saw him turning around a couple of times to see if I was looking at him go. *Not in this lifetime, you meathead!* I would have told him, but I couldn't be bothered. Madame started delivering her instructions.

"Alberto will pick you up at nine. Your client is Richard

Weber. He pays with a credit card, so Alberto will give you cash as you leave. Richard is going to give you a massage, but watch out, because this guy is a tease, so please control yourself."

"I understand," I said, feeling like a secret agent.

I had the world on a string. After all those years trapped in my dead-end job, with my dead-end dates and my dead-end life, I was finally feeling that I could change it all.

"Oh!" Madame added. "And get a good waxing."

"Legs?" I asked.

"Everything," she answered.

"Ouch!" I said to myself.

CHAPTER 13

Brazilians have made at least two great contributions to humanity. The first one is music: the fusion of African, Portuguese, and native sounds that took place in Brazil has no precedents. Half of my CD collection is Brazilian music. Elis Regina, Gal Costa, Chico Buarque, Marisa Monte, Elza Soares, Antonio Carlos Jobim, etc., etc., etc. You hear two notes of a Brazilian song and, no matter if you're burning in the darkest pit of hell, you immediately feel transported to the soft and warm sands of Ipanema Beach, surrounded by swinging palm trees, lying under a bright sun that caresses your skin.

The other great contribution of Brazilians is their waxing technique. They figured out a process that manages to pull the hair painfully out of your coochie, while keeping you from bleeding to death.

Following Madame's instructions, I went to this waxing place in Manhattan that is run by a bunch of Brazilian girls. They're fun, they're crazy, and they're damn good at what they do. As Elisa, my waxer, yanked the paper strips from my body, I yelled, cursed, and screamed over the Brazilian beats and the girls' fast chatter, where every word seemed to end with "*inha*."

After Elisa was done with the painful treatment—and I lay there trying to recover—I noticed that she spent a few seconds looking at my privates. Suddenly she called one of her colleagues.

"¡*Ritinha, vem cá! ¡Olha que coisa mais bonitinha!*"

Ritinha came into our stall, and both girls stood there looking at my hairless genitals as if they were admiring a painting hanging in the Louvre.

"¿*Lindinha, não?*" said Elisa.

"¡*Dá para tirar uma foto!*" answered Ritinha.

I was starting to feel really, *really* uncomfortable when Ritinha grabbed my hand and, with the casual tone that only years of waxing thousands of vaginas can give you, said, "*Você tem a xoxotinha mais bonita que eu já vi.*"

I don't speak Portuguese, but Spanish is close enough for me to figure out that Elisa was congratulating me for the looks of my pussy. This unexpected vaginal tribute caught me so off guard that I must have given her a very skeptical look, so Elisa—without missing a beat—put a hand mirror between my thighs so I could admire it too.

"It's okay, I don't need to see it," I said.

"¡*Não, olha! ¡Olha só como é linda! ¡Olha!*"

She insisted and insisted, to the point where I finally had to give up. Leaning on my elbows, I looked down between my knees, and I saw it.

It's hard to talk about your own vagina—and I don't know enough about other vaginas to be able to compare mine with anybody's — but I do have to admit that it looked kind of pretty. It looked like a smile — like a fresh, pink, vertical smile. I spent a few seconds staring at it, its clean lines and lovely proportions, before realizing that it was the first time I had looked at my own genitals. Thanks to the insistence of my Brazilian waxers, I was finally reconnecting with an old friend.

As I walked out I left a twenty-dollar tip for Elisa, but I wondered if the vaginal homage was just an act they performed for every customer in order to get a good tip. Later, I decided to dismiss that idea. As far as I could tell, an independent committee had determined that my pussy was pretty. All I needed to do was say "thanks" and walk through life proud of myself.

The Brazilian experience inspired me to go on a fast but effective shopping spree. Afterwards, I walked out of the store a few hundred dollars poorer, but rich with confidence that my closet was finally catching up with me.

It wasn't until I got home later that it dawned on me that waxing everything, as Madame requested, surely meant exposing everything to tonight's customer, and that's when I started to panic. I immediately picked up my red cell phone and called Madame.

"Madame, what exactly is going to happen tonight? Is this guy going to see me naked? What does he want? I told you from day one, no sex, and you said no sex. But if I had to wax everything for him, that means —"

"Honey, relax, this guy is just a tease!" she said, trying to interrupt my hissy fit.

"But is he going to see me naked?"

"He's going to give you a massage. Have you ever got a massage before?"

"Yes, many times."

"And what were you wearing?"

"Nothing."

"Point made," Madame said, ready to hang up the phone.

"Wait!" I pleaded. "What do I do if he tries to have sex with me?"

"If he asks for sex twenty times, you say no twenty times, even if you want to say yes."

"What?" I replied, offended. "I would never say yes. It's one thing to have sex with a man that I'm dating, but I'm not a hooker. I would never even think of having sex with one of your clients."

"Wait till you meet him."

And with those prophetic words she left me. According to her, she had somebody else waiting on the other line, but I suspect that it was just an excuse to stop my whining.

I checked myself one last time in the mirror before I left the apartment. I was wearing one of my new outfits: a black low-cut dress with a soft gray suede coat fitted at the waist. It looked sexy and classic at the same time. I accessorized it with these cool earrings that I found in a vintage shop in the Village. They consist of a long, thin gold chain, with a little puff of mink that hangs at the very end. Finally, I added my virginity pendant to protect me from the unknown, and rushed downstairs, where Alberto was already waiting for me.

The appointment was just a few blocks away from my apartment, but he insisted on driving and, naturally, waiting for me outside. He drove down Seventh Avenue, blasting a merengue-mix CD on the stereo while I took deep breaths on the backseat, trying to convince myself that I was seasoned enough to handle any challenge in my new profession.

I'm a girl of the twenty-first century, I told myself. *I went to a nude beach in the Bahamas once. I took my top off in Ibiza every single day for a whole week. I've been to the doctor countless times. I can be naked in front of a stranger without freaking out.*

Alberto looked at me through the rearview mirror and offered me his usual line of support. "If you need me, I'll be outside waiting for your call."

"Thanks." I exhaled one more time before stepping out of the car.

I climbed up the front steps of a brownstone in the West Village, situated in a block where Gwyneth Paltrow was rumored once to have a house. It wasn't a cheap block, that much I can tell you.

I rang, and Richard Weber opened the door.

"Woooooooow," he said as he shamelessly stared at me up and down. That's when I said to myself: "Houston, we have a problem."

Richard Weber was hot. Super-freaking-hot. He looked a lot like a famous actor, like one of the Wilson brothers — the blond one to be precise. Blue eyes, thick lips, pretty face, and a dangerously sexy body. This is the kind of guy that should charge *me* for a date. I thought about Madame's warning: "This guy is a tease, so please control yourself." If that was the case, he had a lot to tease me with.

He welcomed me with a smile that spoke volumes about his sexual drive. I must have been his type, because he was clearly thrilled to see me.

"Helloooo!" he said, stretching his vowels. "I'm Reeeeechard."

"Hello, my name is B."

Richard's brownstone was sparsely decorated with impeccable metrosexual taste. It was a gorgeous house, but it had that impersonal feeling of a home where nobody lives: too clean, too organized, too—I don't know—too perfect. Just like him. He looked good, smelled good, but there was something about him that sent a chill down my spine. I just didn't know what it was quite yet.

"Thank you for coming, B. I'm taking a course on massage therapy—you know, to make ends meet..."

To make ends meet? What a pile of crap. His brownstone alone was worth about eight million dollars, and every single chair in that house had a last name. He had original furniture by Le Corbusier, Marcel Breuer, the Eameses—you name it, he had it.

"...so it's really great to have someone to practice the strokes with." He finished with his lie and then smiled at me. When he smiled, he looked straight into my eyes for that extra second, which in the international language of seduction means, "I'm so shagging you if you let me."

"I have a massage table down in the basement. Why don't you follow me?" he said, giving me a quick wink and another smile. Sexy bastard.

Richard was like one of those Italian sausages that they sell in the street fairs—I always want to eat them, but I know that if I do I'll regret it. Nevertheless, there was something to my advantage: he was a customer, and that was a boundary. I wasn't there to do what I wanted, I was there to play his game, and according to Madame, his game was to tease me, and my job was to say no. That's what I was getting paid for. So, following my intuition—and Madame's instructions—I secretly vowed celibacy.

Clutching my cell phone and overcoming a mild phobia for basements, which started after I saw *Silence of the Lambs,* I followed him downstairs, where a big surprise was waiting for me: a sex chamber.

"What do you think of this room? I designed it myself," he said proudly as he gave me a tour through his dungeon.

Despite how it sounds, his sex chamber wasn't creepy at all. Like everything else in the house, it looked like something that Phillippe Starck would have carefully designed for an airline. It was a dungeon, but the dungeon of a spaceship. It was all covered in black tiles, and it had concealed closets behind the walls that hid anything from a stereo and a plasma TV, to a vast collection of sex toys. The centerpiece was a stretcher covered with a red latex sheet.

"Nice, huh?" he asked.

"Very nice," I lied, semi-horrified.

This is the thing: I like sex, but I feel that certain people take it way too seriously. For them sex is like a hobby, like golfing or woodworking. They have the tools, they have the trade magazines, and sometimes even a special room in the basement. And that was the case with Richard. He was a professional at it, and that's what freaked me out. I could smell that sexual intensity in him.

While he showed me the restraints, the rubber suits, and the latex goods that he carefully kept neatly in a closet, I closed my eyes and thanked God for this saving grace. Yeah, Richard was gorgeous, the kind of guy that I would masochistically like to have walking all over me. But the sex room was a huge turn-off. Who knows? Maybe I would be able to exercise the promised self-control that I had been ready to throw out the window the moment I saw him.

"Weeeeeell, maybe I should take my clothes off so they don't get staaained," he said, with a fake innocence that almost made me laugh.

With slow and calculated movements he stripped, giving me sexy looks as he took off each and every piece of clothing.

He was in spectacular shape. Up, down, and around, there was nothing missing in this man. Let me repeat that: *nothing*. His butt was particularly well put together. I bit my lower lip.

"Soooooo, what do you think?" he asked me with a wink as he posed, wearing only a big smile.

"Nice," I said, trying to keep myself from howling like a she-wolf.

He tied a latex apron around his waist, put on rubber boots, a swimming cap and goggles. He looked like the mad scientist of a pornographic sci-fi movie.

"And nooow . . . it's your tuuurn. You can cover yourself with this towel if you want to . . . but it won't be for loooong." He winked.

I took off my clothes fast and, facing the wall, then covered myself with the towel and lay belly-up on the massage table with a mix of excitement and embarrassment, ready to call Alberto for help if I thought that things were getting out of hand. But where could I keep the phone when I certainly had no pockets nearby? I took a deep breath and tried to relax, while Richard started putting on his rubber gloves.

"Oooh! Such delicate earrings," he said, admiring my mink puffs. "Let's take them off so they don't get stained."

Stained with what? I thought, but I couldn't utter a word.

"Soooooooo, B . . . do you like . . . chocolate?"

"Umm . . . actually, I do."

"Greaaaaaaat!" he replied.

He stood next to the table for a moment, took a deep breath, and yanked my towel off in one motion. Out of nowhere he pulled out a squeezable bottle filled with a chocolate paste and started pouring it all over me.

"There's nothing better than chocolate for your skin. Do you like how it feels?" he asked.

"Yeah...I like it," I said, trying to sound casual about it.

The soft sensation of the chocolate over my skin felt delicious. As I looked up to the mirror on the ceiling—did I mention that he had a mirror installed on the ceiling?—I saw my ample body covered with a thick layer of glistening chocolate, and his lean and muscular shoulders hovering dangerously over me. I felt so turned on that I had to close my eyes and pretend that I was having my appendix removed. I desperately needed to remain calm.

After pouring the smooth sweetness all over me, Richard started with the massage. He began with my neck and shoulders, and it felt great. He certainly knew how to touch a woman. While standing behind me, he bent over until his face was on top of mine and I could smell his fresh, minty breath.

"Now say 'aaaaaaah'!"

I said "aaah" and he quickly poured a bit of chocolate in my mouth. It was Nutella, a chocolate and hazelnut paste that I find simply irresistible.

As I savored the delicious squirt of chocolate that he gave me, he looked long and deeply into my eyes with such intensity that I had to close mine for fear of being swept off my feet. With my eyes closed and my face turned away from him, I felt his disappointment. But his despair quickly turned into an even more desperate need to seduce me.

His strokes became broader and more intense; he massaged my torso as if he were creating a sculpture, firmly but sensually at the same time. Then he walked slowly around the table while letting his right hand caress me from head to toe.

"My, my, myyyyyy..." he said.

I took a deep breath.

He positioned himself at my feet and started massaging my legs up and down...up and down...That's when he started panting.

"Ooooooh my Goooooooood!" he said, clenching his teeth.

I said nothing, because I knew that anything I said could get me in trouble. That man was damned hot, but he would never hear it from me, because any word of encouragement on my part could turn the whole situation exactly into what I was told to avoid. So I kept breathing while he kept moaning.

"Ooooooh! Oooooh my!!!" he said, over and over.

Little by little my breathing became heavier and heavier, I couldn't help it. This guy was irresistible, and he knew how to use his hands. How could I defend myself from the temptation? Maybe by thinking unhappy thoughts I could distract myself from this seductive force.

I tried to concentrate on the most unpleasant things I knew. I thought about the skinny lady who chain-smokes outside my office building; Dan Callahan puking on my carpet; cleaning Dan's puke afterward; Bonnie and all the nights and weekends I worked late to prove myself to her. I thought of my servile attitude, standing like a puppy on my back legs, begging her to throw me a bone. I thought of that bathroom conversation to remind myself how it didn't matter what I did, she hated me, she despised my body, the same body that Richard Weber, the hottest man on earth, was worshipping at that very instant.

Maybe he noticed that I was mentally elsewhere, because he started breaking his pattern of motion, to bring me back to the present. He would rush—and then slow down. He would stop—and then restart, teasing me to death, over and over. Respectfully—or strategically—he kept his hands off my most sensitive spots. I thanked him and cursed him silently.

"Could you bend your right arm?" he said.

I followed his instructions, and suddenly, in a totally unexpected movement, he flipped me over. His strength made me feel defenseless. Then he started working on my back, thighs, and buttocks, and he must have seen something that he liked, because he let go a deep and heartfelt "Oooooooh my Goooooooood!"

He took a bite of chocolate right off my left calf. I jumped, but he didn't stop.

"Beeeeeee...!" he said, stretching the last vowel like a little lamb calling his mother. "Those legs...! That aaaaaaaaaass...!"

One thing that I was never into was dirty talk. In other circumstances, I would have laughed at his chatter. But the massage was so good and he was so gorgeous that—I hate to acknowledge it—he was turning me on *big-time*.

He took a quick bite of chocolate from my right cheek and I started shaking. He kept moaning, and finally I started moaning too. Suddenly it became a bit of a contest. Who was going to moan harder? I realized that, the harder I moaned, the easier it was to control myself. It was the vocal release that was keeping me from losing the battle.

"Beeeeeee, I have never, ever, touched a woman like you. Never. I think I'm going to lose control. I'm going to loooooose it...I'm going to loooooose iiiiiit!"

"Please...don't..." I whispered as I tightened my muscles. I felt him shaking in a short spasm, then he laughed softly, and I relaxed my muscles again. He was probably wondering what the hell was wrong with me. Why wasn't I on my knees already, begging him to make love to me? I forced myself to remember the wise words of Madame: "If he asks for sex, twenty times, you say no twenty times."

"I'm looooosing iiiiiiit..." he said.

"Doooon't..." I begged.

Frustrated by my self-control, Richard's expert hands flipped me back up again, and he started working on my legs, getting closer and closer to the forbidden zone. He bent my knees and started massaging my thighs with circular motions, starting at the knee, and diving down toward Pleasure Valley. The hand motion became more and more intense; his whole body arched on every turn. He took a bite of chocolate from one of my knees, and I howled softly. Before I knew it, Richard's face was taking the dive with his hands. I felt his breath between my knees, his ears caressing my thighs.

At that point I heard myself moaning softly. I let go a faint little "Nooo..."

He replied with a deep and lecherous "Yessssss..."

I said no again, and he said yes again. I kept saying no, he kept saying yes, and the whole yes-no thing started escalating in volume and seriousness until I firmly said, "No! Stop it! I think we've both had enough chocolate!"

That did it. Richard — who had seemed to be on the verge of something for the last five minutes — stopped, tensed his muscles in ecstasy, and arched his back, grabbing the massage table as if he was about to collapse.

I lay on the table feeling horny, disgusted, ecstatic, and freaked out, all at the same time. Richard laughed with relief as he slowly recovered.

"Wow!" he said. "Wow, wow, wooooooow!"

I guess it was a compliment, but I knew that I shouldn't address it. "Can I take a shower now?" I said, trying to remove myself from my chocolate bed.

"Of cooooourse, my dear!" He helped me up, and, flipping a panel on the wall, revealed a small bathroom with a shower stall.

"These towels are clean. Please take your time, and I'll meet you upstairs." He kissed my hand, looking me in the eye, and let go one final "wooooow" before leaving the room.

I showered as fast as I could, while my mind was racing at a million miles per hour. I had never been in such an intimate context with a stud of this caliber, so I was obviously excited about it. Still, there was something that just didn't feel right. A part of me wanted to ask him: "Is it true? Do you really find me sexy? Can a *Playgirl* centerfold like you enjoy touching someone who is far from being a *Playboy* centerfold, like me?" But another, more cautious part of me decided to keep my mouth shut, play it cool, and follow Madame's instructions.

I got dressed and went upstairs, where he was waiting for me. He was barefoot, wearing just a pair of jeans and a sweatshirt — enough to look like he belonged on the cover of an L.L. Bean catalogue.

"There you aaaaaaare!" he said, smiling.

I smiled briefly and continued walking toward the door. He followed me all the way to the exit and stopped me before I could step out.

"Listen, B . . . I just wanted to tell you that you are amaaaazing. I have never, *ever,* felt anything like this before."

"Thanks," I said, wondering if my ears were serving me right.

Then he held my hand, and, while gently pulling me

toward him, he looked me in the eye and—with a flattering tone of desperation—said, "Soooo...when can I see you
again?"

"I'm not sure. I need to think about it," was the best I
could answer.

He looked down, biting his lip, and gave me one last,
longing look as I stepped out onto the street. Alberto opened
the door for me to hop back in the car, and we immediately
took off.

"Is everything okay?" Alberto asked.

"Just give me a second," I told him while I pulled out my
red cell phone and called the Madame.

"Madame! It's B. Can you talk?"

"Sure, honey, but try to make it fast. I'm in the middle of
something."

When wasn't she in a hurry? Anyway, I showered her with
questions. "Why is Richard Weber so hot and so creepy at
the same time? Why would this guy—who could have any
woman in the world—hire someone like me? Why was he
so turned on every time I said no?"

"Honey, I have no time for all these questions; choose one,
and I'll answer that one."

I thought hard for a moment, and finally posed my
question.

"What would have happened if I had said yes?"

"He would have run away," she pronounced.

"But why? Does he like me or not?"

I could almost hear Madame rolling her eyes on the other
end of the line. "Honey...he's a compulsive seducer: he wants
to chase but he doesn't want to catch. There's plenty of men
like him. They work you like pizza dough, they make you soft

and smooth until you're ready for the oven, and then, when you're finally willing to go into the fire, they lose interest."

"But does he like me or not?" I asked anxiously.

"Does he like you? He cannot even see you! He sees a body that he likes, but you are just an object to him. And by the sound of your voice, I wonder if he's just an object to you too."

"He's not an object to me!" I replied.

"If you could really see him as a person, you'd see a guy who will never be able to have a meaningful relationship in his life. That's what you would see. If you could see him as a person, you wouldn't be lusting after him, you'd feel sorry for him."

Before I could say, "What the hell are you talking about?," Madame cut the whole thing short.

"I have to go. We'll talk tomorrow," she said, and hung up, leaving me overwhelmed by my own thoughts.

Was I objectifying Richard? Let's face it, the guy was gorgeous, but, truth be told, the whole concept of someone who chases something that he doesn't want to catch is kind of disturbing. Could you imagine spending your life in pursuit of something that in the end you don't even want? Always longing for something that is useless once you get it?

The ancient Greeks wrote about a character called Tantalus who was punished by the gods. He was up to his neck in water, and dying of thirst, but every time he tried to bend over to drink it, the water level would drop, so he kept being thirsty and yet surrounded by liquid. Richard was somehow like that, surrounded by women he could have, but as soon as he had them, he wouldn't want them anymore. No one and nothing could quench his thirst.

Suddenly I couldn't think of him as the hot stud with the

perfect body, I just saw him for what he was: someone who would be terribly lonely for the rest of his life. I felt sympathy for him, but the sexual attraction disappeared. Yes, he was an exceptionally handsome man, but he had the same psychological twists and turns that we all have. Women always complain of being objectified by men, but that night I realized that I had objectified Richard—and probably many others who had passed through my life before him.

"We're home," Alberto announced "Are you okay, Miss B?"

"I'm hanging in there," I sighed.

"It's been a tough day for me too," he said, letting go a deep sigh himself. I understood that he wanted to chat, so instead of getting out of the car I moved to the front of the limo.

"Would you like to go for a ride?" I asked him.

"Sure!"

We rolled down the windows so he could smoke a cigar. I don't smoke, but I love the smell of Cuban cigars, and his were Montecristos, courtesy of his brother in Miami.

The night was clear and fresh, and the Brooklyn Bridge looked like a Christmas ornament, hanging over the East River with its bright lights reflecting on the water.

"What's going on with you?" I asked.

"My wife and my daughters are in Florida with my mother-in-law." He made a short pause before simply adding, "I miss them."

He pulled out the picture of his wife and kids. All three of them were chubby and adorable. They had the smiles of people who know they're loved.

"How cute!" I said.

"Rosa is five, and Margarita is seven. They're good kids."

I almost cried. I know, it's silly, I barely knew this guy, but the fact that a big man like him would acknowledge something so tender and personal in front of a stranger moved me a lot.

We took the long way back home. He told me about his mother in the Dominican Republic, and his grandmother who was turning one hundred this year. He told me about the kids growing up, the lack of privacy at home, and how he and his wife could only have sex while doing the laundry in the basement. It was all so simple and sweet.

"Do you have a boyfriend?" Alberto asked.

"No," I replied, somehow embarrassed.

"Why?" he asked, surprised.

Every time I hear that damned question, I feel like there's no way to answer it without being sarcastic. *Let's see . . . why don't I have a boyfriend? Maybe I'm ugly, or fat, or stupid. Maybe nobody likes me. Maybe I'm unlovable.* What the hell can you answer to that? But in this case, probably because I was feeling much better about myself, or because Alberto asked it in a genuinely surprised way, it didn't feel like a threatening question, so I answered as honestly as I could.

"I don't know."

"I bet you're picky," replied Alberto, winking at me.

Before I had time to reply with something like "I'm *so* not picky, and I've been so desperately lonely, that I've even considered dating sex offenders that are currently serving time on Rikers Island," Alberto offered his matchmaking services: "Do you ever go to Miami?"

"Every once in a while. My parents retired down there," I replied.

"Next time you go, you have to meet my brother. I think you two could hit it off. He needs someone like you."

That was the sweetest compliment I had ever heard in my life. The fact that Alberto felt that someone he loved needed someone like me in his life was so kind and flattering that I was terribly moved.

Every once in a while — usually when I most need it — I get a little message from God, but these messages are never delivered by people who claim to speak on God's behalf. Priests and televangelists don't do anything for me. The moment I see that they make money out of the faithful, I lose respect for them.

My messages come usually from obscure and subtle sources. Sometimes God's messages are delivered by a book that I'm reading, by a song that I heard at the right moment, or even by a stranger on the street. One day I was walking down Fifty-ninth Street, with all my office worries swirling in my head like a Midwestern tornado, when a homeless lady — out of nowhere — told me, "Let go and let God!" and — having said that — kept going. Corny as it may sound, that's exactly what I needed to hear to stop my self-flagellating thoughts and realize that I was obsessing over things that were way beyond my control.

I suspect that that night God spoke to me through two people, Richard — the loneliest man on earth — and Alberto — the luckiest one. Thanks to them, I finally realized what I wanted: to fall in love with someone, but from the inside out. Someone I could love the same way I wanted to be loved.

When I got home, I had the urge to play one of my favorite songs, "A Sunday Kind of Love" sung by Etta James. There was something warm and fuzzy about those lyrics that made me feel great. It says that "Sunday" kind of love is the love that lasts past the sexy thrills of a Saturday night. And that is exactly what I wanted: a very Sunday kind of love.

Now it was just a matter of finding it.

CHAPTER 14

I've always been fascinated by words. I'm particularly tickled by the emotions and feelings that they can trigger, and how they sometimes translate, and sometimes don't. One of my favorite examples is the word "blue."

In English, blue is a color but also a state of mind. Whoever came up first with that association was a genius, because the color blue chromatically represents sadness like no other. "Feeling blue" paints a perfect picture of your mood.

But in Spanish "blue" is just a color. We call it *azul,* and there are no depressing feelings associated with it. When I say "blue" I think of sadness, but when I say *azul* I think of the sea or the sky: wide, open, beautiful, but never sad. It's funny, because, even though it's the same color, the word doesn't have the same feeling.

In Spanish we have an expression that doesn't translate well into English, but it reflects the type of prejudice that the "weight-challenged" have endured through history. If you like a woman you may say, *"Me cae bien."* It translates roughly as "She falls nice on me." But when you don't like a woman you say, *"Me cae gorda,"* meaning, "She falls fat on me." It doesn't matter how skinny the woman is, if she's a pain in the ass she feels *gorda*. For obvious reasons, it's not the kind of expression that I use lightly (pardon the pun), but the morning after my rendezvous with Richard Weber, *"Me cae gorda"* was the first thought that came to my mind when I had to deal with Lillian at the office. She is quite slim, but she was starting to fall really *gorda* on me. She showed up early at my cubicle, looked me straight in the eye, and asked point-blank, "Are you avoiding me?"

"Of course not," I said casually, while organizing my pens in a coffee mug as if I were putting together a prize-winning flower arrangement.

"Why aren't you returning my phone calls?" she fired, immediately adding, "I love that top—where did you get it?" In case I haven't explained it yet, Lillian is known for her short attention span.

"Barney's. By the way, I did return your phone calls. I told you that I wasn't in the mood to go out," I said, removing the remains of last night's chocolate from under my fingernails.

"You're freaking me out. Are you, like, staying home and feeling sorry for yourself? Did you change your makeup?" Again she rapidly switched topics, while examining the contents of my handbag.

"It's Susie May," I explained.

"Susie May? You gotta be kidding me! That's what my mom wears. Why the hell are you using Susie May?"

"I prefer Susie May. And to answer your question, no, I'm not staying home feeling sorry for myself. I've been hanging out with an old friend," I said, hoping to end the discussion then and there.

A week ago, I would have reacted very differently to Lillian's questions: I might have been docile and apologetic. But today she was pissing me off. While still looking at my makeup kit, she continued in a half-concerned, half-superficial tone.

"B, I can see that you're not in a good place, you're isolating yourself, and if you fall apart—I love this color; what is it called?" she interrupted herself, referring to my new lipstick.

"Temptation Red," I said, pointing to the label.

"Anyway, so if you fall apart I'm your best friend and I'm gonna have to pick up the pieces."

Correct me if I'm wrong, but I believe that this is the most condescending bullshit I've heard in my life. I looked at Lillian, trying to control my fury.

"Do I look like I'm falling apart?"

"I know you well. You are up to something. You can't fool me," she said.

I realized that Lillian probably had no idea that any honest concern she was showing was overshadowed by her patronizing tone, but at that moment I didn't feel like making my usual excuses for her narcissistic behavior. Just as I was gearing up to send her to hell in a handbasket, my cell phone rang. Lillian grabbed it and, looking at the caller ID, immediately asked, "Who's Natasha Sokolov?"

Beyond angry, I snatched the cell phone and my handbag away from her.

"She's nobody. And don't worry, I don't have any plans to fall apart. And if I do, I certainly won't be asking you to pick up my pieces. Now, if you'll excuse me, I have to take this phone call."

I couldn't tell if she was hurt or offended. A sudden cramp in my stomach indicated that maybe I had been too hard on someone who ultimately cared about me, but I chose to ignore it and answer my daily call while Lillian quietly disappeared down the hallway.

"Madame?"

"Alberto will pick you up at nine-forty-five p.m."

"Who's the client?"

"Guido. You'll have fun, he's quite a character."

"Any special instructions?" I asked.

"I'll fax you the instructions later. I'll call you beforehand, so you can wait by the fax machine."

I was still wondering what could be so complicated that it required faxed instructions when Bonnie called me to her office.

"B, I want you to set up a mandatory brainstorming this afternoon."

"With the copywriters?" I asked.

"With *everybody*. We need ideas for the UK Charms slogan."

"Have you seen the slogans we submitted already?"

"I've been too busy. Just set up the brainstorming and e-mail me the results. It's urgent."

It was urgent, but she hadn't taken the time to read the ideas that she already had on her desk. How typically Bonnie. The general brainstorming probably looked like an innocent request. She wanted to give everyone the chance to come up with the million-dollar idea. Very fair, very democratic, right? Well, bullshit.

These general brainstorming sessions are useless for several reasons:

First, the other departments couldn't care less about being included "in the creative process." They just want to leave the office at five-thirty—or five-fifteen, if possible.

Second, it's a slap in the face for the whole creative department, whose job is actually to come up with the damn slogans.

Third, nothing gets accomplished. Half the people don't show up, and those who do, come mainly because we cater the session with chocolate-chip cookies. The copywriters are too pissed to give any ideas, and the others just sit there staring at the wall while chewing chocolate morsels.

I always end up running the meeting with a room half full of summer interns who will not stop playing with their cell phones, some graphic designers who became designers precisely because they care about images — not about words — and a bunch of copywriters who resent Bonnie's assumption that anyone in the company can come up with a better slogan than they. The only thing that these open brainstorms accomplish is to piss off my group.

And to top it off, all of us know that if we come up with a half-decent idea, Bonnie will twist it and mangle it before we have the chance to show it to the client. But, as with everything Bonnie does, there was a secret evil purpose behind it. I just didn't know what it was quite yet.

"Okay, guys, let's go through it one more time: we need something young, something British, something catchy and irreverent. The target audience is fourteen-to-twenty-four-year-old girls. Anything, anybody...? Anything...?"

After an hour of trying to pull ideas out of them, I gave up and started coming up with something — pretty lame — myself, so I could prove to Bonnie that I went through with the meeting.

"How about 'da bomb'? 'UK Charms...da bomb' — they look like firecrackers anyway, right?" I said.

But my group didn't even respond. The interns chewed

their cookies absentmindedly, and the creatives looked at me
with profound disdain.

"How about 'gag the rag'?" Joe Peters finally said, and the
whole room burst into laughter.

"Okay... it's a little graphic, but I'll write it down," I said,
trying not to discourage anyone from participating.

But once the cookies were gone, almost everybody was
gone as well. As I was wrapping up these two hours of nothing, my red cell phone—which was carefully stored in my
cleavage—vibrated, so I excused myself and, skipping like a
schoolgirl, rushed to the fax machine to pick up my instructions for that night's customer.

I waited by the fax machine for a few seconds until the
page came through. Then I read the short text three or four
times, trying to make sense of it:

> ...you will find a set of ankle weights in a box placed in
> the backseat. You must fasten them to your legs before
> you leave the car. Wear a long skirt or pants to conceal
> them. Walk slowly and be careful not to trip on them...

Ankle weights? Why? What for? I folded my instructions
carefully and placed them in my brassiere, next to my red
cell phone, for safekeeping.

I left the office without saying goodbye to anybody. I was
too busy thinking about the scenario I would encounter that
night.

"Ankle weights?" I muttered to myself on my way to the
subway. This was weird.

Very, very weird.

CHAPTER 15

That night I decided to wear a cotton-Lycra bodice, a dark-purple bolero jacket, and a new pair of black silk Palazzo pants that I bought on the way home from work that same afternoon. The pants were so ample that from afar they looked like a long and flowing skirt. If I needed to hide something underneath them, they should do the trick. I took one last look in the mirror before I left the apartment.

"Good," I said to myself, approving of my outfit, "pretty damn good." If it didn't sound immodest, I would say that I looked like a million dollars. Half a million at least.

I rushed downstairs to meet Alberto, but before I could enter the car he stopped me.

"Wait! Wait, Miss B," Alberto said when he saw me. "Can I take a picture before you come into the car?"

"Of course," I said. Using the sidewalk as an improvised runway, I pranced and posed for him while he took a few stills with his cell phone.

"Wait till my brother sees you," Alberto said with a big smile.

I was just about to thank him for his matchmaking services when I found the box on the backseat. As Alberto drove north toward the Upper East Side, I opened the box and found a set of ten-pound ankle weights.

"Miss B, walk slowly with those. I've seen girls trip and fall in them."

"I'll be careful," I promised, while I strapped them to my legs.

Alberto pulled over in front of an elegant condo on the Upper East Side, and I descended from the car with considerable difficulty. Turned out that the "walk slowly" advice was totally unnecessary. It was impossible to walk fast on high heels and with those twenty extra pounds anchoring me to the ground.

The load was so heavy that I couldn't really walk. I just dragged my feet across the lobby as if I were escaping a chain gang. On every step you could hear the loud clinking-clanking sound of the weights. The doorman didn't seem intrigued by my odd walk, making me think that I wasn't the first fat chick dragging her feet around that lobby. Soon I confirmed that I wasn't the first, and wouldn't be the last one either.

As I dragged my feet into the elevator, I heard a woman's voice behind me.

"Hold it!"

You should have seen my face when a black woman, my size, came into the elevator dragging her feet as well, and making the same clinking-clanking noise that I was making. I looked at her, first surprised, and then mistrusting. She looked back and mirrored my attitude.

"Penthouse, please," we both told the elevator operator at the exact same time.

Who was this chick? Was she coming to the same apartment? For a split second I thought that by some mysterious coincidence we were going to different apartments on the same floor, but as the elevator door opened at the top floor, and I realized that at the end of the long hallway there was only one door, my doubts vanished. She was going to Guido's too. At that point I should maybe have introduced myself, but I was too nervous, so, with a competitive attitude that was completely out of place, I started racing her to the door. We must have looked like two fat idiots running a sack race at a company picnic.

We both got to the door at the exact same time, and we both reached for the buzzer in unison. That's when I finally confronted her.

"Look," I said, "is this going to be a lesbian scene? 'Cause if that's the case I'm not staying, okay?"

She looked at me briefly with an attitude that only black girls are capable of. "Girl, you need to chill," she said, and rang the doorbell.

Before I could say anything, I heard a familiar clinking-clanking on the other side of the door. A big red-haired woman opened the door with a broad smile on her face.

"About time!" said the redhead.

What the hell was going on here?

"This way, ladies, watch your step . . ." she welcomed us.

I didn't have time to question the presence of the third girl, because a new piece of the puzzle immediately made my head spin. That fancy penthouse on the Upper East Side was a gigantic mess. There were piles and piles of newspapers and magazines everywhere. There was so much crap in there that the absurd mass of stuff created a labyrinth, literally, which we had to venture through to get to the living room. There, in a small open area, we found our customer: a short Italian guy with a bad case of hair plugs, who wore a ratty bathrobe and a set of gold chains that would put a gangsta rapper to shame.

"Hawyadoin', girls! Come right in!" Guido greeted us with his charming New Jersey accent.

"Puchy," said the black girl — addressing him by his nickname, I supposed.

"Myrna, I don't know how ya manage to look hotter every day," he told her.

"Oh, stop it!" she answered back.

"Yer B, aren't ya?" he asked me. I nodded, virtually speechless.

"Yer gorgeous!" he said. "Just like Madame said."

"Oh really? And what did Madame say about me?" asked the redhead.

"She said that ya were a big red pain in the ass, that's what she said," joked Guido, and they all laughed.

"I'm Lorre," said the redhead finally introducing herself to me.

"I'm Myrna," said the black woman politely, but keeping her distance.

"Lemme apologize for da mess," explained Guido. "See, my wife, she has OCD, and she won't throw anything away. Just gimme a second to prepare a place for you to sit."

He gave us a collective wink and disappeared into the bedroom. The three of us were left alone in the crammed living room. I thought about saying something, but I was too tense and embarrassed to make small talk with the girls. After a second of uncomfortable silence, Myrna turned to Lorre and asked her about an old acquaintance.

"Whatever happened to that Greek girl who used to come here all the time? What was her name?"

Feeling excluded from the conversation, I shied away from them and started looking at the piles of magazines left around the apartment, while discreetly eavesdropping on their chat.

"Anastasia?" said Lorre. "She got married and moved to Chicago. They bought a nice house in Oak Brook. She's pregnant with twins!"

"Good for her!" Myrna said with a laugh.

A girl who used to do this got married and moved to the suburbs? Interesting . . . I thought to myself. I guess I never stopped to think that the comfort providers were just regular women who were hoping to get married one day and have a house and a few kids. I was happy to hear that story, and it made me feel that we were all in the same boat, and that maybe what I was doing was not a mortal sin after all.

While I was entertaining these and other thoughts, I started discovering a few little treasures in the piles of old magazines that Guido's wife had all over the apartment.

"Wow! Check this out, girls!" I said, picking up a dusty issue of a *Life* magazine with Eva Gabor on the cover. "Doesn't she look like Madame?"

"Yeah, a bit," Myrna agreed, "but Madame reminds me of this other actress, the one who did that movie with Elvis Presley . . ."

"Ann-Margret," I offered.

"That one!"

"Well, check this out," said Lorre, digging up yet another *Life* magazine, this one with Ann-Margret on the cover.

Next thing you know, the three of us were going through the mountains of periodicals trying to outdo each other's archaeological efforts. These were some of our most valuable findings:

- The original *Cosmo* magazine with the Burt Reynolds nude centerfold.
- A *Playbill* of the first staging of *My Fair Lady* on Broadway.
- A graphic brochure on sexually transmitted diseases issued by the Ministry of Health of Guatemala.
- Napkins from the old Horn & Hardart Automat restaurant at Forty-fifth Street and Fifth Avenue.
  Vanna White paper dolls.

We could have spent the whole night digging up treasures in this pop-culture mausoleum, and, surprisingly enough, we did, because it in no way interfered with our duties.

A few minutes later, Myrna, Lorre, and I were sitting on the bed in Guido's cluttered bedroom. The entire perimeter of the bed was flanked by more books, more magazines, more everything.

"This place is a mess. But I have to confess that it's fascinating," I said.

"You are a Gemini, right?" asked Lorre.

"How did you know?"

"You have that double-thing thing—the child and the adult, the virgin and the whore—you're very Gemini," Lorre explained while browsing a French magazine from the sixties. "Wasn't Sophia Loren gorgeous?" she asked.

"Beyond gorgeous," I said, and we all sighed.

Feeling more comfortable with the girls, I ventured an apology to Myrna.

"By the way, I didn't mean to come across as homophobic out there."

"Don't worry, Mama, I'm not a lesbian," she replied. "But

if you find me a woman who's got a nine-inch dick, I might give it a shot."

We laughed as if we were stoned, until we were interrupted by a mournful groan.

Myrna propped herself up, looked at the spot she was sitting on, and asked, "Honey, can you breathe okay?"

"Dontcha move!" moaned Guido.

Oh, wait a minute. I forgot to tell you something fairly relevant: all along, as we talked and laughed·on the bed, Guido had been lying underneath us, facedown, on a feather mattress.

I know, it's crazy, but Guido seemed to be turned on by heavy burdens. So the three off us, with clinking-clanking weights and all, were parked right on top of him for about two hours. I was going to volunteer the phone number of Dr. Goldstein, my chiropractor, but I didn't want to put Guido on the spot.

Myrna sat back down on his shoulders and went back to her magazine. That's when we heard another muffled groan from below.

"What did he say?" asked Myrna.

"Grind, I think," replied Lorre.

And so we did. We kept grinding ourselves repeatedly to increase the pressure on Guido. Each time, he screamed in ecstasy. He was as happy as a pig in shit. Who knew that someone would get off on something so ridiculously simple?

"A Carmita como que le gustan los hombres sin culo," my mom used to say about my aunt Carmita, who always dated the same type of men, with broad shoulders and no ass. "I think she has a fetish," Mom said, and that was the first time I heard that word: fetish.

As the years went by, I ended up associating fetishes with creepy guests on daytime talk shows, but after that night in Guido's apartment I started seeing the other side of the coin.

The most obvious fetishes are well known: shoes (especially stilettos), leather clothing, dungeons, military uniforms. But I have learned that fetishists can be turned on by pretty much anything. Some people are irresistibly attracted to veiny arms, soft elbows, bulging eyes, hairy backs, and even big front teeth. What has to happen in your childhood to make you crave the company of a bucktoothed lover? I have no idea, but I wonder if God decided to create fetishes to make sure that the bucktoothed guy found a girlfriend too. I've heard that some people are even turned on by sneezing. I can be a bit of a sneezer when the seasons change, so for a minute I wondered if I could find myself a nice "sneezophiliac," but, knowing how insecure I can be, I know that I would constantly be questioning if I sneeze too much, or not enough, or if he's seeing another woman on the side who sneezes better than me.

When I see these young girls who marry rich old men, I wonder if they have a money fetish. Would they marry the same senior citizen if he were poor?

But when I see someone like Guido, who's turned on by such a simple pleasure as having three fat girls sitting on his back, I can't help feeling a little envious. For me sex is not so simple. In my case, sexual attraction is based on a mix of feelings, fantasies, and expectations. Even at my horniest, I need to think that the man I'm with is "the one." I can't just randomly pick three bodies and place them on my back. I need someone with a certain personality, a nice smile, a good job. Is it better to be like me, or to be like Guido? I honestly don't know. He will always find someone who'll make him happy. But me? I wasn't so sure. Maybe Alberto was right when he told me that I was picky. Maybe that's why I had such a hard time finding my match.

But let's go back to the story. After two hours sitting on Guido's back, Myrna, Lorre, and I decided to go to a Greek diner for a quick bite. While our respective chauffeurs smoked cigars outside, we looked at the menus and decided to indulge in comfort food.

A super-young, super-skinny, super-gothic waitress with black lipstick and piercings all over her face came over to take our order.

"I want a hamburger...make it a Cheddar cheeseburger deluxe, and a Coke," said Myrna, while still browsing the menu.

"Diet Coke?" asked the waitress innocently.

There was a dead silence while Myrna lowered the menu with a menacing look on her face.

"Did you hear me say 'Diet'?" she snapped.

"I...I didn't hear it..." the waitress tried to say apologetically, but Myrna interrupted her.

"You didn't hear it because I didn't say it. So bring me a full-fat sugar-coated carb-loaded motherfucking soda, all right?"

Understanding the screw-up, the girl blushed and turned to me, trying to change the subject.

"And for you, miss?"

"Same thing."

Lorre indicated with a smile that she wanted the same, and the waitress left in a hurry.

We all laughed at the incident. What's up with people

assuming that just because you're fat you have to drink a diet soda? Let's face it, if we're having cheeseburgers deluxe, we're not in a hurry to lose any weight.

"So how long have you been in the business?" asked Myrna. "A week?"

"Yes. How did you know?" I said as I smiled, a little embarrassed. "Is it that obvious?"

Myrna and Lorre laughed out loud.

"We can tell," said Lorre. "It's great money, right?"

"Oh, it's fantastic money, but for me..."

Before I could finish the sentence, Myrna stepped in, completing my thought. "You're doing it for the thrill, right?"

I nodded, and they laughed again.

"Getting paid to be worshipped? How did this happen?" said Lorre.

"First I did it for the thrill too," said Myrna, "but then the thrill went away and I got hooked on the money."

"See...that's my problem. I'm not a prude, but I feel guilty about making money out of this. Being with someone because he paid me, it makes me feel weird, it makes me feel like I'm a..."

"Whore?" Myrna completed.

"Exactly," I whined.

"That's just social bullshit. What's the difference between marrying for money and having sex for money?" Lorre asked.

"Sex? I wish this was sex!" Myrna added. "My husband loves this, because I make a ton of cash and I come home horny every night. Do you have a boyfriend?" she asked me.

"Nope."

"Well, you better get one, because you're gonna get very horny very fast," predicted Myrna.

I must have blushed to a deep purple, because both girls laughed so hard at me that I was afraid they were going to have a stroke.

Yes. I needed a boyfriend, because I was getting restless, and impatient, and — truth be told — I was also getting very horny, very fast.

CHAPTER 16

*M*y friend Rodolfo was a seriously talented advertising producer, and he did tons of commercials for my agency. But he had a bad habit: every time someone in the crew made a mistake, he would call him an idiot to his face. It was kind of embarrassing to witness that, because he would yell and scream things like "How stupid can you be?" or "What kind of retarded asshole are you?" The guy was smart and gifted, but his social skills truly sucked.

Obviously, he wouldn't treat his clients the same way. However, though he never insulted them to their faces, privately he would tell me anecdotes that proved their hopeless idiocy. I confess that, for me, it's sometimes fun to trash certain people, like Bonnie. But Rodolfo really took it to another level. He dwelled on it.

At some point, his company, which used to be extremely successful, went down. Unable to attract clients, he felt the need to leave expensive New York City for a more forgiving environment. He moved to Mexico, where he produced a few commercials and a documentary about the shamans of Tulum. I lost track of Rodolfo, then a year later he came back to New York and took me out for dinner.

I noticed that he had mellowed out quite a bit. He wasn't describing in detail the stupidity of mankind anymore. He talked a lot of about Tulum, where he was living now, making videos for some New Age company that promoted spiritual healing and such. I was pleasantly surprised to see that he was in a less negative mind-set, and I told him so. He heard me and smiled. Then, after looking around as if we were being spied upon, he told me something I never forgot.

"B, after I lost my business I realized that not only should you not call people stupid, you shouldn't even think it, because they can hear you."

"Okaaay," I said to myself, thinking that maybe he'd gone a little crazy. I guess that, after you'd been chewing peyote for a while with the shamans of Tulum, something was bound to happen. But, crazy or not, after this spiritual awakening he was a much nicer person. His confession always stayed with me, and the morning after my Upper East Side adventure, I caught myself thinking about Rodolfo's statement. *Not only should you not call people stupid, you shouldn't even think it, because they can hear you.*

Can people actually read your mind? I must confess that I have seen men running away from me every time I got into my desperate-spinster funks. Just like dogs that attack you when they smell fear, men run away from you when they smell an agenda. I know that there's a generalized complaint that men are afraid of commitment, but when women show up with an agenda — be it *marry me,* or *buy me a house* — men have very few options other than doing it, or running away as fast as they can.

But that Friday morning, as I pondered all these things in my cubicle, a mysterious phone call brought me back to reality.

"B?"

"Hi, Mary!"

"I think you need to go to the bathroom."

"What?"

"I think you need to go to the bathroom right now."

That's when it clicked. Something had happened in Bonnie's office that required my immediate presence in the ladies' room. Without hesitation I grabbed my recorder and went to sit in the toilet with my legs propped against the wall, dying to hear and register whatever the hell was going on.

Bonnie stormed into the ladies' room bitching and moaning, closely followed by Christine. I felt her checking for any visible legs under the stall door before — convinced that they were alone — erupting in an endless tirade against the Chicago Boss. Apparently, she was having a disagreement with him about the UK Charms pitch, but, being the two-headed monster that she was, she would keep up the smile in front of him, and then use Christine to blow off steam.

"I can't stand that asshole!" Bonnie said. "But he is digging his own grave, that much I can tell you."

"Are you sure that you want to pick a fight with him?" Christine asked.

"Oh, I'm not going to fight with him. I don't waste my time fighting. But he's going to come in next Friday and he's going to find himself in the middle of a minefield. And you can write that down."

Actually, there was no need for Christine to write it down, since I was recording the confession of her master plan from my stall. The only good news was that, this time, I wasn't her prime target. She had her eyes on someone bigger. Even I had to acknowledge that she was brilliant. Rotten, but brilliant. And the problem with brilliant, rotten people is that, much like serial killers, after they get away with murder over and over, they get cocky, and they start thinking that they are invincible. That's probably why Bonnie wasn't smart enough to realize that when you brag about your killings in a public place, someone — like me — can be recording every word of it.

Back at my desk, I finished working on the brainstorm notes that I had to e-mail to Bonnie. I kept even the stupidest slogans from the disgruntled creatives, including "Say hello to Aunt Flo" and "Parting the Red Sea." The fact is that all the ideas sucked, but it would make no difference to Bonnie. It would probably facilitate things for her.

Two hours later, I was at the copy machine when she walked by.

"What are you doing?" she asked.

"I'm putting together the reports for the UK Charms presentation."

"I didn't have time to go through the stats that you gave me, so you *have* to write me some bullet points," she said in her usual military tone.

"And by when do you need this?" I asked while examining my cuticles.

"By the end of the day. I'm going to leave early, so drop it with my doorman tonight so I can read it during the weekend."

Great. So I *did* the research, I *gave* it to her a week ago, I *offered* to write her bullet points then — but she refused them — and now I *had* to stay way past midnight on a Friday so she could look good in her meeting. And, naturally, she expected me to drop it at her home, because, even though

I had to work late, she was leaving early. Correct me if I'm wrong, but this lady's *cojones* should be on display at the Museum of Natural History.

But timing is everything, and at that particular moment my red cell phone rang loud and clear. I pulled it out of my cleavage. Bonnie looked at me as if I had burped in the middle of her wedding. Her nasty look encouraged me.

"I can't work tonight," I said.

"This is *very* important," she threatened me.

"Well, this is a *very* important call, and I will not work late tonight, so if you'll excuse me..."

I just walked away from her, knowing that I would piss her off beyond reason, and that was exactly what I wanted to accomplish.

Once out of the reach of her claws, I answered my cell.

"Madame?"

"Honey? Alberto will pick you up at ten. It's going to be a mellow night. Bring a book to read."

Knowing that Bonnie was leaving early, I left a bit early myself, and I rushed home to get ready and to go through the pile of books that I'd been buying but, because I have never said no to Bonnie, I hadn't had time to read in the last three years. I chose a book of short stories by Gabriel García Márquez that a friend had recommended months ago. I threw it in my bag and went downstairs to meet Alberto.

Alberto took me to Tribeca, one of the most expensive neighborhoods in the city. We stopped in front of a renovated warehouse. I rang the bell, and a female voice answered.

"Who is it?"

"It's B," I said, wondering if my client could be a woman. Would Madame send me to see a woman?

The woman buzzed me in, and I walked into one of

those private elevators where you need a key to access the floor you're going to. Someone called the elevator up, and the door opened in a photography studio. Turned out that the whole warehouse was the studio and residence of a fashion photographer.

I stepped out of the elevator to find a very active photo shoot in progress. There were a handful of assistants, hair and makeup stylists, and several super-skinny models dressed up in haute-couture gowns, posing in front of a very complicated set made out of pink leather. Some of the models looked familiar, probably because I had seen them on the covers of fashion magazines. These were the kind of girls who fly first-class from New York to Milan to work on the big fashion shows.

The photographer was tall, skinny, and scruffy, and he wore thick eyeglasses. I immediately knew who he was. I had seen him mentioned in the newspapers as the fashion photographer of the moment. He was none other than Simon Leary.

"Put your right hand on your hip...Okay...you are bored...You are so bored you can hardly stay awake...Now look at me!" said Simon while snapping a few shots of a blonde who was lying on a chaise longue.

He switched cameras, got rid of the chair, brought over two more models, and started snapping a new batch of pictures. The girls stood in languid poses, looking away from each other as if they had been forced to stand together. I've worked in advertising for several years, but I'm always involved in unglamorous projects where we have to photograph a box of cereal or a jar of peanut butter. This was my very first time watching fashion models at work. I'm not crazy about the whole anorexic-model aesthetic, but I couldn't stop watching them. It was one of the most interesting things I've ever seen.

When the models were not posing, they just looked like emaciated teenagers. But the moment they made their "model face," they would turn into sex goddesses. They would stretch their necks, relax their shoulders, lower their faces, open their eyes really wide, and—very subtly—suck in the sides of their mouths to enhance their cheekbones. They managed to look real and fake at the same time.

Watching these girls working it for the camera made me realize how much effort and energy it takes to look naturally pretty in a photo. It looked exhausting.

"Sandra, you either look at her or you don't, but right now you're giving me this three-quarter look that is totally useless," Simon said to one of the girls, without even making eye contact with her.

I studied Simon. There was an extreme awkwardness about him. His lips were tightly pressed together, as if he was fighting a smile, and he spoke so low that catching his words was like trying to catch a bullet with your teeth.

At some point the Sandra girl tried to adjust the strap of her shoe, but she lost her balance and attempted to grab Simon so that she wouldn't fall. Before she even touched him, he jumped away from her as if she were trying to stab him, knocking over one of the lights and causing a small commotion.

What's wrong with him? I thought. She had barely touched him, and he jumped back as if the devil were coming to take his soul. The oddest part was that Simon didn't even apologize to her.

"I'm so sorry," said a confused and embarrassed Sandra.

In my opinion, it was Simon who should have apologized. But Simon didn't say a thing. He stood back for a few seconds, looking at the floor, while Sandra recovered from the incident — she would have fallen on her face if it weren't for the model next to her, who stepped in to help. The studio assistants quickly replaced the light, and then Simon continued taking his pictures, but standing at a safer distance from the girls and avoiding their eyes. I'm telling you, the guy was odd. Very odd.

Romina, Simon's young, slim, cute, and Italian-accented assistant, approached me.

"May I help you?"

"I'm looking for Simon."

"He's busy right now. May I take a message?"

"Well, I believe that he's waiting for me, but if he's busy..." I replied, tempted to use that as an excuse to leave. This guy's attitude was totally rubbing me the wrong way.

At that moment, Simon noticed me, and he walked right up to us. He looked me up and down, and, without addressing me, told Romina, "Take her upstairs," as if I were an additional piece of lighting equipment some delivery man had just dropped off.

Okay, how rude was this guy? Very rude. As Simon walked back to his models, I couldn't help asking Romina, "Is he in a bad mood?"

"He's always like that," she answered.

Great! A grumpy one, I thought, and followed Romina back into the elevator. She took me to the third floor, where Simon had his apartment. For someone who supposedly had a lot of money, his place was terribly humble: a couch, a coffee table, a TV, a couple of chairs, and tons of books and CDs. What was very cool, though, were the photographs he had on display. Even though Simon was a famous fashion photographer, there was not one fashion shot hanging on any of the walls;

instead, he had a beautiful series of huge portraits featuring commuters sleeping in trains. I immediately remembered seeing a couple of them at some famous SoHo gallery. They were in a book called *Sleeping Beauties* that came out a few years ago.

"Did Simon take these too?"

"Of course," said Romina, and she excused herself to go back to work.

I remained in the apartment, mesmerized by those photos on the wall. They were the portraits of working people who had fallen asleep in the trains during their commute. If you've ever been in the New York subway during rush hour, you know there's a good number of people who snore their way to work every morning. When I lived in Brooklyn, I had a longer commute, and I would share close quarters with quite a few sleeping passengers; almost every single day, I ended up with someone drooling on my shoulder. Not only is it a real annoyance, but it's gross as hell. The fascinating part is that all the sleepers managed to wake up automatically when the train arrived at their stations. It's as if they had built-in alarm clocks in their heads.

Watching the sleeping commuters was an enormous voyeuristic pleasure. Young and old, men and women, they all had the innocent expression of sleeping babies. These photos made you feel like it doesn't matter how old you are, there's an innocence that seems to overcome all humans when we sleep. I was impressed that this rude guy could be capable of capturing such delicate beauty.

The sound of the door pulled me out of my trance. Simon walked in, avoiding eye contact at all cost. I decided to avoid it too, since—as Madame used to say—the customer is always right.

"Sorry for making you wait. I just needed to finish something downstairs," he said.

"Don't worry, I was admiring these pictures. They're wonderful."

"Yeah, I wish they could pay the rent," he said, dismissively.

I didn't know what to reply to that, so I just said, "Well—I love them anyway." And when he heard me say that, he stilled.

"Thanks," he said without looking at me.

"My name is B." I extended my hand, but Simon avoided the handshake. *Okay, he doesn't shake hands,* I said to myself while trying to figure out what to do with my hand suspended in the air. But after seeing the way he treated the models downstairs, I had no reason to take this personally. Whatever made him act like that was entirely his problem, not mine.

To avoid the awkwardness of the moment, Simon turned around and started shuffling magazines from one table to another. While doing this, he said in a low but audible voice, "Nice to meet you."

I smiled at no one, since he was still avoiding my eyes.

"Do you need anything? A glass of water? The bathroom, maybe?" he offered.

"I'm fine," I replied.

"Okay, so let's start."

Here's where the big mystery began. Simon took a large pillow and put it against the armrest of his couch. Then he pulled out a measuring tape and carefully measured sixteen and a half inches from the pillow.

"Can you sit over here?" he asked me.

I walked over to the couch and sat near the spot he was marking.

"Closer," he said. "Your right leg should be right here."

He tapped his finger on the sixteen-and-a-half-inch mark. I hesitated, but finally managed to slide down the couch to the exact mark he had measured. Apparently satisfied with the placement, he asked: "Did you bring a book?"

"Yeah, it's in my bag ..."

As I made an attempt to get up to reach for my bag, which I had left by the entrance, Simon jumped: "Don't move!"

I froze. What a control freak! I rolled my eyes and remained in place while he nervously brought me my bag. Without looking at him, I pulled out my book and waited for additional instructions. But he didn't say one more word. He just picked up an alarm clock, set it to ring in three hours, and put it in front of me on the coffee table. Then he took a couple of steps back to look at the scene, as if he was going to take a picture. I could almost hear him thinking: *Clock in place, pillow in place, fat girl in place* ... I just sat there witnessing this, waiting for something to happen. And it finally did.

Simon came over and squeezed himself into the tight sixteen and a half inches that were left between the pillow and me. He took a deep breath, let out a sigh, closed his eyes, and — almost immediately — fell asleep. That was it.

I sat there wondering if anything else was going to happen, but after ten minutes or so, I realized that my job was to sit there and read a book while he slept. And so I did.

He slept for three hours and I read for three hours, interrupted only by his peaceful snoring.

Thank God my book was great. Gabriel García Márquez is — in my very humble opinion — a genius. He wrote my favorite novel ever: *One Hundred Years of Solitude*. But this book, lighter than that novel, was a collection of short stories called *Strange Pilgrims*. One of my favorite stories was about an aging prostitute who was so lonely that she trained her little dog to go weep at her grave, thinking that no one else would miss her when she died.

The story made me think about my recent adventures, and myself. Was I going to be like her? Would I ever find love? On a night like this, sitting next to this strange guy — who couldn't even give you a decent handshake — I very much doubted that love was anywhere in sight. The novelty of my new profession was starting to wear off. I could appreciate the small changes that it had inspired in my life, but how long could I continue doing this?

Lost in the book and my thoughts, I barely noticed when Simon's head started resting comfortably on my shoulder. I thought about shaking him off, like I have often done with subway commuters, but I was getting paid here. So I let him lean over comfortably. That's when I realized how long it had been since I'd had anyone sleeping peacefully next to me. It's a wonderful sensation. We are so vulnerable when we sleep, I believe that sleeping next to someone is the ultimate proof of trust. I was surprised that this guy, who barely knew me, could feel so comfortable next to me. Then again, I was hired as a "comfort provider."

After three hours, the alarm clock went off. It took a few seconds for Simon to react. When he was fully awake, he realized that he was leaning on me, and — abruptly — he took his head off my shoulder and got off the couch in a hurry.

Without saying a word, he reached for his wallet, paid me, and showed me to the door. I went back to the limo, where Alberto was patiently waiting for me.

"How did it go, Miss B?"

"Ugh..." I answered.

"What do you mean?"

"This guy is so...I don't know...he's weird." And that was saying a lot, considering the guys I had met recently through the Madame.

"Was he rude to you? Do you want me to have a talk with him?"

"No, he wasn't intentionally rude...He...he's just very guarded."

Alberto dropped one of his favorite lines, "There's a lot of lonely people in New York."

"Yes, indeed," I said.

As Alberto drove me home by the riverside, I mumbled his words once again: "There's a lot of lonely people in New York." But at that point I wondered if I was referring to Simon, or if I was referring to myself.

CHAPTER 17

The morning after my sitting stunt at Simon Leary's studio, I went shopping for lingerie. I wanted to treat myself, because the previous night had been kind of depressing. Hanging out with that guy brought me down big-time.

So I was browsing through these pricey negligees, and when I asked for an extra-large to try on, the clerk looked at me as if I had asked for a spare kidney.

"I don't think that we carry your size."

Inspired by Myrna and the Diet Coke incident, I just gave her a nasty look and said, with my best New York attitude: "You *don't think* you carry my size? Well, stop thinking and start checking, because I want to try it on."

Realizing that I was "big" trouble, the clerk retreated. "Let me see what we have in the back."

The clerk momentarily disappeared, and I turned my attention to an embroidered push-up bra without padding. That's when I started feeling weird. I remember once in school a teacher reading the fairy tale "The Princess and the Pea" to our class. From then on, whenever something didn't feel right to me, I imagined I was just like the princess feeling a pea under a tower of mattresses. That pea usually hinted that I was avoiding my feelings.

I'll never forget something I saw years ago on one of the shopping networks. They had a caller who was asking about some fantasy jewelry collection. The woman in question was calling from Hawaii. She was out there on her honeymoon.

I could picture the view from the balcony of her hotel room: the red Hawaiian sun setting in the ocean, the palm trees softly bending under the tropical breeze, the gentle volcanoes blowing their pink smoke on the horizon, her brand-new husband taking a hot shower, preparing himself to exercise his recently acquired love rights...So why the hell was this woman glued to the TV, making a long-distance call to discuss a pair of amethyst-nugget heart-drop earrings? I could be wrong about this, but my feeling is that this lady was in denial. She was afraid of the unknown: the married life, the tropical island, even the body of her husband must have felt like a foreign object. So what did she do? She looked for comfort in something she knew very well, her shopping channel.

I thought about her at that particular moment because I suspected that I was doing something similar. I was shopping to avoid my feelings. I was using my credit card as an antidepressant.

At that precise moment, my cell phone rang between my boobs.

"How was last night?" asked Madame.

"Mellow," I said.

"Well, I don't know what you did to that man, but he wants to book you for the next five nights in a row."

"What?"

"Five *whole* nights, starting Sunday. Are you okay with that?"

"I guess."

"You guess? You can buy yourself a Jaguar with the money you're going to make. Are you crazy?"

Madame had a point. Though five nights of sitting on that sofa with that guy sounded like a major pain in the butt, turning down such an absurd amount of money was insane, right? And I clearly needed that money to buy unjustifiably expensive negligees from stores that didn't want to sell them to me in the first place.

"Okay," I sighed, "I'll do it."

If nothing else, a mellow client like Simon would give me time to figure things out. It's not often that I have time to sit down and ponder why, if everything in my life is moving in the right direction, I still feel a pea hurting the small of my back. I left the store—without buying anything—and headed home to prepare myself to earn the first payment on my Jaguar.

CHAPTER 18

On Sunday, Alberto drove me back down to Tribeca. That night, I didn't even stop by Simon's studio. Romina came down in the elevator and took me straight to Simon's apartment. She seemed nice, and I would have loved to talk to her a little, but I really didn't know how to engage her. "Hi! I'm a fat escort and your boss hires me to sit next to him on the sofa" could have been a hell of an icebreaker, but I wasn't going to open that can of worms.

As I waited for Simon, I observed the portraits on the wall. Once again I was fascinated by the images of the *Sleeping Beauties*. I remembered what he'd said about those photos: "I wish they could pay the rent." It was an interesting choice of words. Simon's apartment was in one of the most expensive buildings in one of the most expensive neighborhoods in Manhattan. Why would this guy be worried about paying the rent?

On the coffee table in front of me, there was a *Vogue* magazine opened to the middle, and a dirty coffee mug on top of it. I lifted the mug and noticed that there was a story about Simon and his fashion photography. He'd carelessly left the coffee mug on top of the very page that praised his work. Either he was incredibly sloppy, or he didn't buy into his own fame.

As I was entertaining these thoughts, Simon showed up.

"Hello..." I said.

He said nothing.

"Hello?"

"Huh?" he mustered.

"How are you doing?" I said with a smile. The least I would expect from someone who's going to spend five nights with me is to say "hi."

"I'm sorry, I'm thinking about this job that I'm doing tomorrow."

"It's okay," I replied, even though it really wasn't. And then I started to feel stupid for agreeing to five nights with him. Something about this guy made me very uncomfortable.

He was wearing a pair of partially destroyed jeans, with a plain white T-shirt that was in pretty bad shape too. Some rich people like to dress in carefully chosen rags, but he was just wearing totally random rags. There was nothing stylish about what he had on. I also noticed that he looked older than the night before, but maybe he was just tired, because he did look exhausted. He sat there without making eye contact with me, set the alarm clock, put the pillow in place, measured the sixteen and a half inches, and squeezed in next to me for the next seven hours.

But something very interesting happened that night. Even though I wasn't a fan of Simon's, the moment he sat next to me, let go a couple of sighs, and dozed off, his energy changed. Awake, he was as dry as a piece of Sheetrock, but when he was sleeping he had the same angelic quality as the people he photographed in the subway.

I must have read until about three in the morning, but then, at some point, I fell asleep, and I had an extremely strange dream.

I saw myself in bed with a man and a woman. The three of us were there kissing and caressing each other, but the weird thing was that it wasn't really a sexual dream. I can't remember the details, but what I do recall is that I had a very pleasant sensation of being physically accepted by these two people who were in bed with me. Now, here's the weirdest part: I looked over the edge of the bed and noticed that the bed was on top of a tall tower of mattresses, and the whole tower was floating on the sea. The tower was so high that there were clouds around us, as if we were up in the sky. The dream was strange but beautiful—so much so that I made the effort to remember as much as I could and find out what it meant. Maybe I could ask Madame, I thought. She had a few doctorates in psychology. She should know about these things.

At 6 a.m., Simon's alarm clock woke us up. That's when I realized that my head was resting on his shoulder.

"What the fuck!" he said, jumping off the couch.

Okay, I never expected him to wake me up with a kiss on the forehead, or by tenderly caressing my face with his fingertips. I understand that he must have been a bit surprised when he found a stranger's head snoozing next to his, but he could have said "Oops," or even "Excuse me, can you take your head off of my shoulder?" I felt that "What the fuck" was uncalled for, and it deeply pissed me off. I might not be a Miss Universe, but I'm not the Creature from the Black Lagoon either.

Simon stood next to the couch, looking at the floor and frantically searching for something in his pockets—my fee, I suspected. In the meantime, I gathered my book and my purse with a deep frown that I didn't even try to hide.

"Don't worry about the money. You can send it to Madame later," I said, throwing my book in my bag and getting up from the couch without looking at him.

He stood there like a statue as I walked up to the exit. When I tried to open the heavy metal door that protected the elevator, I realized that it was locked, so I stood there, took a deep breath, and looked at the ceiling.

"It's locked," I announced through a clenched jaw.

"What?" he mumbled.

"The door is locked. I can't get out."

He rushed to the door and proceeded to unlock it. For about ten never-ending seconds he fumbled with the key—still looking at the floor—while I kept looking at the ceiling. If he had looked at the ceiling I would have looked at the floor. *Anything to make it clear I had no interest in making eye contact with this idiot,* I thought to myself.

What did he think? That I had put my head on his shoulder on purpose? Oh, please! I stepped into the elevator, wondering whether he would cancel the rest of the nights that he had booked with me, and, truthfully, hoping he would.

He hid behind the main door as the elevator's doors started closing, and that's when I heard a barely audible word coming from him.

"Thanks."

I looked up to make sure that he'd actually said that, but the doors closed completely.

"What the fuck?" I said to myself. "After that stupid scene

he thanks me?" I shook my head, and left his building convinced that I would never come back to that place.

Alberto was waiting outside in the car. He had bought fresh coffee and a croissant for me. He's such a sweetheart.

"How was it, Miss B?"

"This guy is so weird!" I said.

"There's a lot of weird people out there," he said, shrugging.

I sat in the back of the car feeling cranky and confused. Maybe it was the fact that I had slept on a sofa and not in my bed, or that I only got three hours of sleep that night, or that stupid reaction of Simon when he found my head resting on his shoulder, but something was irritating me about that night. Didn't know what it was, but something about this guy was pushing my buttons.

"What the fuck?" I said to myself one more time as the limo rushed down the West Side Highway.

CHAPTER 19

*T*hat Monday morning—after the "What the fuck?"—I went home, changed clothes, and hopped on the subway to go to the office.

"When you are hysterical, you are historical," my AA-ex used to say. I wasn't hysterical, but I was exceptionally angry—considering how trivial the "What the fuck?" incident was. According to my AA-ex's theory, my anger had nothing to do with what Simon said, but with something older and deeper than that.

As I sat there pondering my AA-ex's theory, I noticed a couple sitting on the other side of the car. They were tenderly holding hands. It was eight-thirty in the morning—which in my opinion is the most unromantic time of the day—but they were all lovey-dovey, and I noticed that she was sporting a rather large engagement ring.

That's when I connected the dots that led from "what the fuck" to that diamond ring. I wanted that "Let's hold hands and look into each other's eyes at eight-thirty in the morning" thing. I was about to turn twenty-eight years old, my clock was starting to tick, and I was having serious New York City single-girl issues.

I didn't like this Simon guy, I swear. He was not my type at all: too tall, too skinny, and I'd noticed that hair grew on his back and spilled over the collar of his T-shirts—eeew! Trust me, I didn't like him. But just suppose for a second that I did: he was single, straight, and fairly successful. Why couldn't I corner this guy in his apartment and tell him, "Listen, Simon, enough with this couch-sitting bullshit. Let's go have dinner at a swanky place in Tribeca, drink a nice bottle of wine, and get to know each other a little better"?

If I wanted to get laid, it might work, but at this point in my life—when I needed something more meaningful than a one-night stand—I still couldn't allow myself to make that move. Blame it on my upbringing, "society," or whatever, but the way I see it, women are in a limbo where we are independent enough to be alone, but not liberated enough to aggressively pursue a husband. Men are still supposed to take the initiative. If you want to date a guy, he still has to ask you out. If you want to marry him, he still has to propose. Obviously, there are exceptions, but it's not often that you see a girl kneeling in front of a guy and asking for his hand in marriage.

And then, to make things more complicated, there are men who feel terribly uncomfortable making all the moves. I believe that these guys would be perfectly happy with women taking the initiative, but society would label them as emasculated or "pussy-whipped." I'm convinced that singleness is a modern social problem because neither party knows who should take the initiative anymore. As a consequence, nobody is taking it. Men and women are running around desperately trying to find the love of their lives, and it just doesn't show up. Why can't we connect? Have we become too demanding? Too specific about that ideal love that we're after? At the sight of the first defect, we run away, encouraged by friends who keep telling us, "You can find someone better than him."

After a long and deep analysis, I have decided that there's only one thing to blame for the sentimental state of our nation: Chinese takeout. Yes, you heard correctly. Chinese takeout is keeping us single. Let me explain.

My friend Fran's grandparents met in New York City in 1905. They met on Tuesday, she cooked for him on Wednesday, and they got married on Thursday. Every time Fran's grandfather talked about their short courtship, he explained the whole thing in one line: "She was Jewish, she was a hardworking woman, and she could cook." That's all he needed to know about her.

I'm sure that the Jewish and the hardworking parts were important, but I guarantee you that the cooking closed the deal. Why? Because he knew that he would be eating her food for the rest of his life. In 1905, there was no McDonald's, or Wendy's, or Hunan Palace. Nowadays you don't need anyone to go buy the chicken at the market, pluck the feathers, and feed logs to the fire. Now we all can live independently, and we have the luxury of choosing our better halves very carefully, and maybe that's why we're all so lonely. Fran's grandparents — who took a chance based on necessity — stayed together for sixty-five years, until they both passed away.

But here's a second problem. Let's suppose that you find

a guy and get married. How do you make that relationship last? Life for a married man might be tough, but life for a married woman is hell. Women have to work and take care of the house and take care of the kids and stay young and stay thin and stay pretty. Nowadays we have to be housewives, mothers, professionals, and models: that's four full-time jobs right there. Oh! And please try to save an hour a day for yoga, so you can alleviate some of the stress of this insane lifestyle. I see women walking in and out of the gym with a baby in one hand and a BlackBerry in the other one. I have yet to meet a man who can juggle all the responsibilities that we handle.

After women's lib, our duties increased while men's decreased. Women have been Stepford-wifed into thinking that all we do is never enough: make more money at work, raise your kids to go to Harvard, keep the house looking like a Pottery Barn catalogue, be a gourmet cook, and make sure that you know how to walk around on those damned Manolo heels while you do all that, because you can't afford to be a sloppy mom in your own home anymore.

And while women drive themselves crazy with work and increasing responsibilities, we're so stupid that — instead of complaining — we brag about our insanely busy routine, flaunting our madness like a badge of honor. We're like slaves showing off our shackles. "Look," we seem to say to each other proudly, "mine are heavier than yours." It seems like if you're not stressed out of your mind and ready to commit suicide, you're not working hard enough.

Anyway, where was I when I started talking about all this?

Oh yes. I was in the subway, on my way to work, watching two people in love and wondering when I'd be a part of that type of couple.

The morning of the "What the fuck?" moved painfully slowly, and by noon I received my daily phone call from Madame.

"So you're on for tonight, right?"

"He wants to see me again?" I asked, surprised.

"I told you, he reserved five nights in a row."

"But I don't understand what this guy wants. He squeezes himself onto the sofa—between me and a pillow—but if I accidentally touch him, then he runs away as if I had some contagious disease!"

"Do you want to cancel?" she asked impatiently.

"No, I just want to understand—"

"Don't bother trying to understand him. Trust me, it's useless."

Before I could say, "But I need to understand these things because I'm a compulsive thinker," Madame came up with an excuse to change the subject: "Want to come shopping with me on Wednesday, after work?"

"Sure," I said. Perhaps I could get her to answer my questions in person. We agreed to meet at a fancy department store on Fifth Avenue, and I went back to work.

That night, I took a shower and hopped into Alberto's car to head down to Simon's place, where Romina, his assistant, had a surprise for me.

"I won't be around tomorrow, so Simon asked me to give you the keys so you can let yourself in."

Okay, so I went from "what-the-fuck" to "let-me-give-you-a-copy-of-my-keys"? I'm telling you, he was totally unpredictable. At least he was consistent about that.

While waiting for Simon, I set up the alarm clock, I put the pillow in place, and I measured the mysterious sixteen and a half inches that I had to leave for him. I had started carrying my own measuring tape in my purse to speed up the process.

I sat in my spot and waited patiently. The coffee table was a little messy. It seemed like he had been going through his mail. He had a small trash can where he had thrown a bunch of ripped papers and junk mail. I knew that opening other people's mail is a federal offense, but I hoped that going through someone's garbage wasn't — because I just couldn't help myself. I'm a Gemini — and we're as curious as cats — so that bucket full of fascinating information about this guy was just too strong a temptation.

While checking some of the discarded items, I found a few surprises. This guy had been invited to every single high-profile event in New York: film festivals, charity dinners, fashion events. But all the cards were in the garbage.

"Very interesting," I said to myself. Here's a super-famous guy who throws out every single perk that comes with fame. How come? Did he think he was better than all these people? Did he just not care for parties and cocktails? It was hard to guess his reasons for passing on all these exclusive invitations. But I guess it was also impossible to imagine someone like him feeling at ease in any social environment. He was one of the most antisocial guys I had ever met.

Half of New York would give a limb to be included in the exclusive mailing lists that Simon was on but, clearly, Simon didn't care about it. A part of me wondered if he was crazy, but another part of me thought, *Good for him!* After all these years in New York, I'm sick of people who would do anything to belong to the A-list.

While going through his mail, I also discovered that he set aside some fund-raising mailings from Doctors Without Borders, National Public Radio, and a bunch of other charities and institutions that I happen to support myself. He threw out the party invites, but picked up the charity bills. *Interesting.*

I heard the elevator coming up, and before Simon could open the gray door that led to the apartment, I managed to hide all evidence of my little garbage study. He was wearing the same raggedy jeans as the previous night, and a T-shirt with a caption that simply read "Fuck the Hamptons."

He seemed surprised when he noticed that I had arranged everything, including the sixteen and a half inches for the desired spot, but he didn't say a word. I started to feel terribly guilty for going through his trash. This time I was the one avoiding eye contact.

He looked much better that night. He looked rested, and he had shaved. For a second, I even found him vaguely attractive, but his stubborn silence still annoyed the hell out of me. Maybe all the sleeping he was doing around me was having a positive impact on his appearance, or maybe I was just getting used to his big nose, his thick glasses, and his bald spot.

Once again, with a big sigh, he dived into a deep sleep in the narrow space between the pillow and me. But this night, while Simon slept like a baby, I was restless. It didn't help that this time it was Simon who draped over me. Maybe I was tired, or stressed, or who knows, but I was antsy. I felt trapped and annoyed at having to sit there the whole night. At some point I tried to reach for the remote control of the TV, but he held on to me in his sleep, as if he was hanging on for dear life. It was virtually impossible to move without dragging the six-foot-plus photographer with me, so I decided just to stay there. Thank God I didn't need to go to the bathroom.

I tried to go back to my book, but I couldn't concentrate. Without anything better to do, I reviewed the information that I had of Simon. Why was he always in a bad mood, when he had the most glamorous life in the world? Why did he jump back when that model held on to him? Why would he throw out invitations to the most exclusive parties in Manhattan? Why was he paying me to sit sixteen and a half inches away from a pillow? And why the hell would he push me away when he was awake but then hold on to me in his sleep?

"What the fuck?" I mumbled pensively.

I was exhausted for the lack of sleep. That was probably why my mind kept grinding the same thoughts over and over, so I closed my eyes and started doing a visualization. Visualization is a relaxation technique that I learned in a holistic weight loss center. You just close your eyes and meditate on your favorite place on earth. It never helped me to lose weight, but it always helped me to relax. So, taking a deep breath, I thought of my favorite place on earth: the top terrace of Hearst Castle, on the coast of California.

Hearst Castle is the most wonderful place in the world. I'm not necessarily a big fan of William Randolph Hearst personally, but his former vacation house is just awesome. He built it on top of a hill overlooking the Pacific Ocean. The house is enormous, packed with antiques, and it was the coolest party scene of the twenties and thirties. Charlie Chaplin, Carole Lombard, Clark Gable, Johnny Weissmuller — everybody who was somebody in the arts, sports, science, or entertainment — was invited to spend as much time as they wanted at Hearst Castle.

Hearst hired a female architect named Julia Morgan to build it. Morgan was one of the first female engineers in America, and the first woman ever accepted to study architecture at the Ecole des Beaux-Arts in Paris. Hearst—who had a very eclectic and eccentric taste—would buy European antiques and expect Julia to build the house around them. Most people make the furniture for the house; Hearst wanted to make the house for the furniture, and Julia Morgan managed to accomplish this Herculean task. In some cases she had to rebuild entire rooms so they could fit a fireplace from a Scottish castle, or the engraved wood ceilings from a Spanish monastery. She built a couple of swimming pools, one indoors—the Roman Pool—and one outdoors—the Neptune Pool. I don't exaggerate when I tell you that I would gladly give all my savings for the privilege of swimming in the Neptune Pool.

Some art critics think that Hearst Castle is just the corny mansion of a millionaire who bought antiques at wholesale prices, packing his house with disjointed pieces of art from all periods, but I don't care what they say. This place—unlike most museums—was a home, a home that was thoroughly enjoyed. The whole house is soaked in a very special energy. And to top it all, it has an amazing view of the Pacific Ocean.

Felicia—my voice teacher from my third semester in college, when I briefly considered acting—told me that it has been scientifically proved that the sound of an instrument that has been played well is better than the sound of one that has been played poorly. In other words, the violin that Itzhak Perlman plays sounds better than others simply because a great musician has been playing it all along. The good sound purifies the object. Maybe something like that happened to Hearst Castle. All the smart, beautiful, and talented people that stayed there purified the atmosphere of the house. I wonder if love can do that for your body too. Maybe love makes you purer and prettier. Maybe love makes you better.

My mind kept jumping from the view from Hearst Castle, to Felicia, to Simon snoozing on his couch. Then I thought about Simon's grip. There was something in the way he unconsciously held on to me that made me feel — I don't know — wanted, needed. My other customers had made me feel desired, but, as flattering as that was, I had a much more intense and warm feeling spending the night with Simon.

But I was probably doing way too much thinking. My AA-ex used to say. "Don't go into your head alone. It can be a dangerous neighborhood." And I'm pretty sure it's even worse when you've had three hours of sleep in two days. The next day I had to prepare for the UK Charms meeting, and I couldn't afford to be brain-dead for that.

I finally fell asleep, and, though I couldn't remember what I dreamt of, I know that it was a very peaceful dream.

CHAPTER 20

The following morning, there was a tense calm at the office in preparation for the Chicago Boss's visit on Friday. I had met him only once, and I thought that he was a pretty cool guy. So cool that I couldn't understand how he could allow a harpy like Bonnie to run the New York office.

What I liked about the Chicago Boss was that he had created the company from the ground up. He was your quintessential maverick. Smart, creative, and talented, he refused to wear suits, picked up his own phone, and until very recently had still directed some of our commercials. He was a black inner-city kid who didn't finish high school. He started working when he was young, and worked his way up to the top. Unfortunately, as the company got bigger and bigger — and finally went public — a board of directors was instated, and bureaucracy stepped in. The Chicago Boss built an empire by breaking the rules, but now his empire had more rules than dinnertime at Buckingham Palace. As a consequence, the energy that had made him a success was nowhere to be found in his own company. It's pretty sad, but not uncommon.

Bonnie was the direct result of this type of corporate mentality. As much as I disliked her, I have to acknowledge that her managing strategy was very smart and effective. I believe Machiavelli called it "divide and conquer." Her trick was to build an invisible wall around the Chicago Boss, so he couldn't befriend or communicate with any New York employee who could hint to him of her evil ways. That's why she insisted—wait, let me rephrase that—that's why she *demanded* that everything had to be run through her. You were not allowed to talk to him on the phone—even if he called you. It happened once to Gregory, one of our producers. Bonnie went berserk at him because the Chicago Boss called him directly, as if Gregory had provoked the phone call. What the hell was he supposed to do? Tell the president of the company, "Please don't call me, or the bitch that I have for a boss will fire me"? As you see, there was no way around her.

The agency had lost a lot of clients and was in pretty bad shape since she took over, but Bonnie—who was an expert bureaucrat—knew that as long as she stood in everybody's way and controlled communications, she could take credit for whatever worked and blame others for whatever didn't. How could anybody tell the Chicago Boss what was going on if we couldn't even say good morning to him without having our eyes poked out?

After the copy-machine incident—when I refused to work late on Friday—Bonnie had stopped talking to me, but I knew that the wise thing to do was to lie low and wait for the next shoe to drop. On Tuesday, I stayed out of her way and did everything correctly from 9 a.m. to 5 p.m. Then

I went home to prepare myself for the third full night at Simon's.

At 9 p.m. sharp, Alberto picked me up and dropped me at Simon's studio. I let myself in, prepared the couch, and waited for him to show up. But that night something completely unexpected happened. That night Simon couldn't sleep.

He arrived looking more stressed than usual, sat next to me, and closed his eyes, but twenty minutes later he was huffing and puffing, trying to get comfortable.

I looked at him from the corner of my eye: his eyes were closed, and he was fighting to fall asleep.

Sitting there next to him, I couldn't help noticing that Simon had really long and dark eyelashes, the kind that women wish for, that seem to be wasted on men. His nose was big, but elegant — one of those Greek noses, descending in a straight line down from his forehead. I had never noticed any of this before because his heavy-framed eyeglasses covered his face like a mask. Then I focused on Simon's lips. He had a robust pair of kissers. You could hardly notice them when he was awake, since he was always biting on them, or pressing them together in a tense grimace. But as he sat there next to me, his mouth was relaxed, and his lips were broad and rather full. They were nice, very kissable lips. *He's not that bad looking after all,* I told myself.

"Don't look at me like that," he said abruptly.

"What? What are you talking about?" I replied, looking away from him as fast as I could and faking total surprise.

"I don't like it when you look at me like that."

I blushed to a deep shade of purple. Of course I was checking him out, but I did it for barely a split second, and his eyes were closed! Was he a mind reader or something?

"I could feel you staring," he said with his eyes still closed.

"I don't stare," I lied. I would rather die than acknowledge that I was lusting after him.

There was a minute or two of uncomfortable silence, while he changed positions three more times in his narrow sixteen and a half inches. Now I was uncomfortable, and when I'm uncomfortable, I talk.

"Can't sleep tonight?" I said.

Silence.

"Do you want me to leave?"

"No!" he ordered.

I didn't like the tone of his voice, and he must have noticed that, because he immediately softened it to an almost apologetic whisper and added, "Please don't leave."

His voice carried a tone of desperation that I had never heard before.

"Do you want me to count sheep for you?" I joked.

He chuckled. He actually chuckled, and getting that reaction out of such a serious guy made me feel as if I had won the lottery. I noticed that he looked very cute when he smiled, and I wished that he did it more often.

"Wanna talk?" I asked.

"About what?"

"Anything — art, local news, the weather . . . But I must warn you, I'm bit of a talker, so if I start I might not be able to stop."

He chuckled again, and for the first time looked me in the eyes.

"I'll take the chance. What do you want to talk about?"

"It's your money, you tell me what you want to talk about," I joked.

"Well, money is one thing I don't want to talk about."

I extended my arm, gesturing at his elegant apartment, as if I were presenting a brand-new convertible on *The Price Is Right*.

"You have money problems?" I asked, incredulous.

"A lot of money brings a lot of problems," he answered.

"Damned if you have it, damned if you don't," I said.

"That's life."

"My grandmother used to say: *That's life—no one gets out of it alive.*"

Simon laughed again.

"That should help you relax," I joked.

"I wish," he said.

"Well...would you want to try a visualization?"

"A what?"

"It's a technique that I learned to—" I stopped myself in the middle of the sentence. There was no need to tell him that it was a weight-loss method. "It's a relaxation technique. Wanna try it?"

He said "sure," and I immediately adopted the tone of my shamanic teacher.

"Okay, close your eyes, and think of a beautiful beach..."

"I don't like going to the beach."

"Why?"

"It's a long story," he said, and by the tone of his voice I knew that he wasn't planning to share it.

"Okay, let's think of a mountain, then. A mountain by the sea. I'm sorry, but I do love the beach."

He laughed again, and I felt good. Making him laugh was no small victory with someone as guarded as Simon.

"Okay: picture a mountain by the sea. Have you been to Big Sur in California?"

"Sure."

"Have you been to Hearst Castle?"

"I lived in San Simeon for two years. I worked in the Castle's archives."

My jaw dropped all the way to the floor. "Did you get to swim in the Neptune Pool?" I asked, trying to control my excitement.

"Twice," he said.

Parenthesis. I've learned that sometimes coincidences are just that: coincidences. But sitting there, with Simon telling me that he pretty much lived in my favorite place on earth, was too much of a thrill.

Back to the couch. I didn't want to go any deeper into the Hearst Castle conversation, because otherwise neither one of us would sleep that night, and this guy was paying me to help him sleep, so, biting my lower lip, I asked him to close his eyes again, and I started with the visualization.

"It's a bright-blue day. And we're at the patio next to the big house."

"By the pool?"

"No. We're at the back of the house, and we're going to enter through the kitchen door. We cross the kitchen . . . and we get to the spiral staircase. We walk up the steps all the way to the second floor . . . To the right we have Marion Davies' bedroom . . . but we are going to make a left, to enter the small living room that connects it with Hearst's bedroom . . . Do you know where that is?"

He nodded, his eyes firmly closed.

"Okay, we stop in the middle of that living room, and we walk to the window . . . we open it . . . There are a couple of steps that climb out to the terrace . . ."

"Are there really steps by that window?" he asked, his eyes still shut.

"Trust me, there are steps by that window. Now we're going to climb them—one...two...three—and now we're stepping out to that little terrace. Feel the breeze. Breathe in. We're going to sit right by the edge. Look, the patio is down there, and if we look to the right we can see the Neptune Pool. Now we're going to look at the horizon. The ocean is light blue, and it turns into silver at the horizon. You can hardly see the difference between the sea and the sky in the distance. There are seagulls flying slowly above us. And there's nothing to worry about. The past is gone, and we don't know anything about the future, so all we have is the present. And now, right now, we are happy. Completely happy. Now we are happy...and all we have...is now."

It was the first time that I had conducted a visualization for someone else, and I must have done something right, because at that moment I turned around to ask him if it was working and I realized that he was already sleeping like a baby.

But here's the best part: now that he was finally sound asleep, I could look at him for as long as I wanted without his knowing. And that's exactly what I did. And that was the night I realized that Simon was cute. Very cute.

Then I picked up my book and read it until I fell asleep on his shoulder.

CHAPTER 21

y mother is a workaholic. I'm not embarrassed to say it, because she is not embarrassed to be it. She works proudly, like a mule, and she raised me to work like one as well. She worked full-time with my father in the family business, and still managed to make sure that not one particle of dust could settle on her furniture. She could catch an atom of filth in midair. We could eat three meals a day directly off the floor knowing that there was not even a slight chance of swallowing a germ. I saw my first cockroach when I was ten years old and had spent the night at my friend Victoria's home — her mother was a poet and a midwife with very little time or interest in household chores. Roaches wouldn't even come near our house. They knew better.

I believe that this obsession with labor is the remnant of my mother's immigrant experience. Like so many others, she came to America to work hard, and she would not stop, no matter what.

My brothers and I grew up brainwashed by a quite unreal

image of Christmas—inspired by TV shows like *Family Ties* and such—where everybody gathered around the piano, singing Christmas carols and gazing lovingly into each other's eyes. In these fictional families, parents had time for their kids and they sat on the bed to have heart-to-heart talks with them while a very moving soundtrack played in the background. Their conversations always ended with lines like "Whatever happens, just remember that I love you and that I'm proud of you."

Well, we didn't get any of that at home.

On Christmas Eve—or Nochebuena, as we called it—my mother spent the whole day cooking and the whole night cleaning. The kitchen door never stopped swinging, and my father never stopped yelling at Mom, "Can you please sit down for a second and eat?" But resting and enjoying the moment was never part of her agenda.

I often tried to help her, but she always sent me back to the table. She didn't want to share the burden. She kept compulsively bringing dishes in, and taking dishes out. When she finally sat down—if she finally sat down—she would do it for five minutes, just to complain about how tired she was. Having said that, she'd get up and start cleaning the table, insisting on hand-washing everything. God forbid she should ever use her dishwasher. The bigger the sacrifice, the better she felt.

We've tried everything to sabotage her Christmas routine, from demanding reheated pizza for dinner, to threatening not to come home for the holidays ever again. But for Mom, work is like a bottle of Scotch, and we have no right to pull that away from her. My theory is that she's afraid of intimacy and she needs to put something between you and her. And if that something is hard work, how can anyone complain?

Bitching aside, I've learned to love her the way she is, because the one thing I know above everything else is that she loves me truly — she just has an odd way of showing her affection. And since there's no chance that she will ever sit on my bed to tell me, "Whatever happens, just remember that I love you and that I'm proud of you," the best time to have a heart-to-heart with her is when she's busy. Actually, let me rephrase that: the only way you can talk to her is by following her around when she's busy. She's at her best when she's multitasking. Her advice and intuition are right on the mark, but if you want a piece of either, you have to chase her around while she's cooking, cleaning, or gardening. Don't even try to corner her or make her slow down: it won't work. The best of Mom's wisdom is shared while she's scrubbing the bathroom tiles, or replanting a young willow, so just follow the rules and don't take it personally.

I bring all this up because this is precisely one of the things that Madame has in common with my mom. Madame is always busy, always in a hurry. "I have a business to run," she told me one too many times, until I understood that she came from the same school of immigrational trauma that trained my mom. The only difference is that Madame came from the Russian chapter.

So, when Madame asked me to go shopping with her, I realized that it was not just a mission to find clothes. She was using this field trip as an excuse to catch up. I met her after work on Wednesday at a very fancy department store around the corner from my office.

"Hi, honey!" she said, kissing me on both cheeks. "Is everything good?"

"Yes," I said.

"Great. Then let's look for summer blouses," she instructed.

Shopping with Madame was like taking a course at Harvard. Calling her picky would be an understatement. This woman took the store apart with a scalpel. No garment was left unturned. Utterly unimpressed by brand names or designer labels, she analyzed clothing from every possible angle — fabric, cut, stitching — she would actually turn things inside out to see how they were made.

It was a bit embarrassing for me, because every time I was attracted to something flashy or trendy she would simply dismiss it by whispering, "garbage," as she walked right by it.

"Clothes are an investment that has to be made very consciously," she explained. "Oh, look! This is decent," she said, picking a skirt from a rack. Not even once did she look at the label.

"See?" she told me, showing the hand-rolled inseams of the chosen skirt. "I like designers who invest in their clothes, not in advertising. Advertising is for stupids," she said, frontally attacking my line of business. "How can anyone buy a product because its manufacturer tells you that it's good? Of course they're going to tell you it's good, they want to sell it to you."

"How are things at work?" she asked, referring to my actual day job.

I took a deep breath and started explaining the complicated web of intrigue that Bonnie was knitting around everybody: "Well, I discovered that my boss, who is this horrible woman, has been sabotaging not only my career but..." I went on to babble every unnecessary detail of my personal soap opera: "...and then I heard her in the bathroom explaining that she has this evil plan to oust the big boss, who's a really nice guy, but I had a tape recorder with me and..."

Madame, who — visibly bored by my yapping — was

examining a silk scarf, finally interrupted me mid-sentence
to close the case with a simple piece of advice.

"Just choose your boss."

"What?" I had no clue what she was talking about.

"You're good at what you do, right?"

"I guess..."

"Well, then, anyone you work for would be delighted to
have you as an employee. You are not going to change that
woman, so stop wasting your time, and find someone you
want to work for, someone who has ethics, and who doesn't
feel threatened by your talent."

It never crossed my mind that I had that power to choose
my boss. Same as in love, I always waited to be chosen.

"I know you are right, but first I have to settle one piece of
business with this bitch."

"Don't hurt yourself trying to hurt others," she finished.

She left me speechless with that line: it was short and
direct, and it explained with frightening accuracy my previous experiences with revenge. She noticed my reaction,
smiled, and dived into a rack of summer blouses.

"Tell me something fun. Tell me about your customers,"
she asked.

I told her everything about every client: Lord Arnfield
and his socks, Mr. Akhtar and his gowns, and the seduction
battle with Richard Weber. She laughed and nodded, listening carefully — though acting as if her true concern was the
thread count of the Egyptian-cotton sheets.

"Can you interpret dreams?"

"I can try," Madame replied.

"Well, I had this dream where I was having sex with a
man and a woman, and the bed was on top of a tall tower of
mattresses floating on the sea."

Madame looked at me for a second as if she was studying me and finally declared, "In dreams I always interpret the sea as love. That tall tower of mattresses that separates your bed from the sea would be the distance that you put to separate sex and love."

Immediately I began making free associations that began all the way back with Monique in second grade and took me all the way to Richard Weber's sex chamber. If sex was a despicable activity, it could only be practiced with despicable people (Dan Callahan included).

If Madame was right about my dream, then my Russian pimp could have saved me thousands of dollars in psychotherapy. But before she could continue with my analysis, she found something on sale and left me in the middle of the cosmetics department trying to cope with my suppressed memories.

"Smell this," she commanded, bringing a bottle of some new, trendy perfume endorsed by some dubious celebrity.

"Hmmm, it smells a little like bubble gum..." I said.

"What woman in her right mind would like to go around smelling like bubble gum!" she exclaimed, disgusted.

It didn't smell so bad to me, but, then again, I do like bubble gum.

"Women are deep, mysterious, profound. We are life givers. Why should we go around smelling like candy?"

"What perfume do you wear?" I asked, intrigued.

"I make my own."

"Really?"

"I use a base of Eau Impériale from Guerlain, but I add a few secret ingredients."

"Secret ingredients like what?" I asked.

"Honey, if I told you the secret ingredients, they wouldn't

be secret anymore," she said, smiling. "I don't like these new fragrances that are made by committee. A parfumeur is an artist, and no artist can perform with twenty executives breathing down his neck and telling him what to do. And don't even talk about these celebrities who put their names on the bottle not even knowing the difference between vetiver and bergamot. There's no tradition anymore. There's no artistry. Everything is a scam," she concluded.

Inspired by Madame's strong views on the subject, I picked a perfume from the vintage shelf.

"What do you think of this one?" I asked her.

"Shalimar? That's a classic. They've been making it since the 1920s"

My grandmother Celia had a bottle of Shalimar. It was her favorite perfume, and she wore it all the time. When my mother left Cuba, my *abuela* wanted to give her something to remember her by, and she gave her that bottle. They never saw each other again.

My mother kept that bottle of perfume in her special drawer, with her fine lingerie, and every time she missed her mother she would pull the bottle out and take a whiff. It must have felt like having her mother back with her for just a second.

I've seen my mother crying very few times in her life, but I could swear that every time I saw tears in her eyes she had that perfume bottle in her hands.

It has never crossed my mind to try Shalimar on. For me it isn't just a perfume, it's a family heirloom. But as I recalled these memories while holding the tester in my hand, Madame approached me with her two cents' worth.

"Are you going to try it on?" she asked.

"I'm not sure if it's for me. It's too intense." I hesitated.

"Just try it on. Your chemistry will change the scent. But, honey, don't try the cologne, try the extract."

Madame ordered the clerk to bring us a tester of "pure" perfume. She came back with a minuscule bottle that I picked up respectfully in my hands. When I was about to splash my neck with it, Madame stopped me. "Honey, wait a minute. Let me explain something to you. You put a little on your wrist, then you go away for a couple of hours — look at bags or shoes — and then you smell it again to see if it feels right. Fifty percent of the perfume is you — your scent, your body — and it takes time for the chemical reaction to take place."

Then, smiling, she added, "It's just like a man. It doesn't matter how good it looks at first: you have to try it on and take it for a long walk before you decide if it's worth keeping."

While she dabbed a tiny amount of perfume on my wrist, she fired a question, and I wondered if it was connected to her recent statement.

"So how are things with Mr. Five in a Row? Still sleeping?"

"Like a baby."

"Good!" she replied.

"He's so mysterious. He never talks, he hates the beach, and what is it with the sixteen and a half inches?"

"Don't ask. It's the kind of thing that even if he explained it to you it would make no sense, trust me. Is he attractive?"

"Well, he's tall . . . skinny . . . scruffy."

"Is he attractive?" she asked again.

"I guess he is kind of cute in a tall-skinny-scruffy way, but . . . he's so serious, and so quiet . . ." I replied.

Madame shook her head, smiling, and mumbled something in Russian.

"What did you say?"

"I said, 'Tight face, loose ass.' I know that type."

"Oh no!" I defended Simon. "I don't think that he's a Jekyll-and-Hyde type. He's just very hard to read, he has a hard time letting his guard down. It's just that it's so quiet in there that..."

"...you are bored," she completed my sentence.

"Well, I'm getting a little restless, I guess."

"Do you want me to send somebody else?"

"No!" I replied abruptly. Madame stopped what she was doing and gave me an inquisitive look. "It's good money," I added, trying to change my tone, but I could tell that she wasn't buying it.

"This is the thing, and I know it's totally silly," I started, "but I feel that he needs me and..."

"...and you like to feel needed," she completed with a smirk.

I couldn't take one more analytical remark from Madame, so I stopped her. "No, I just wish I could—I don't know—maybe watch a movie while he sleeps."

"Honey, if he wants to keep you around he's going to have to compromise. Bring in a movie tonight, and if he has a problem with that, just call it quits and I'll send another girl."

"But I feel sorry for him!" I pleaded.

"And you don't feel sorry for yourself, bored to death on that sofa? Look," she continued, "I have no time for this, I have a business to run. Do whatever makes you happy."

Okay, here's what kills me about Madame. She can make the most casual comment, and the thing sticks in my head like Velcro. *Do whatever makes you happy.* What a concept! You can laugh at me if you want, but I had never—ever—looked at life in those terms. I've complained about not being happy countless times, but very rarely have I actually done what makes me happy. I can say that I've waited for someone to make me happy. I've waited to be recognized by a boss who won't do it, I've waited to be asked out by men who won't ask, but hardly ever have I taken the initiative. The fear of rejection has been too strong.

That fear has kept me from saying things like "I want to work for you," or "I want to be loved by you." The whole idea of "This is what I want, so I'll ask for it" seemed not only foreign to me but actually unattainable.

As I was thinking about this, Madame, exercising her well-developed psychic powers, turned around and—out of nowhere—delivered the following line: "The opposite of love is not hatred. It is fear."

Madame ended up buying a pair of leather gloves, a box of Teuscher champagne truffles, and a bottle of Mitsouko, for Alberto's wife, whose birthday was apparently coming up soon.

I bought a little something for myself: a small bottle of Shalimar. Turned out that it smelled delicious on me—especially after I'd had it on for a little while. Now, every time I use it, I feel that I'm invested with the strength of my mother, and the wisdom of the grandmother whom I never met.

I said goodbye to Madame on the street, and, clutching my precious perfume as if I were carrying my grandmother's ashes, I hopped on the subway to go home to prepare for my fourth full night with Simon.

As I sat in the subway, I recalled Madame's words: *Do whatever makes you happy.* What would make me happy? I was so used to thinking about how to make others happy that I feared I might have lost the capacity to please myself. As my mind was navigating these turbulent waters, the woman sitting next to me fell asleep on my shoulder. She reminded me tenderly of Simon, so I let her snooze for a couple of stations, until I got to my stop.

As long as there was no drooling, I could take it.

CHAPTER 22

*P*reparing for that night at Simon's, I decided to stop by a cool video store on Greenwich Avenue to pick up a movie that I could watch while he snored.

I went to this particular store because it was kind of funky. Each employee had a shelf with movies that he or she recommended, and in addition to regular categories like "Comedy" or "Action," they had a bunch of less traditional categories that could match the strangest interests, from "Spaghetti Westerns" to "Vintage Erotica."

There was also a shelf labeled "Chubby Chasers." In the past I had deliberately ignored that shelf. Picking one of those movies would be like buying clothes in a store for the fat and the ugly. But with my self-esteem in advanced stages of reconstruction, I felt that it was the right shelf to pick a movie from, so I started checking out the titles and I noticed that most of the "Chubby Chasers" films were foreign. I guess American movies hardly ever present anybody chasing a fatty.

Anyway, they had movies that I had never heard of, like *Seven Beauties, Georgy Girl, Bagdad Cafe*, and a few Fellini films like *Amarcord, La Dolce Vita*, and *Nights of Cabiria*. I'd heard about Fellini in a film course I took in college, but I had never seen any of his movies, because I assumed that they would be too artsy for me. For some reason I felt that it was the right moment to give Fellini a shot. Maybe being trapped on the couch would make me relax into those old films.

A couple of hours later, after a particularly slow and fulfilling session of exfoliating and moisturizing motions, I showed up at Simon's wearing jeans, a sweater, and a few drops of Shalimar behind my ears. He was busy downstairs, so I just took care of all the details, including the sixteen and a half inches, and I sat there to wait for him while reading the booklet on the movie I'd rented.

Simon walked in, looked me straight in the eye for a second, and smiled.

"Hey!" he greeted me.

I was pleasantly shocked. Maybe that conversation we had the night before had had a positive impact on him.

As he was getting ready to sit down, I gathered the courage to mention that I wanted to watch a movie. Would he be pissed off? Would he throw me out in a rage? Would I freak out like I did that infamous night when Ludwig Rauscher — the Nazi officer — rejected me?

Enough thinking, B! I ordered myself. It's one thing to be mortified when a loved one rejects you, but being rejected by someone you hardly know should mean absolutely nothing.

"Simon...I'm getting tired of reading every night. I need to do something else..."

He was shocked — and for a second I thought that he was

the one who actually felt rejected by my words — so, to avoid a misunderstanding, I continued with a soft and honest tone. "If you want me to stay tonight, I need to watch a movie."

There was an uncomfortable silence.

"Do you want to see what's on TV? As long as you keep the volume down..." he finally said, reaching out for the remote control.

"I brought a movie," I said.

"What is it?"

I handed him the DVD of *La Dolce Vita*.

"Have you seen this one?" I asked. "It's supposed to be a famous Italian movie."

He looked at the DVD and shook his head.

"I don't like subtitles."

Shit. I made the wrong choice, but it was too late to back out.

"Well, I really wanted to see it."

"Just keep the volume down," he finally said as he placed the DVD in the player. He sat next to me and closed his eyes while I started watching the movie.

It took me a bit to get into the story, but finally I got hooked on it. In the meantime, Simon kept moving around in his seat, trying to fall asleep.

La Dolce Vita is the story of this journalist, played by Marcello Mastroianni, who hangs out with "the rich and the beautiful" in Rome. Marcello has to choose between these shallow friends and the simpler but more honest people in his life. I wondered if, to a certain extent, that had been Simon's life.

There was a great scene where Marcello stepped into the Fountain of Neptune with Anita Ekberg, who was at the peak of her beauty then. Anita at her prettiest was kind of chunky. Prancing around on the screen with her humongous bosom and her thick legs semi-covered by a fabulous gown, she reminded me of someone.

Yep, she looked a lot like me.

Give or take a few pounds, Anita looked like me on that night when Mr. Akhtar had dressed me up. She had that type of hourglass figure that you only see on a big girl, with those generous and voluptuous curves that, at that time, were the highest expression of sensuality.

"Can you raise the volume?" Simon asked me as we saw her standing under a stream of water in the Roman fountain. Turned out that he was awake. I should have said something like "excuse me, I thought you didn't like subtitles" but I kept it to myself. I was glad that he was enjoying the movie too.

The film ended, and I turned off the TV. Simon's eyes were wide open.

"I'm so sorry—the movie kept you awake, right?" I apologized.

"It's okay. It was good," he said.

We were silent for another minute, and then—surprise— he asked me something.

"Where are you from?"

"New York."

"New York?"

I knew what this was about. "Do you want to know where am I from, or where are my parents from?"

"Yeah, that's what I meant—I guess."

"My parents are Cuban."

"Huh..." he said.

"And where are you from?" I asked.

"Miami."

"Cool. All my cousins are in Miami."

"Wait—not Miami, Florida; Miami, Arizona."

I laughed. "You gotta be kidding me! Is there a Miami in Arizona?"

"Yep. They call it Miami-Globe, because there's a twin town called Globe next door."

"Oh," I said, "big town?"

"Well, last time I checked, the population was about eight thousand—make that seven thousand nine hundred and ninety-nine since I left. So you're Latin?"

"Yes, and you?" I replied jokingly.

"Me too."

"Oh, really!" I said sarcastically. Latinos come in all colors and sizes, but that this big white guy could actually be Latino was pushing it. He was probably a mix of German, English, and Polish—or maybe even Russian—but I just didn't see much Latin flavor in his features.

"I was raised by Mexicans."

"How come?"

"It's a long story."

"I have time," I said.

He took a second before he started talking.

"My mother...she died when I was a kid. My father was a miner, so the woman next door raised me...Her name was Teresa, she was from Rosarito."

He looked away and then added, "She was a great lady."

There's nothing sadder than when a kid loses his mom, and I could tell by the way Simon was talking that it was a painful memory.

"Can you speak any Spanish?" I asked, to lighten things up.

"I understand some, and I can say a couple of things."

"Go ahead."

"¡*Hiiiijo de la chingada!*" he said with the purest Mexican accent.

I laughed really hard. To hear this white guy speaking like a Mexican was so incongruous, it was truly hysterical.

"¿*Hijo de la chingada?* Son of a bitch? Is that all you can say?" I joked.

"I had to learn all the bad words. I had to defend myself. It was a tough town."

"But did you learn anything nice to say?" I asked.

"Yeah. There's a word . . . it's my favorite word in Spanish."

"Which one?"

"You're gonna laugh," he said.

"Come on, tell me!"

He made a theatrical pause and finally said proudly: "*Sacapuntas.*"

"¿*Sacapuntas?*" I asked surprised. "You love the Spanish word for 'pencil sharpener'?"

"I just like how it sounds," he replied. "*Sacapuntas,*" he repeated, taking a deep breath and exhaling with a smile.

So cute! I watched Simon sink softly in his tight corner of the couch, his favorite word still resonating in the air.

"I feel guilty for keeping you awake. What can I do to help?"

He kept his eyes closed for another second, and then said,

"Take me back to Hearst Castle, please."

CHAPTER 23

*T*he alarm clock woke us up at six in the morning that Thursday. But instead of jumping off the couch, Simon sat there for a few minutes. Not knowing what to do or say, I sat next to him in peaceful silence.

"Did you sleep okay?" I finally asked him.

He nodded.

"Do you still want me to come in tonight?"

He nodded again.

"Can I bring another movie?" I ventured to ask.

He looked away, and took a second before answering. "No action movies and no scary movies."

"Are subtitled films okay?"

"Yes"

"Cool," I mumbled, knowing already what movie I was going to bring for my last evening with Simon.

In some cultures people kiss too much. The Spaniards always kiss twice—on both sides of the face—and I've heard that the Belgians kiss up to three times—going back and forth from right to left to right again. Cubans kiss only once, but they kiss everybody: friends, family, even strangers once they've been introduced. I know that in America greeting someone with a kiss on the cheek is less acceptable, so I only kiss hello and goodbye with my close friends.

So it came as a surprise — even to myself — when, after Simon escorted me to the door and I was about to step out, I gave him a kiss in the cheek. He jumped slightly, and I jumped too, realizing — a second too late — that I was stepping over the line.

"Sorry!" I said. "I do that automatically sometimes."

"It's okay," he said in a barely audible voice, as he closed the door behind me.

I stood in the elevator, my heart racing.

It was Thursday — the day before we had the big UK Charms meeting — but I couldn't care less about those damned tampons. I just kept thinking about meeting Simon that night.

After Alberto took me home, I dressed up and took the subway to go to the office, where Bonnie had scheduled a meeting to prepare for Friday's event.

There were about ten of us, including a couple of creatives and a slew of managers, directors, and VPs of other departments. Bonnie presided from her chair, avoiding eye contact with me at all cost.

"Creative will go after the media planning presentation," Bonnie determined while Mary Pringle took notes of every word that came out of her mouth.

Bonnie had a very specific strategy for these meetings. The heads of all the other departments always presented their groups' ideas, but Bonnie would never do that. See, when you pitch an idea you are asking for approval, and Bonnie would never ask for approval from *anybody*. She always found ways to transfer that dirty duty to someone below her. Then she would sit next to the Chicago Boss and act as if she were hearing the ideas for the first time too. By doing so, she could distance herself from the whole thing. If the ideas worked, she would step in to take credit; if they stank, she would pretend that she'd had nothing to do with them.

Since we didn't have a creative director on the project, there were only two people who could present the ideas on behalf of our department: Bonnie and me. The logical solution was to let me present them, but she would rather die a slow death than let me speak in front of the Chicago Boss. She'd prefer to bring in someone else — even someone who was not in the creative department. "You'll present the slogans, Mark."

She was referring to Dan Callahan's friend, Mark Davenport, an account executive who had been transferred from the London office about a month ago, and who had been assigned that very morning to the project.

"Me?" pleaded Mark.

"You are perfect for this," Bonnie said. "You have a British accent, which is most appropriate for this project." Mark was new to the office, but he already knew that there was no point in trying to argue with Bonnie.

"B will write it all for you," Bonnie offered without even looking at me.

"It's written already, Mark. If you want, I'll sit down with you after the meeting to go through it," I said.

"Thanks." Mark smiled at me.

After working with Mark, I left the office early to stop by the video store and prepare myself to meet Simon for our last night together. I picked another Fellini movie from the "Chubby Chasers" shelf: *Amarcord*.

I went home, threw on a miniskirt, a light sweater, and a pair of knee-high boots, and went downstairs to find Alberto waiting for me.

I have to confess that the film we saw that night was so good I almost forgot that I was with Simon. That night I redis-covered the joy of watching movies that move you, and change you, and make you understand things. I'm not trying to come across all intellectual and artsy-fartsy. It's not like now I only like foreign films with subtitles — as a matter of fact, *Clueless* is still one of my favorite flicks. But I finally understood the trick with foreign movies; you have to ease into them. You have to assume that there's stuff that you are not going to understand and let go of it. Think of the people in Bombay watching something like *Booty Call*. You think they get all the jokes? Of course not. For them it is as much of a foreign film as any Japanese movie is foreign to us.

But back to Simon and Fellini. *Amarcord* is about this lit-tle town in Italy where all the schoolboys are always lusting after the older women around them. Now, the beauty of this movie is that all those ladies are gorgeous...and fat. You see them walking up and down the street of their tiny town with their voluptuous curves swinging from left to right, like Grandpa's old pendulum clock.

And — not to sound conceited — almost every woman in that movie looked a little like me. There was the Gradisca, who had a tiny waist and an extensive ass. There was the tobacconist, whose boobs were so enormous that they could easily suffocate a lover. These women didn't hide their curves with blazers or tunics: they walked around wearing skin-tight sweaters and short skirts, showing off their bodies with pride, as if there was no one in the world more attractive than they.

The more I saw of the movie, the better I felt about my body. To think that a smart guy like Federico Fellini saw beauty in a big ass, or a gigantic pair of boobs, made me proud of my size, and that doesn't usually happen when I see movies starring Jennifer Aniston.

As I saw Gradisca prancing around on the screen, I fully understood what Madame told me on the first night: "It's not what you have, it's how you feel about it."

Maybe I was getting more comfortable in my own skin, or maybe Simon was getting to know me and letting down his guard, but, little by little, we ended up leaning very comfortably on each other. It happened naturally, I swear to God that I wasn't planning to make a move on him or anything. We were so close to each other that it simply made sense to intertwine our limbs a little. To make a long story short, by the time we got to the sad part of the movie, Simon was holding my hand.

I must have some unresolved issues with my mom, because, ever since I was a little girl, seeing a mother dying in a movie — even in *Bambi* — makes me cry uncontrollably. In *Amarcord* there's a death of a mother, and, as expected, I started silently weeping. What I did not expect was Simon's reaction. Out of the corner of my eye I caught him wiping a tear off his face.

I like manly men, but I also like a guy who's man enough to allow himself to drop a tear when it's necessary. It takes a lot of courage to let your feelings show.

When I met Simon I never imagined that he could be that kind of guy, and I'm not embarrassed to admit that I was wrong. It takes time to get to know somebody, and if I had dismissed him on that first night, I would have never been able to witness this side of him.

I've been to a bunch of singles events in New York where you sit with a stranger for a couple of minutes to talk about yourselves, and then a bell rings and the guy leaves and a new one comes in. I'm not saying that you should court someone for years before you decide to take the plunge, but for me, fast dating is like fast food: it doesn't fill me up.

Women go through men, and men go through women, as if we were going through shoes: too high, too low, too tight, too loose, too white, too dark. We're not taking the time to get to know anybody.

Simon was not my physical ideal, but that single tear he shed watching that scene said more about him as a person than a thousand words, than a million personal ads, than a gazillion profiles on the Internet.

As the movie ended, we relaxed more and more, and our breathing became one. I can't remember when we fell asleep, but I know that it was smooth and peaceful. In less than twelve hours I was having the big meeting with the whole marketing team, Bonnie the bitch, and the Chicago Boss, but nothing else seemed important to me that night. I felt for the first time in a long time that I was living in the present. And being in the present made me realize that I was falling in love.

That Friday morning, when we woke up, I could tell that he felt no shame anymore when I found his arm around my shoulders. I looked at him and smiled, and he smiled back. As I was looking for the words to tell him thanks, or you're welcome — or whatever you say to bid farewell to someone who paid you an insane amount of money for sitting next to him for five nights in a row — he took an initiative that swept me off my feet.

"Would you like to come back tonight and watch another movie?"

"Sure," I said. But I actually wanted to hug him and scream, "Yes! Yes! Yes!"

My passion horse was running out of control.

CHAPTER 24

That Friday morning, I went home tired but walking on air. I took my shower, applied my makeup carefully and lovingly, and started the complicated process of choosing what to wear for the big meeting with the Chicago Boss.

"Should I wear something simple—something to blend in—or should I dress up like a vamp and steal the spotlight?" I asked myself.

Blending in would be safe. No one would notice me, I would sit, take notes, and before I knew it the meeting would be over. On the other hand, I could wear something sexy and fabulous, be acknowledged, and piss Bonnie off. It was a tough decision.

I instinctively reached out for one of those boring pantsuits that I've been wearing for the last three years. The cut was conservative, the colors were muted, it was the perfect outfit to pass unnoticed. But when I saw myself in the mirror wearing that stupid suit, I felt disgusted. I felt that I was betraying myself.

"Who am I kidding? I don't have a muted personality. Why the hell do I have to wear muted colors?" I concluded. "Fuck that," I said, and I went back to the closet and picked the coolest outfit I could come up with. Once you taste freedom, there's no way you can ever go back into slavery.

I arrived at the office fashionably late, and as I entered the big conference room I got a few compliments on my appearance from some of the girls in Media Research.

"I absolutely love that dress," said Caroline Connors.

"Thanks!"

I wore a red vintage-looking dress with a sweeping skirt and shaped bodice that made me look like an ample Grace Kelly on the way to a 1950s Hollywood party. To top it off, I accessorized it with a rather excessive necklace made of Swarovski crystals that trickled playfully between my boobs. Let's face it, I have great breasts, and now that I'm proud of them, why not show the road to paradise with a long path of shiny stones?

I combed my hair back, but left the natural curl in, so I had a big head of hair over my shoulders. I'm telling you, hair alone, I was traffic-stopping. I did wear my glasses, though, to add a little intellectual flair to my look, but even with them I was a knockout.

At the office, all the departments had gathered to present and discuss the creative and marketing ideas to the big man on campus. I sat with my notebook ready to take notes that I would transcribe and distribute afterward. Yeah, I have a B.F.A., and a master's in communication arts, but my life had been reduced to taking notes in meetings. Welcome to corporate America.

The Chicago Boss was sitting at the end of the table, and Bonnie — being the ass-kissing snake that she is — squeezed herself in at his side. If he said yes, she would nod; if he said no, she would shake her head. It looked like a ventriloquist act. The purpose was to convince us all that she had the Chicago Boss by the balls, but anyone who can read body language could see that the Boss was vaguely annoyed by having her next to him at the narrow end of the table, and — knowing what I knew — that made the whole scene more repulsive and amusing for me.

Group after group, the plans were laid out in front of him.

"We've planned six cities — New York, Miami, Los Angeles, Chicago, Dallas, and Seattle. We're talking billboards, bus stops, phone booths, even phone cards!"

"Tampons on phone cards?" asked the Chicago Boss with a frown.

"Of course!" said Larry from Media Planning. "The average age of the phone-card user is —"

"Phone cards?" the Chicago Boss asked again. He had a very subtle way of letting you know when he wasn't crazy about something. I personally thought that the phone cards were a bit excessive too. You see, great minds think alike.

Finally came our turn to pitch the slogans. "Go ahead, Mark, blow us away," said Bonnie, trying to distance herself from our presentation.

"We've come up with a very exciting and eclectic list of possible slogans," Mark said.

Bullshit. We came up with a few lame lines that were downgraded to "pathetic" by Bonnie.

Poor Mark leaned over the computer, controlling the sad PowerPoint document that was being projected on the wall.

"...and the last one: 'UK Charms...to the rescue!'" Mark finished.

The Chicago Boss remained silent through the whole presentation. Then he spoke.

"To the rescue? Is that your grand finale?"

Mark stood there frozen.

The Chicago Boss took his glasses off and covered his eyes for a second.

"There's nothing here," he told us somberly. "We are trying to attract young girls. Come on! The product is fun, sexy, new! This is not your mother's tampon! You don't sell tampons to girls and old ladies with the same language," he said. "You gotta give me something to work with, guys!"

This came as no surprise to me. Our original ideas were nothing to write home about, but anything decent that we came up with had been carefully destroyed by Bonnie. Acting as if she were fixing our lousy work, she mangled all the concepts, turning funny into boring, and surprising into predictable.

"You gotta give me something to work with, guys! This is the backbone of the campaign," he pleaded.

But nobody said anything, because we all knew that opening our mouths meant getting instantly fired by Bonnie. She didn't allow any cracks in her power structure. That is the problem with many of these big companies: they have turned into royal courts where your boss is the undisputed king. You can see these bureaucrats single-handedly sinking the business, but nobody can do anything about it. The hierarchy is so rigid that they are untouchable, unapproachable, unquestionable. If the company goes down, then everybody praises the whistle blower, but try to blow the whistle to stop the company from sinking and you'll get fired in a New York second. Isn't that insane? And if you happen to have your retirement invested in stock from that company, then you're double-screwed.

The Chicago Boss was huffing and puffing. Bonnie sat there completely undaunted, watching her plan come to fruition. She couldn't imagine that I had an ace up my sleeve.

"All these slogans are crap," said the Chicago Boss. "They're not smart, they're not direct, and they are *not funny*. We need to put ourselves in the shoes of our demographic and say, how would a fourteen-to-twenty-four-year-old girl describe the product in a short and direct way? We have to come up with that: something simple, easy, organic. One line, give me one line," he begged, surrounded by the most solemn corporate silence.

I waited patiently for the right moment to drop the bomb.

"We need a line that is fun, irreverent, and direct. One line that says 'tampons,' that says 'England,' that says 'quality,' and that screams 'young.'"

No one said a word.

"One line, please!" he asked one more time as he collapsed on his chair, putting his hands on his face in deep frustration.

Finally, my voice bounced against the walls.

"Bloody awesome."

Everybody turned to look at me as if I had gone nuts.

"What?" the Chicago Boss jumped in.

"Bloody awesome," I proudly repeated.

"Who said that?" asked the Chicago Boss.

Bonnie extended her bony finger in my direction.

"She did," barked the harpy, hoping that I would be publicly scolded.

Knowing that I was in the spotlight, I automatically straightened my back, relaxed my shoulders, and assumed the beautiful pose that Madame had taught me. If everybody was going to stare at me, they should see me at my best — I thought — so I lifted my head proudly, as if they were about to cut it off in the French guillotine.

The Chicago Boss looked at me with his mouth open.

I looked back at him and repeated myself one last time: "UK Charms... Bloody Awesome."

Then the Chicago Boss leaned over the table toward me, his eyes fixed on mine. Everybody held their breath, there was a tense silence, and finally he said the two most beautiful words I have ever heard in my whole professional career:

"*Fucking* brilliant!"

The Chicago Boss started clapping; everybody else started clapping. Even Bonnie was clapping — she was pissed but clapping. Ha! To make matters worse — or better — my red cell phone started vibrating, and in the process it started sliding right between my boobs.

"Sorry, it's an important phone call," I said, digging deep into my cleavage to rescue my cell. Everybody laughed, and I left the room while bowing at the adoring crowd.

"I'll be back in a minute," I said, leaving my fans waiting for more, as I closed the door behind me.

I walked outside the conference room and answered the phone.

"B?"

"Yes, Madame?"

"I got a frantic phone call from Richard Weber. He needs you there tonight at..."

"Wait, wait. I have plans. I'm seeing Simon tonight," I confessed.

"Aren't you done with Simon? We agreed on five nights — Sunday through Thursday."

"Well, he asked me to stop by tonight to watch a movie. I guess I should have told you."

There was a short silence, and finally the Madame spoke.

"Were you keeping this a secret?" she asked suspiciously.

"It came out of nowhere. I didn't like the guy at all, remember? I swear I didn't plan this! I didn't even find him attractive to begin with!" I bit my tongue.

"It's not a crime if you liked him all along. I'm just curious, because so many people say that they hate something and then go running after it."

I didn't want to argue. Like Madame, I didn't have time for this so I cut to the chase. "Is it okay to have a date with a client or not?"

"Of course it's okay, but . . . are you sure that it's a date?"

"Of course it's a date! It's a date—first—because he didn't call you to book me, and—second and most important—because he and I really connected last night. We were holding hands!"

"Are you sure that you want to date this guy?" she asked.

"Yes," I said, convinced.

"Then do it. I want you to be happy," she said.

Getting Madame's blessing felt good. Everything was working exactly the way it should. I got a surge of energy and happiness, and I strutted my way back to a second round of applause in the conference room, which made me feel like one of those teenage girls that we were trying to sell tampons to: everything was "bloody awesome."

But the day wasn't over yet. As matter of fact, the best part of my day was only beginning.

CHAPTER 25

*R*ight after the lunch break, I wasn't surprised or scared when Mary popped her head into my cubicle.

"This is it, baby. Are you ready?" she told me, knowing that I knew exactly what she was referring to. Bonnie wanted to see me immediately, so it was time to pull out the big guns. I prepared myself and headed for Bonnie's office.

I walked with my head high into her chamber of horrors.

"Good afternoon," I said with a big smile.

She didn't answer. She pretended to be busy looking at some papers, but I knew that it was just an act. She wanted to create tension, and have an excuse not to make eye contact with me, so later on she could use her Medusa eyes to turn me into a stone statue or something of that sort.

Regardless of her intentions, I sat down very comfortably in front of her; actually, I was almost disrespectfully comfortable. After a moment of calculated silence, she dropped the papers and looked me straight in the eye. I smiled again, defiant. She started her speech. "As you are well aware, the meeting that we had this morning was *not* a brainstorm. It was a presentation. I specifically asked you to schedule a brainstorm several days ago, for a good reason."

I listened to her with my best puppy face, pretending that I was genuinely concerned and repentant.

"You have no authority to present ideas directly to the president of the company without getting previous clearance from me. I don't need to explain that this qualifies as gross misconduct and it's an immediate cause for dismissal that I will bring up personally with Human Resources, to issue an official warning."

She made a small pause, thinking that that was my cue to start begging forgiveness. I just smiled at her and placed my tape recorder on the desk. She looked at me as if I had two heads. I smiled again and pressed PLAY. Then we both heard her voice from the conversation with Christine in the bathroom.

"... she's too fat to work here. That's reason enough."

"You can't say that!"

"Oh, I'll set her up. I've done this before. How do you think I got rid of Miller and Jessica? Nobody, I repeat, nobody fucks with me."

Just to annoy her for an extra minute, I faked surprise and said: "Oh, I'm sorry, that was the wrong tape."

I popped another cassette in the machine, and we heard her distinctive squeaking, setting the ultimate trap for the Chicago Boss.

"Kevin is so stupid he doesn't even know how stupid he is. If we don't get UK Charms — and trust me, I'll make sure that we don't — he better start looking for a retirement home in Florida."

"Do you have that much pull with the board?" asked Christine.

"Watch me! I've got those idiots of the board in my back pocket."

The plan was finally unveiled. Bonnie was actively sabo-

taging the tampon presentation to kick the Chicago Boss out
of his own company and—most likely—take his position as
the president of the agency. I used to think that she was evil,
but I was being too nice: she was the Antichrist.

I stopped the recording. For once she was speechless. I
leaned over the desk—still smiling—and very carefully
explained my intentions:

"Bonnie, now I'm going to go back to my 'dungeon,' and
I'm going to pack up all my things. And you have half an
hour to decide if I'm in fact leaving the company, or if I'm
moving to the window office with my new title of creative
director. Got it?"

She tried to utter a word, but I stopped her with another
line.

"Oh, by the way, if I'm not at my desk by the time you
make up your mind, I could be at the post office, sending
copies of this tape to a couple of friends in Chicago, so don't
hurry, but keep me posted."

I smiled one more time. I could tell she was grinding her
teeth. I was hoping that they would fall out.

Before I left, I turned around one last time and left her
with one more line: "We have one thing in common, Bonnie.
Nobody fucks with me either." I know. I overdid it—I'm
such a drama queen—but how could I miss such a Bette
Davis moment?

I walked out triumphant and felt like the queen of the
world, but before I got to my desk—just like the princess of the fairy tale—I felt a pea hurting the small of my
back. Could I be feeling guilty about blackmailing Bonnie?
"Nonsense!" I told myself, ignoring the pea, and I started
packing my belongings in my green trash can for recyclable
paper.

Needless to say, Mary came over to my cubicle fifteen minutes later with a big smile and announced that Bonnie wanted me to move my things to the window office.

"The official reason is that she wants you to work in a more comfortable environment so you can concentrate on the UK Charms campaign, but everybody in Facilities is saying that you got the job." Very discreetly, Mary high-fived me before she left.

But the pea was still hurting my back. I'm telling you, there's something about revenge that doesn't sit right with me.

Bonnie deserved to get screwed. She deserved it for all the damage she had done, for all the pain she had inflicted. But blackmailing her felt weird. "I'm not used to standing up for myself; that's why I feel like this," I mumbled while I crossed the hallway, my arms full of manila folders, and pushed the door of my new office with my butt.

The news of my unofficial promotion spread like wildfire that afternoon, so I wasn't surprised when a blast from the ugly past stopped by my new office. There he was, none other than Dan Callahan.

He stepped in without knocking, leaned on the archway, and watched me unpack as if I were stripping for him. What a moron.

"Wow! Congratulations!" he said.

I was busy arranging my things and dealing with the pea stuck on my back; the last thing I wanted to do was engage Dan in any type of conversation, so, without turning around, I replied with a simple "Thanks."

Then, giving me a master demonstration of masculine stupidity, he threw the following line: "So let's go for a drink tonight to celebrate."

The nerve. I stopped for a second, turned around ready

to send him to some place where the sun never shines, but something in me kept me from being a bitch. It was the pea on my back, and the pea was warning me that I was turning into a Bonnie. So, hiding my recently developed claws, I decided just to answer to Dan with complete and profound honesty: "Dan, I'm sorry, but I can't go out with you."

I guess he didn't understand complete and profound honesty, because he came back with another stupid line.

"Let's do it tomorrow, then..."

I was shaking my head no, but he wasn't even looking at me. He was writing it down in his BlackBerry, while probably admiring himself for being the suave swinger that he thought he was. So, convinced that the date was a fact, he started giving me instructions for tomorrow's rendezvous.

"I'll pick you up at eight, and we'll go for a quick bite—"

I had to interrupt him. "Dan, I don't want to go out with you."

Okay, parenthesis: I never had sex with Dan, and I'm sure I never will. But either he has a huge penis or he thinks he does, because he looked at me as if I were just insane. He went from disbelief to anger to sarcasm, while trying to process the fact that I was turning him down.

"What's wrong with you?" he asked, still in shock.

"There's absolutely nothing wrong with me," I replied, knowing that my words had more relevance than he could even imagine.

He tightened his lips and finally uttered, "Well, congratulations again."

And I just replied, "Thanks again," and continued unpacking my stuff. Sorry, Dan, no time for this crap. The world is a big place, so good luck in all your endeavors, and may you find a woman who puts up with your narcissistic bullshit.

As I was preparing myself to fill my cabinets and go back to the silent biopsy of the pea on my back, Lillian — on the verge of a nervous breakdown — stepped into my new office.

"B, I need to talk to you *right now*."

"About what?"

Lillian closed the door — it's a good thing I finally had a door — and then moved close to me and, in the lowest and most dramatic tone of voice that she could find, announced, "I Googled your friend Natasha Sokolov. They call her 'the Russian Madame.' Did you know that she's been in jail?"

Oh, shit.

CHAPTER 26

*A*wareness is a bitch.

I'm not a psychic, but I'm going to tell you something about your personal past: you were a little kid, and you were running around in the backyard, or the playground, or the living room, and your mother warned you, "You're going to trip and fall," and, like magic, you did. Your mother said it, and it happened, right?

Was your mother a psychic? Maybe — I suspect all mothers are — but that's not the reason why you fell. You fell because suddenly you became aware that you *could* fall.

When we were kids, we all did stupid things. I remember being in Miami, and, while trying to impress the friends of my cousin Virna, I walked on the ledge of a sixteen-story building. Pretty stupid, huh? It never crossed my mind that a sudden gust of wind could send me over the edge. But I'm convinced I didn't fall — mainly — because I didn't realize that I could. If my mother had been there, she would have screamed, "You're gonna fall!" and there would be no more

B, just a crater in the asphalt, and a bunch of Cuban relatives saying things like:

¡Pobrecita! She had her whole life ahead of her!

She was so nice!

Chubby, but, yeah, nice, very nice.

Why would she jump off that building?

And inside my coffin I would be yelling, "I didn't jump, you idiots! I fell off because my mother told me that I could!" Nothing jinxes you faster than common sense. When you do something stupid but you don't know how stupid it is, you are somehow protected by your imbecility. As my aunt Carmita used to say: "God protects the drunks and the idiots."

That's exactly what I was thinking about when Lillian took me downstairs to the smokers' corner in front of the building. I knew that she was probably right to warn me, but I was afraid that she was going to make me aware of things that I wanted to be completely oblivious to, and jinx the hell out of me.

Good old Lil was so frantic that I had to drag her to the park across the street, where we sat on a bench to discuss my life of crime. I don't know exactly how we got to it, but at some point I heard myself presenting a rather lame argument. "For God's sake, Lillian! Even Martha Stewart has been in jail!"

The truth is that Madame had been arrested in the past, but she had not been convicted—just as she confessed that first day in Coney Island. But for Lillian the fact that I knew about it and still willfully joined her comfort-providing service was a sign that I was going slowly mad and I needed professional help. She may have been truly concerned for my well-being, but—that moment, to me—it just felt like she was raining on my parade.

"Stop it, B! You've been keeping this a secret because you know that I would never let you go through with something like this. Are you insane?"

Okay, I could appreciate her concern, but I could do without the condescending attitude. So, without fighting, I tried to turn the tables around.

"Lil, you were the one who told me, right here—actually, over there by the ashtrays—that I was going through all this shit with Dan Callahan and Bonnie and my ripped pants to learn a lesson, and that nothing was an accident, and blah, blah, blah..."

"But I didn't expect you to become a prostitute!"

When I heard those words, my blood pressure dropped, and an acrid taste of bile filled my mouth. I didn't have a mirror handy, but I suspect that my face must have turned white like a bathroom tile.

"Lillian, first of all, lower your voice," I managed to say without strangling her. You see, it's one thing to be a prostitute, but something very different to be *called* a prostitute in public. Screw sticks and stones, certain words can totally break your bones. I felt cornered, and angry, and judged. In the back of my head, I heard the words of my aunt Fronilde: *If you don't want people to know what you did, then don't do it.* Too late for that advice, right?

Half of me wanted to send Lillian to hell, while the other half wanted to make her understand my reasons, and yet a third half—if that is possible—realized that the priority was to shut her up to prevent serious and well-founded rumors. I didn't like the idea of having a hysterical Asian model revealing the nasty details of my secret life across the street from my office. So—trying not to get carried away by the anger—I took a deep breath and explained in my lowest audible voice, "All I can tell you is that, yes, I've been working for her, but I haven't done anything illegal, and I haven't had sex with anybody."

"You haven't had sex with anybody *yet,* but that's the next step!" she replied, pissing me off even more.

"Lillian, you don't know what you're talking about. These guys pay me just to be there."

"They pay you?" she said with the most annoyingly high pitch that human ears have ever registered. "Can you hear yourself? You've turned into a hooker!"

This time she'd really done it. I was ready to kill her, so I looked her straight in the eye and — with an exaggerated overbite — I spelled it out.

"Listen, Lillian. Men pay good money to spend time with me, and they pay good money to spend time with you too, okay? You and I are not different, so get off your high horse and face the facts."

"What?" she asked, putting her right hand over her chest to underline her shock and awe.

"Come on, Lillian, you bounce from bed to bed, and you don't even look at their faces, you just look at their bank accounts!"

"That is not true..." she said, on the verge of tears.

Driven by an anger that might be illegal in some states, I slashed her with one more comeback: "Lillian, you're always looking for a boyfriend with a bigger car, a bigger dick, or a bigger wallet."

Lillian started crying quietly. I started crying too. I was embarrassed about what I had just said. I tried to put my hand on her shoulder, but she brushed it off. That gesture made me understand how unfair I had been with her, so, with my hand on my heart, I spoke with complete honesty.

"I'm sorry, Lil, I shouldn't have said that. I'm confused. I'm excited, and afraid of all this at the same time. But I can tell you that I've learned to love myself more in these few days than in all these years of psychotherapy."

She kept crying in silence. The only way to make her understand was to get her to put herself in my own shoes. So I spilled the beans.

"Lil, I've always envied you. I love you, but I've envied the hell out of you — if that makes any sense. Every time we go out and I'm neglected while you're surrounded by all these men who make you feel desired, I...I...I want to die. These guys I have met through the Madame have made me feel sexy and wanted. Some are young, some are old, some are handsome, some are ugly, but they've opened my eyes. I have learned that I have an audience, and I didn't know that!"

The funny thing was that as I was talking, a very good-looking guy walked by and gave me one of those looks that can burn through twenty layers of pantyhose. It was so obvious that he was checking *me* out, and not Lillian, that even she had to acknowledge that I was on to something.

"But, B," she said, "I've always told you that you were beautiful!"

"Yeah, but I didn't feel it! Now I feel it! And it's making me look at life in a completely different way. I needed this, I needed to meet these guys who are dying to admire me — who would pay a lot of money just to have me sit next to them, or give me a massage, or even smell my feet!"

"Eeeeew!" she said, disgusted "Is that what they do?"

"Yeah," I sighed, "some of them."

"Listen, B" she said softly, "so maybe I've had more men after me than you've had, but I go out with them a couple of times, and if I have sex, I never hear from them again, and if I don't, I don't hear from them again either. So what is all this attention good for? I don't need hundreds of men. I only need one, a good one.

"They come after me because I'm skinny, right? And they go after you because you're fat... So what's the difference? They just look at the outside. And the one thing I've learned is that I'm never going to find true love with someone who only looks at the outside. I want true love. What is it that you want? Dates? Flings? One-night stands? What do you want?"

I thought for a moment, and finally replied.

"I want...a Sunday kind of love."

I guess that Lillian also knew that old song, because she smiled and hugged me.

Now that I had the capacity to feel attractive and desired, I could go from man to man, gorging on these attentions, or I could use my recently acquired powers to find the one love that could make me truly happy. Gorging on attentions sounded really tempting, but...Who the hell was I kidding? I wanted to find one good guy too.

"Yep," I said, hugging Lillian, "I want a Sunday kind of love"

"Then maybe it's time to put your heart where your mouth is," she whispered.

"I'm afraid of being rejected," I confessed.

"Fear is the opposite of love," Lillian said, delivering the exact same advice that Madame had given me just hours ago.

Was I brave enough to follow their advice?

CHAPTER 27

*S*aying that my day had been hectic would be a hell of an understatement. However, in case you haven't guessed it already, the biggest thrill was yet to come. That same night, I was meeting Simon for our first "date."

I was halfway ready when Madame called me.

"So are you going through with the date?" she asked.

"Of course I am! I'm getting ready right now. Why?"

"I just want to make sure that you know what you are doing. I don't want you to get hurt."

What the hell was going on? Was it "kill-my-buzz" day or something? Here I was at the top of my game, getting the credit I deserved at work, putting my evil boss in her place, and actively pursuing the man I liked. I had never been so positive and assertive in my life.

"I know what I'm doing! I'm not going to get hurt!" I tried to calmed her down.

"If you say so," she said, not sounding terribly convinced. "So what happened at work?"

I briefly told her about my victory over the evil empire.

"Isn't that great?" I finished, convinced that she would applaud my bravery.

"Great? You are still working for that crazy bitch, who now hates you even more, and who'll do anything to destroy you."

"But the human resources department…" I tried to cut her off.

"The human resources department is neither human nor resourceful," she said. "They are there to protect the biggest fish, not you. All they care about is preventing lawsuits. From this moment on, somebody is going to go through your e-mails, your phone calls, and even your trash can. And if they can't find anything, they will plant it. If you are lucky — in a month or two — they'll promote you to a higher position in a different city, or in a worse department, and your new supervisor will be confidentially warned against you."

"Oh, shit," I said to myself, realizing what I'd gotten myself into.

"Honey, they could call it 'a bunny race,' but they call it 'a rat race' for a reason."

"But, Madame," I said, trying to defend my point, "I can't let her win! I have worked my ass off for years, and I have invested all this time…"

"You can't invest time! You can put money in the bank and get more money five years later, but If you say, 'I'm going to be miserable for five years, and then I'm going to be very happy in the sixth year,' guess what? A truck can run you over after those five years of misery, and you won't see a second of happiness. You have to choose happiness, not more years of misery working for that same woman."

"But she deserves this. She's a monster," I said.

"Yes, she is a monster, but now you are a blackmailer."

"How do you think she got where she is? Blackmail!" I replied.

"So if she jumps off a cliff are you going to jump after her too?" Madame said, making me feel I was ten years old.

There was a second of uncomfortable silence.

"B," she said tenderly, "my favorite writer, Jorge Luis Borges, used to say, 'Your revenge will never be better than your peace.' You are smart, talented, and hardworking. Choose happiness, not revenge."

That was the pea that was stuck at the small of my back. But just like the night when I went on my first date, with Mr. Rauscher, I didn't want to hear Madame. So, for the first time, I was the one in a hurry to get off the phone.

"Madame, I'm sorry for cutting you short, but I have to get ready."

"Do what you have to do, and call me if you need to talk," she said.

"Thanks."

"You are welcome," she said affectionately, and we hung up the phone.

I remained on the couch for a few seconds, trying to analyze my feelings. I felt volcanic and powerful, but childish and vulnerable at the same time. That was a sign that my passion horse was pulling too hard. And as much as I enjoyed riding that stallion — just like the ancient Greeks advised — it was wise to restrain it. But how could I do that when I was getting ready to see Simon? I felt savagely tormented by my own thoughts.

"Fuck thinking!" I said, and went back to my bedroom to get ready for my date.

CHAPTER 28

The first time I saw Simon, I didn't like him at all: his nose was too big, I couldn't see his eyes — covered by those thick glasses — his shaven head made him look like a refugee, and his tall, skinny, slouching body just seemed out of proportion with the world around him. But what can I say? By the end of night number five, all I could think of was having those long and skinny arms wrapped around me.

Hoping for that, I fixed myself up to look spectacular. I was wearing a see-through blouse with rather long and flowing sleeves, over a cute skin-tone tank top. I chose a trendy peasant skirt, and bought new sandals that were both stylish and comfortable. I wore just a drop of makeup and gelled my hair to have that wet-curl look that makes you look as if you just stepped out of the shower. I added a touch of Shalimar behind my ears, and I headed to Simon's house in a taxi.

That night I brought another Fellini movie, *Nights of Cabiria*. For those unfamiliar with the plot, it's the story of a prostitute who's always looking for love. What can I say? It sounded like a familiar theme to me.

When I got to Simon's place, I noticed that he wasn't wearing the same old paint-stained jeans that he wore all the time. He was wearing a different, slightly less destroyed pair of jeans, and a button-down shirt instead of a worn out T-shirt. It might sound silly, but that small detail made me very excited. He had been anticipating my visit. Good.

"Would you like something to drink?" he asked.

"Do you have red wine?"

I'm not sure what he usually drank — if he drank at all — but it certainly wasn't red wine, because he started running around as if I had asked for a pint of blood. After walking back and forth a few times scratching his head, he started digging in a closet where he kept winter coats, skis, a pair of Rollerblades, and varied sports equipment.

"Somebody gave me a bottle last year," he mumbled. "Here!" he said triumphantly, pulling a bottle out. "I hope it's still good. You are gonna have to try it, 'cause I wouldn't know." He must have been nervous: he just gave me the bottle as if I could open it with my bare hands.

"Do you have a corkscrew?" I asked innocently.

"Oh my God!" he said, realizing the faux pas. He ran to the kitchen, brought two glasses and the corkscrew, and proceeded to open the bottle.

The wine was good — very good, as a matter of fact. Simon went back to the kitchen for a couple of minutes and came back with a bowl of popcorn; then he sat next to me, in the narrow space that he was accustomed to, and we started watching *Nights of Cabiria*.

I didn't know it then, but the musical *Sweet Charity* was based on the same story. The difference is that *Charity* is lighter, and funnier. *Cabiria* was funny at times, but when it got sad, it got really sad. We sat there mesmerized. We didn't hold hands, but we held each other's arms very tenderly throughout the whole movie, and at the end we were both in tears. Then, in the last few seconds of the movie, I saw something totally unexpected on the screen.

"Did she look at us?" I asked Simon.

"What?" He'd been busy crying, so he'd missed the spot I was talking about.

I was convinced that, at the end of the movie, Cabiria looked at the audience and smiled. To double-check, we went back to that scene to see the ending one more time.

Yep. She smiled. This was particularly strange because this is a very realistic drama, not one of those MGM musicals where actors look at the camera and smile. In a movie like *Cabiria* the actors never acknowledge the audience to keep the illusion of reality.

But Cabiria does it.

I don't want to ruin the movie for you if you haven't seen it, but toward the end, just when you think that she'll be alone and bitter for the rest of her life, she smiles again. She looks at you and she smiles. It's as if she was trying to tell you, "No matter how many times you've been hurt, you can't lose hope. Keep smiling. Life goes on. It'll get better." I still get goose bumps just thinking about it.

"Yes, she looks at you," Simon acknowledged. Then he looked at me tenderly through his thick glasses and asked with a tiny thread of voice, "Would you see it again with me?"

Naturally I said yes—one, because I loved the movie, and, two, because who could say no to that big boy from Arizona, with his Coke-bottle glasses and his refugee haircut?

So we ended up seeing the movie twice—from beginning

to end—and then we went back and started picking up scenes that we particularly liked, watching them over and over.

Cabiria was petite and cute, but Wanda, her best friend in the movie, was more my size. There're a couple of show-stopping scenes in the movie where you see Wanda walking with her voluptuous legs, boobs, and ass across the screen. Wanda had a feminine magnetism that no Hilton sister could ever achieve in her lifetime. As we were watching Wanda in action, Simon froze the image, and then he suddenly turned to me.

"Could I take your picture?" he asked.

"My picture?" I gasped.

The number-one fashion photographer in the world wanted to take my picture? Holy shit!

"Yeah. I'd love to," he said with an intensity that I had never seen in him before.

"Sure," I said, flattered.

In the meantime, Simon's eyes were studying me with the detail that a surgeon dedicates to a patient.

"But would you mind if I..." he started saying, and then he stopped while still analyzing my features.

"Would you mind if I..." he started again, leaving the sentence in half one more time, and looking at me with that mad sparkle that artists have when they come up with a great idea.

"Would I mind if you... what?" I asked, trying carefully not to interrupt his thought process.

"If I..." he started again. But there was no need to continue, because I knew exactly what he was trying to ask me. A deep chill went down my spine, and I felt that I was standing by a sharp cliff.

"You want to take my picture naked, don't you?" I asked.

He nodded, but I could tell that he wasn't with me anymore. He was in his head, planning it all, setting the lights. We were still in his living room, but in his head he was taking my pictures already. In my head, I was fighting every ghost of my childhood, every fear, every cause for shame, and every single perception of my body as a despicable and embarrassing object.

But that night I was strong. That night I could fight them all. Yes, I pictured my father having a heart attack, and my mother banning me forever, but this whole thing wasn't about them, it was about me. If they truly loved me, they would understand that I needed to exorcise my demons, that — once and for all — I needed to feel proud of my body, proud of being big, thick, and voluptuous.

Proud of being the way I am: fat.

So, having said that, it was time to put my ass where my mouth was: naked, and in front of a Rolleiflex 2.8.

I followed Simon downstairs feeling nervous but excited. Simon's studio was huge, and it changed constantly depending on the shoot he was working on. Every day he had a different contraption built by prop masters and stage designers to use as a background for his models. That night he had a beautiful mountain landscape hanging by strings from the ceiling, a grand staircase that climbed up to nowhere, and an impossible room made out of silks and plywood. In a corner he had a pile of absurdly modern chairs that no human being could sit comfortably on. He took a chaise longue from that corner and asked me to lie on it. He thought about mimicking the *majas* of Goya. He painted the same model twice in the exact same position, but in one she is completely dressed up, and in the other one she is stark naked — shamelessly lying on her back, with her arms above her head.

But before I could sit on the chaise longue Simon had already changed his mind.

"Wait a minute, can you swim?"

"Sure" I answered, wondering what he had in mind.

His crew had built a huge fish tank for some photo shoot where the models were dressed up as mermaids. The tank was still there, so he proceeded to set it all up. I sat there observing Simon changing the background, turning on the lights, and taking measurements with his light meter. It was fascinating to see a genius at work, and it was incredibly flattering to think that all this work was devoted to taking my photograph, to immortalizing this body that I had hated for so long.

Do I deserve all this attention? I kept asking myself.

When he was done setting it all up, I got up, took off my clothes, and let myself into the tank.

I've heard that our bodies are more than 60 percent water, and it doesn't surprise me. Obviously, I've been in the water many times, but always with a purpose: I was going to bathe or exercise, or I was jumping in and out of the pool just to cool off on a summer afternoon. But this was the first time I allowed myself just to *be* in the water, letting it caress my skin, enjoying the delicious experience of weightlessness. When you are in the water, it doesn't matter if you are skinny or fat. You become part of something bigger than you. It's like stepping into another dimension where the sounds, the light, and the speed of things are completely different. In the water you can't set the pace, you need to go with the flow. "Going with the flow"—what a beautiful thought. That night, the fish tank was a place for introspection, a place to stop the fight against others and against myself.

Next time you go to a pool, take a few minutes and—very

slowly—let the air out of your lungs and allow yourself to sink to the bottom. There's not a more peaceful place anywhere, there's not a safer space in the world. I suspect that the reason why humans can't breathe under the water, is that, if we could, then we would never leave that place. As you lie at the bottom of the pool, try to open your eyes, and just look up, and see the light coming through the bubbles and the ripples of the surface. I don't know if you are religious or not, but then and there you'll see God, I promise.

I don't know how long I was in the water, but Simon must have taken hundreds of pictures of me. I even forgot that he was there. He never gave me an instruction, or a direction. He just stood there taking picture after picture, while I floated in the tank as if I were floating in my mother's womb. When I finally got out of the tank, I felt completely reborn.

When he did his fashion shoots, Simon used a digital camera, but when he did his artwork, he preferred to use his old-fashioned Rolleiflex, his first professional camera.

"When will you develop them?" I asked him while I wrapped myself in a towel that he had set by the tank.

"Right now. Don't you want to see them?" he said, excited.

Like children playing with a brand-new toy, we went into his darkroom, to start the developing process. We stood side by side when he finally inserted the photographic paper in the developer fluid, and we held our breath together as the first image appeared before our eyes. The image was too beautiful to be described. To think that this body that I had hated for so long could look so beautiful through the eyes of this man, gave me a chill.

I was so moved that I spontaneously turned around and kissed him on the cheek. But when I was about to separate myself from him, I noticed that his face followed my mouth, as if he wanted to be kissed again. So I kissed him again. But this time his face followed my mouth again, and turned slightly to the right. Then he placed his lips near mine. Someone had to take the initiative, so I kissed him on the lips. And I kissed him again. And he opened his mouth, and we kissed with our lips, and our tongues, and our hearts. And it was the sweetest kiss I've ever had.

I turned to face him, and I made him face me. And I hugged him while I kissed him. But his arms remained at his sides, as if he didn't dare hug me back. His arms said no, but his mouth kept saying yes. So I held his face in my hands and whispered softly in his ear, "Simon. I want you to lift your arms...A little higher...Even higher...Right around my torso, yes, just like that. Perfect! Now I want you to wrap them tightly around my body. Tighter, tighter, tighter, tighter...Aha! Good. That's a good hug. I want you to remember this...and I want you to hug me like this every time you feel like it."

I don't know how I did it, but I opened the floodgates. Simon hugged me and kissed me as if he had never hugged and kissed anyone in his life. And I hugged him and kissed him back as if he were the only man I'd ever known. And the kisses turned salty with the taste of tears, and I couldn't tell if they were mine, or his.

CHAPTER 29

I vividly remember the first time I heard Madonna singing "Like a Virgin." It wasn't when the song first came out, but when she released her greatest hits album, *The Immaculate Collection.* I was in Miami with my cousin Mariauxy — her actual name is Maria Auxiliadora, but she shortened it because she says that her name was too long and no one could pronounce it (as if "Mariauxy" was any easier). Anyway, we were in her bedroom, we were having fun painting our toenails and trying on crazy hairdos. I wasn't crazy about Madonna at the time, but Mariauxy was her biggest fan. She kept playing that album over and over, to the point where she actually scratched the CD.

When I like a song — don't ask me why — I get hooked by the music first, and much later I pay attention to the lyrics. That first time I heard "Like a Virgin," I thought that it was catchy, but since I didn't pay attention to the words, it took me a while to realize what it really meant.

As I was lying in bed with Simon (yes, I ended up in bed

with him), I felt that I was being touched for the very first time. It's going to sound totally corny, but I felt as if being with Simon made me a virgin once again.

I knew that this was something special because when we kissed I lost track of time. We could have kissed for minutes, hours, or days—all I knew was that I could keep kissing him forever.

If you think I'm going to describe in detail what happened in bed, I'll have to disappoint you. I am not going to get all graphic here, and I'll tell you why:

First, because I think that sex is overrated and closeness is underrated.

Second, because I think that good sex doesn't require extravagant displays of gymnastic skills.

And, third, because what I do in bed is nobody's business. If one day I'm in the mood to talk about it I will, but very likely we will be sitting at my kitchen table, with a bottle of bourbon and a bag of corn chips.

But the point is that having sex with Simon was awesome. Sometimes when you're lying in bed with a guy, your arm doesn't fit right around his back, or your leg cramps under his leg, or he rests his head on your chest and you can't breathe. You don't want to ruin the magic of the moment, and you try to keep quiet about it until you're almost ready to pass out in pain. Well, none of that happened that night. His body and my body fit so perfectly that it truly felt like one breathing, loving being. I caught myself thinking that from above we must have looked like the yin-yang sign: a perfect complement for each other. I heard bells, violins, trumpets, foghorns—you name it, and I heard it.

There was music playing, but it wasn't Madonna's. It was a Rickie Lee Jones album of standards called *Pop Pop*. If one day I meet Rickie Lee Jones I'll have to thank her personally for this fabulous night. We sang along with her, and kissed, and told each other how much we liked this part or that part of each other's bodies, and kissed again and again. I felt that every inch of my body was loved, desired, and accepted.

That night, time stood still. We made love, fell asleep, made love again, fell asleep again… It was incredible. Madame was right once again: I'd thought I had never had bad sex because I had never had good sex.

Later, we were lying there, intertwined, and I felt comfortable enough to ask Simon a question. I moved my mouth close to his peaceful face and whispered in his ear.

"Can I ask you something?"

"Go ahead."

"Why do you hate the beach?"

He laughed, and, burying his head in my hair, he answered: "You don't want to see me in a swimsuit."

"Actually, I'm seeing you without one right now, and I think you look pretty damn good."

"I'm too skinny…"

"Nobody is too skinny," I replied, kissing him.

"Nobody is too fat," he said, kissing me back.

"So what's the problem?"

He made a dramatic pause, and finally confessed, "Well, I have all this hair on my back…"

Yes, Simon had hair on his back. Long, soft, delicious hair that grew—I can't believe I'm saying this—in the most beautiful and artistic pattern. Like every other woman in America, I've always replied "Eeew" to the idea of a man with hair on his back. But once I had a taste of it, I realized that I want it every time.

I remember letting my hand wander from his neck down

to the small of his back, and saying "Oh my God!" every time
I completed the journey. I'm telling you, it was delicious.

"Have I complained about the hair on your back?" I told
him while stroking it one more time.

He replied with a kiss that almost made me pass out in
ecstasy. That's when I felt at ease to ask a second question,
the one that was really driving me crazy.

"Okay, one more thing," I asked playfully. "What is it
with the sixteen and a half inches?"

This time he didn't hide his face in my hair—instead, he
just looked away.

"It helps me sleep."

"Well, I figured that much out, but why?"

He paused, still looking away from me, and finally spoke.

"I stress myself. I start thinking about what would happen
if I screwed up a job and they stopped hiring me...I start
thinking that I'm going to lose everything and I'm going to
be broke again..."

"Simon. It's not like you're simply talented. You are a
freaking genius. You will never have a hard time finding
work."

"This is a very flaky business. Today you're in and tomorrow you're out."

"Well, if being 'in' is killing you, maybe you would be
happier being 'out.' What was the happiest time of your
life?"

He thought about it for a second.

"When I was working at Hearst Castle."

"Were you rich? Were you famous then?"

He laughed. "I was living from paycheck to paycheck."

"So what's better, then, to be miserable with more, or to
be happy with less?"

Simon took a deep breath, and his body relaxed so much next to mine that it felt as if we got even closer.

"I want to be happy, like I am right now," he whispered in my ear.

I held his head against my chest lovingly.

"But why those sixteen and a half inches?" I insisted.

There was an uncomfortable silence.

"It's a long story," he finally said.

I instinctively knew that it was time for me to shut up and stop asking.

"Well, I don't have time for long stories right now, so let me tell you a short one. It's called *sacapuntas*."

He laughed and kissed me, and I kissed him back. And while kissing him — long, sweetly, and deeply — I hoped he could read my mind, so he could understand that it didn't matter if he was too skinny, or he had hair on his back. That it didn't matter what those sixteen and a half inches were about. I was willing to accept him with no further questions. And I believe that he kissed me back understanding this.

CHAPTER 30

*P*eople say that time flies when you're having fun, but I have to disagree with them, because that night — the most memorable night of my life — felt like it lasted forever.

It was Saturday, but Simon had a photo shoot that afternoon, and the sound of his crew hammering in the studio woke us up. I was still half asleep when I saw him rolling out of bed, and stretching his naked body by the window — not to flash the neighbors, but just to own the world and the sunlight pouring in. I dozed off again while he threw some clothes on, but I felt his kiss on my lips before he stepped out of the apartment.

Yes, it was a beautiful morning for Simon, and it was a beautiful morning for me too, for about fifty seconds. I finally got out of bed with a big smile and a glow that you could see from outer space, but then everything came crashing down as I found that Simon had left a check on the night table with a Post-it note.

"Thank you very much," the note said.

For a moment I couldn't breathe, and my vision got blurry. I sat down again and looked at the note one more time.

"Thank you very much."

I didn't look at the amount. I ripped the check in pieces, threw them on the bed — or the floor, who cares — and got dressed in a hurry, feeling so nauseous that I was afraid of vomiting right there. Such irony! To think that the most beautiful night of my life was followed by the most horrible morning I could remember.

In Cuba they say *"Guerra avisada no mata al soldado,"* which roughly means that if the soldier has been warned that the war is coming, he shouldn't get killed in it. That damned Lillian had warned me that sooner or later I would have sex for money, and Madame had warned me not to fall in love with a client, so why the hell did I let this happen? If I was warned about this "war," why the hell did I get shot, and right in the middle of my heart?

How could I allow myself to fall in love with a crazy guy who got off on squeezing himself between a pillow and me? And this time I had no one to blame. I couldn't blame Bonnie, or Lillian, or Ino, or my mother. I couldn't even blame Madame, and, worst of all, I couldn't blame Simon either. He was a customer, and he had done what a customer was supposed to do. I thought of every time I'd made Madame swear that I wouldn't have to have sex with my customers, and I felt even dumber. I'd thought I could play this game without getting hurt. How could I be so stupid?

I was so convinced that this was a "date" and not a "job" that Alberto wasn't there waiting for me in the limo. So I had to face the "walk of shame" to the subway all by myself, and tormented by all the echoes of my Cuban Catholic education: *A woman who has sex out of wedlock is a whore. A woman*

who enjoys sex is even worse than a whore. Men are out to get you. A
woman must defend her virginity at any cost.

I was so upset that I couldn't think straight. If I could, I
would have told myself, "Wait a minute, B, you were not a
virgin to begin with, he wasn't out to get you — you were out
to get him — and, technically, you might not be a whore, but
you've been walking a fine line for the last couple of weeks."
But this was too much reasoning for a woman in my state.
All I could think of — over and over — was that I felt something magical that night, but clearly Simon didn't.

I thought again of how my AA-cx used to say, "When you
are hysterical, you are historical." Maybe that was the case.
Maybe I wasn't reacting to Simon, I was reacting to a whole
life of guilt and remorse. A life filled with the fear of being
used and the fear of being ignored.

To torture myself from a different angle, I started contem-
plating Simon's thoughts:

a) He probably thought that I was a real whore — not a
tourist in the industry.

b) He probably thought that I'd made love to hundreds of
men, the same way I did to him.

c) If his maid — I was sure he had one — cleaned the bedroom after I left, he would never get to see the ripped check,
and he would probably think that I even cashed it.

d) If the maid didn't throw the ripped check in the garbage, and he actually found the pieces, he would probably
laugh, thinking that I was a stupid and sentimental whore,
just like Cabiria.

Great. In Simon's opinion, I was a whore and a loser.

No matter which way I looked at it, the more I thought
about it the more embarrassed I was. I felt stupid, lonely,
cheap, rejected, and needy (and I so hate feeling needy). Just

when I thought that my life was changing — that I was changing — reality was slapping me all the way back to square one. How could I think that someone like him could fall in love with someone like me?

I hated Simon. I hated him for not reading my mind. For not knowing what I thought he should have known. For not feeling what I thought he should have felt. For not doing what I thought he should have done. I cried like a baby — and, worst of all, I felt like a baby. What I didn't understand at the time was that I was acting like a baby too. And I had a whole weekend ahead of me to cry and scream like a child until I turned blue. Yep, there's nothing worse than a whole empty weekend ahead of you when the only thing you have to do is punish your psyche. That damned Lillian was right: Fridays were the new Sundays. I should have stayed home and watched an old movie on cable, instead of going out to destroy my barely sprouting self-esteem.

By noon that Saturday, things had deteriorated considerably. I couldn't read, I couldn't watch TV, I couldn't go out, I couldn't stay home, I couldn't stand up, and I couldn't sit down. I was a mess.

I could have called a friend, but the only one I could call out of the blue was Lillian. Unfortunately, I was still pissed off at her for warning me about what — in fact — ended up happening. I even wondered if she had jinxed the whole thing with her stupid warnings. I still had the temptation to call her, but the fear of hearing anything close to "I told you so" kept me from doing it.

I tried to think about all the positive things that had come out of this — my brand-new window office, the victory over Bonnie — then it dawned on me: maybe God was punishing me for blackmailing Bonnie. I was lost in these and other miserable thoughts when Madame called me.

"Mr. Five in a Row has been calling the whole morning. What happened?"

She tried to be casual and matter-of-fact, but from the tone of her voice I knew that she suspected something.

"I can't talk about it, and I can't see him ever again," I said.

"Let me guess..." she replied.

"Please don't," I cut in. And then I started to cry.

Madame waited patiently while I sobbed on the phone.

"He paid me," I said when I was finally able to talk.

"But, honey, he was supposed to pay you," she answered, trying to comfort me.

"No, not after last night! You don't understand!" I almost yelled at her.

She probably realized at that point that nothing she could say could get me out of my misery. So, in her usual fashion, Madame moved to the next thing.

"So what do you want me to tell him?"

"Tell him that I'm busy. I cannot see him ever again."

Then I had the stupidest idea that had ever crossed my mind, but, being the train wreck that I was, I couldn't help going for it.

"Do you have another client for tonight?"

"Listen, B," she said, concerned, "from the way you sound, I don't think that you should—"

"Madame, please, I want to be busy tonight. I *need* to be busy tonight."

There was a minute of silence. She wanted me to think about what I was asking for, but I couldn't think. I just pleaded one more time.

"Please, Madame!"

She didn't say a word.

"Please," I begged one more time.

Every reasonable argument would have been ignored in my state of mind. Nothing would convince me: my passion horse was running out of control and ready to flip me over.

Reluctantly Madame explained the situation.

"There's a new customer, but I don't know him well yet. You shouldn't —"

"But I want to," I interrupted her.

"Shut up for a minute, will you?"

I finally closed my mouth, embarrassed at being such a pain in the butt.

"This is the deal. I only work with people who've been highly recommended. This guy has a referral, but his referral is out of the town, so —"

"So what do I have to do?" I jumped in.

Madame — sick of me by then — said something in Russian that was probably the equivalent of "Enough already!" and continued.

"Okay. You'll have to ask him the safety question."

"What safety question?"

"If he's a law-enforcement agent."

"Oh! *That* safety question," I said, trying to sound like a seasoned hooker. "Of course, of course, don't even worry about that."

"Are you sure that you're going to remember that? Because you sound like —"

I interrupted her again. "I know what to ask," I said with a nastiness that was totally uncalled for. "I'm *not* stupid."

Turned out I was wrong.

I *was* stupid. Extremely stupid.

CHAPTER 31

*A*ccording to my friend Carmen—who grew up in the Bronx—you know when a woman in the neighborhood has been betrayed by her man because she puts the speakers in the window and blasts songs by La Lupe for the whole barrio. La Lupe is the Cuban Billie Holiday, the Caribbean goddess of *despecho*.

Despecho is a very interesting word. It means "heartbreak" in Spanish. I'm not sure how it was created, but the roots of the word might hold some significance. The particle *des-* translates in English to "un-" or "undo." The second part, *pecho,* translates to "chest." Someone not only broke your heart but also completely messed up your chest, so you'll never be able to hold your heart in it again.

It doesn't matter what type of love trouble you're in, there is always a song from La Lupe that describes the type of treachery that you have been subjected to. Here are a few examples:

He used you for sex.

He used you for money.

He used you in general.

He lied.

He let you down.

He faked his feelings.

He left you to hook up with your best friend.

He left you to hook up with your worst enemy.

And probably the worst of all:

He left you for no particular reason.

The problem with "He left you for no particular reason" is that you cannot even blame a third party for the abandonment, so you'll always carry a little voice inside of you that tells you, "You did it, bitch, it's all your fault. He left you because of who you are," and that is the worst possible form of *despecho*.

That dark afternoon, as I was sitting in the subway on my way home to get ready for my new customer, I was listening to the *despecho* playlist in my iPod, trying to control my tears, and repeating the advice that my aunt Fronilde used to give in this type of desperate circumstances: "*Un clavo saca otro clavo*" — One nail can pull out another nail. If you broke up with a boyfriend, finding a new one will help you get over it.

That night, I wanted to prove to myself that I didn't care about Simon. That I was strong, that I could pretend that I was a real whore. "Come on! Go make some money! Turn a trick!" I told myself. The truth is that nobody in my state of mind should be allowed to make any type of decisions or drive heavy machinery.

I was lost in these absurd thoughts when I noticed that a skateboard-wielding teenager next to me had fallen asleep on my shoulder. I got so pissed that I stood up quite abruptly, and — without my shoulder to lean on — he fell over to his side.

"Shit," he said, still half asleep, as I moved across the car to sit on my own.

"Enough with these people drooling all over me," I mumbled. I kind of felt bad for the kid, but after what I just went through with Simon I couldn't put up with one more sleeper on my shoulder.

I got home and tried to take a long bath, but I couldn't relax into it. Then I tried to exfoliate, but I did it so forcefully that I almost removed a layer of skin. As hard as I tried to pamper myself lovingly — like Madame had instructed — I just couldn't get into it. I didn't enjoy getting dressed or putting on makeup, or putting on perfume. I knew that these were bad signs, but, just like a kamikaze pilot on a suicidal mission, I couldn't stop myself.

In the limo, I couldn't talk to Alberto. I felt angry and jaded.

"Are you okay, Miss B?" he asked.

"I'm fine," I said, wiping off an angry tear. He kept checking on me through the rearview mirror, but I avoided making eye contact with him. I needed my full attention to torture myself.

I was grinding my teeth all the way to the fancy hotel where my client was waiting for me. As I walked through the lobby, it should have been obvious to me that the magic and excitement of my previous adventures had vanished.

I knocked on the door of the room, and Adam — a good-looking guy in his forties — opened. He was well dressed, in a business suit, and said something about being in town from Sioux Falls for business. I can't describe him, because I didn't care and, frankly, I didn't even see him; all I could think of was Simon and what he thought of me.

"Would you like a drink?" Adam offered.

"Sure," I said. I needed some liquor to give myself courage to accomplish my stupid plan of "pulling out one nail with another one." And that's why that night I decided to drink something stronger than anisette.

"Do you have any vodka?" I asked.

"Sure, I can mix it with orange juice, cranberry . . ."

"On the rocks," I interrupted him.

"On the rocks?" He seemed surprised to hear me asking for such a manly drink.

"I'm not in the mood for sipping Cosmos tonight," I said with my best femme-fatale voice.

Allegedly, when you mix sugar and alcohol you get stupid and you pass out fast. But when you drink pure alcohol, before you pass out drunk you actually can achieve moments of clarity. In the Amazons, the shamans get drunk or high before they start channeling spirits and sharing the wisdom of the gods with the rest of the tribe. I'm not encouraging alcoholism or drug use here, but if this is all true, then — at least — I made one right decision that night when I asked for vodka on the rocks.

"Absolut or Grey Goose?" he asked.

"Absolut."

He served me one of those little bottles from the minibar in a glass with ice, and I downed it as if it were water.

"May I have another one?"

He pulled out a few more little bottles from the well-stocked minibar, put them on the table in front of me, and served me one more. I downed it as well, and that's when I started talking.

"What was your name again, honey?" I asked, holding my glass next to my face, as if I were the most jaded street-hooker in New Orleans.

"Adam," he said.

"Can I ask you a question, Adam?"

"Sure," he said, watching with wide eyes as I served myself the third little bottle of vodka.

"Suppose that you meet a girl, the way you're meeting me tonight..." He smiled and winked at me. I looked away and continued, "...and suppose that you pay her a few times to 'be' with you..."

"Which reminds me..." he said, pulling a roll of hundred-dollar bills out of his pocket.

"Thanks," I said, avoiding his eyes. He placed the money on the table, but I didn't touch it. I just continued with my speech.

"But then suppose that one night this guy and this girl share an intimate moment"—Adam chuckled, but I ignored him—"and this girl felt this incredible bond that made her feel...special. It made her feel accepted, it made her feel as if each and every ounce of her body was...loved," I said fighting a tear.

"Talking about love..." he said, winking, and pushed the money closer to me.

"Shhh!" I stopped him. "Let me finish."

I carried on with my story. "And suppose that that 'intimate moment' was the most loving and erotic experience of her life. But then, when they were done, and she was totally in love with him, and he should be able to see it because it's written in her eyes—then he goes and pays her. Isn't that fucked up?"

"Yeah, I guess..."

"I thought so," I said as I poured myself the fourth vodka.

"So...should we get down to business?" he said, pushing the bills even closer to me.

"Wait, I have another question," I continued. "Suppose that this girl that met this guy in this particular situation, has met other men, because she needed to learn that she was attractive in a way that she never could imagine. She needed to see herself through somebody else's eyes to realize that she was beautiful in her own way. If she confessed something like that to him, would he believe her?"

"I don't know," he said impatiently. "Would you like to come with me to the bedroom and get more comfortable?" he asked.

"Wait, I have another question."

I noticed that he rolled his eyes, but I didn't care a bit, so I just went on and on.

"Why is it that sex changes things? Can we look at the person that we had sex with last night without shame? Can we say, 'I did it because I liked you, because I think you like me too, not because I'm a whore, not because I want to marry you—simply because I like you a lot, and it made sense to have sex with you'? Tell me, Alan . . ."

"Adam," he corrected me.

"Yeah, Adam, tell me: why do we have to be embarrassed about telling people that we like them? Can't we just say it without fear of being rejected?"

"I don't know what to tell you," Adam managed to interject in the middle of my monologue.

"You don't have to tell me anything," I replied as if I were a washed-out drunk. "I'm the one who's telling *you:* the world is fucked up."

At that precise moment, my red cell phone rang. I dug it out of my bag and noticed that it was a call from Alberto.

"Give me a second, dear," I said.

I answered, but I only heard a crackling noise.

"The reception is bad in here," Adam said, "must be all the skyscrapers around."

I shrugged, put the phone back in my bag, and took another sip of my fourth little bottle of vodka.

"Where was I?" And with that I continued talking for a long time. I talked about sex, and dating, and relationships, and anything in between. I caught him checking his watch a couple of times, but since I didn't care, I just kept going and going, spilling the beans on my situation with Simon.

I have no idea how much time went by. All I know is that at some point Adam interrupted me. "Excuse me... Are we gonna have sex or not?" he asked, exasperated, placing the stack of bills in front of me.

How dare he? Couldn't he see what I was going through? I could have punched this guy in the face then and there, but I was too drunk to actually attempt that. What I did manage to do was take the money and throw it at him.

"Of course we are *not* going to have sex! Are you crazy?" I said disgusted. "For your information, I'm a 'comfort provider,' not a hooker, you asshole!"

There was a moment of silence. He looked at me, arching an eyebrow as if sizing me up. That's when my instincts finally kicked in, warning me that this guy wasn't just like any other customer. Maybe he was a maniac or a serial killer. I held on to the armrest of my chair to try to get up and leave, or at least to be able to face him on my feet.

As I got up, Adam bent over to pick up the money that had fallen on the floor, and then he pulled the lapel of his jacket close to his mouth. In an unexcited tone of voice, he then said, "Okay, let's pull the plug and watch the game."

At that precise moment one cop came out of the bedroom, another one came out of the closet, and two female cops

298   ALBERTO FERRERAS

came in from the hallway. The shock was so enormous that I
sobered up instantly.

Adam — or whatever his real name was — sat on the
couch, lit up a cigarette, and turned on the TV while the two
male cops in uniform sat on the sofa.

"Dude, I was starting to fall asleep back there. How's the
game?" asked the cop who had walked out of the closet.

"Yanks are up four to three in the top of the seventh."

"Could you guys be more fucked up and insensitive?"
complained one of the female cops giving them a nasty look.
Then, turning to me, she asked tenderly, "Hey, doll face,
would you like a coffee?"

I was still speechless, but somehow I managed to ask,
"Are you busting me?"

"Not tonight!" Adam said, and the guys laughed with
him. The second female cop gave me a bottle of water, patted
me in the back, and with an honest tone of solidarity said, "I
know this is none of my business, but I was listening to your
story outside, and I could totally relate. Why don't you talk
to this Simon guy, and explain the whole thing? He'll understand what happened."

"No, stay away from him. He's an asshole and he ain't
worth your time," said the first female cop, starting a she-
said/she-said routine.

"He's not a psychic! He doesn't know how she feels about
him. He can't read her mind!" the second one replied, and
then, addressing me, she added, "Don't listen to her. Tell him
how you feel. If he understands, he's the guy for you; if he
doesn't, then he's not."

The first lady cop stepped in again:

"Listen, doll face, you're a very handsome woman."

"Elaine, do not address the suspect as 'doll face,'" the second one interrupted.

"Shut up, Carol! She's not a suspect anymore," Elaine replied. "Listen, doll face, no man has the right to treat you like this. Look at you! You are a hot mama! I'm sure there's tons of men *and* women after you," she said, raising an eyebrow. "I'm glad we're not arresting you, but—what the hell—between you and me, I was kind of looking forward to the frisking."

"Elaine, please!" said Carol, frustrated.

"What?"

"She's a lesbian," Carol explained, lowering her voice.

"Carol, you don't have to whisper!"

"Elaine, this is not the place."

"You wouldn't whisper if I was straight. Why the hell do you have to whisper that I'm a lesbian? I'm loud and proud!" Elaine said, fighting back.

"Too loud, if you ask me," said one of the guys, and they all laughed.

"Ha-ha!" Elaine replied sarcastically. "Very funny, you dickless moron!"

"Elaine, one of these days you're going to get busted for harassment."

"This is not harassment, I'm just being honest."

Adam stepped in.

"Can you keep down the girl talk? We're trying to watch a game here!"

"Shut up, you meathead!" Elaine said to Adam, and then quickly asked, "By the way, who's winning?"

The Yankees were still winning. Me, on the other hand, I was feeling like the biggest loser on earth.

CHAPTER 32

I don't want to sound moralistic here, but this is the part of the story where I feel compelled to remind you that you should *not* try this at home. It's fun to read about the secret life of escorts, watch the movie, hear the stories, but not everyone can pull it off. That night I learned that I couldn't. I was just lucky—extremely lucky, to be precise. Maybe I went through this adventure and made it unharmed so I can tell you about it, and you don't have to do it.

All I can say is that there's nothing fun about being arrested, or even *almost* arrested. If you've ever been through anything like it, you know what I'm talking about.

To make a long story short, they couldn't prove anything against me, so I was basically free to go. My crime would have been selling sex, but since I refused Adam's proposal—and threw the money back at him—it became clear that I was selling my time, not my body. Selling time is not a crime; selling sex is.

One of the positive consequences of the whole adventure

was that the lady cops—or the "copettes," as they called themselves—and I really hit it off. Elaine and Carol had worked together for a few years, but they acted more like a married couple than like simple colleagues.

The girls offered to give me a ride home, so we left the hotel through the back door and hopped in their patrol. Alberto was probably waiting for me, but I would call him when I got home to avoid getting him involved in this. In the meantime, I took my first ride in a police car while hearing the sentimental advice of my new cop friends.

"Men have no feelings. They are simply not equipped. That's why women bear the children," pronounced Elaine.

"My God, you are so freaking radical," said Carol.

"It's the truth!" Elaine insisted.

Giving up on Elaine, Carol turned to me.

"I had a high-school boyfriend, and I cheated on him with his best friend. It's been twenty-five years and I still feel guilty about it. You gotta come clean. Do it for yourself," said Carol with her thick Long Island accent.

"Are you still thinking about that moron?" Elaine asked her.

"It's my life, goddamnit! I have the right to feel guilty about my past if I want to."

"You're a lost cause!" said Elaine, and then, turning to me, she dropped a solid piece of advice: "Doll face, if you were dating a woman you wouldn't have these problems. Check this out: good sex, artificial insemination, and you double your wardrobe."

She made me laugh so hard that I almost forgot all about that traumatic evening.

"Stop recruiting!" said Carol.

"Shut up!" said Elaine.

We arrived at my building, and I thanked them both for their advice. I told them that they were the coolest chicks I had met in a long time, and we even exchanged phone numbers.

The moment I stepped out of the patrol, my red cell phone rang.

"Madame?"

"Look to your right," she said.

Alberto's black limo was parking right across the street from us. Alberto had followed us all the way from the hotel. The window of the backseat rolled down, and Madame, wearing a pair of oversized sunglasses, waved me into the car.

I was still shaken by the events, but I wasn't angry with Madame. I couldn't blame her for this — if anything, she'd tried to dissuade me from going out on this date. I stepped into the car and she hugged me.

"I'm so glad you're okay. Alberto saw the police cars downstairs, and we figured out what was going on."

"I'm sorry, Miss B. I tried to call you" Alberto apologized.

"I know, I know," I said.

"Did you ask them the safety question?" asked Madame.

I looked down, embarrassed.

"I knew that it was a bad idea to send you to a new guy."

"I'm an idiot. I put your business at risk," I apologized.

"Don't worry. They've been after me for a long time, but they don't have a case. It's you that I'm concerned about," she said, holding my hand.

"I'm okay. It was a little scary, but I'm fine now. It's not even worth talking about. But I need to tell you something. I don't think I can do this anymore."

Madame looked me straight in the eye and — without trying to talk me out of it — she simply asked, "Is it because of these stupid cops?"

"No."

"It's Mr. Five in a Row, isn't it?"

I nodded, and started crying. Madame held me like a child in her arms.

"Why don't you just talk to him?"

"No way. He thinks I'm a whore."

"A whore!" she said, rolling her eyes. "That is such a stupid word!"

"But it is the truth! He must think that I'm a cheap, pathetic whore. That I had sex with him just for the money," I cried.

"Honey, first of all, this is not about sex, this is about love. And who do you think is more pathetic: someone who charges for love, or someone who has to pay for it?"

Madame was right — as usual — but I just couldn't think anymore that night. I kept my head down as I wept. She took my hand with true tenderness and continued.

"Honey, I don't know if he thinks that you are a whore, or if he thinks that you are a saint, but I do know that you really like this guy, and he's dying to talk to you. Let me get out of the way so you two can talk directly and figure it all out."

"No," I said stubbornly. "He should have known."

"Should have... could have... I hate those words," she said.

No hay peor ciego que el que no quiere ver, we say in Cuba: The worst blind man is the one who doesn't want to see. In this case, the worst deaf woman was the one who didn't want to hear. And that was me.

"All I can tell you," added Madame, "is that, if you feel so strongly about him, he's one lucky guy."

"Please don't tell him anything," I whispered.

"I won't."

"Swear?" I asked.

"Over my children."

I gave her a long, deep hug and left the car.

I took two steps into the street before I turned around to ask her one last question.

"Madame, do you have any children?"

But she couldn't hear me, because the car had left and was about to turn the corner.

CHAPTER 33

*T*he day after my "bust" was a Sunday, and — surprisingly — I woke up serene, almost in a good mood. I decided to call Lillian, and invite her out for brunch down in the Village.

We strolled down the street, chatting about anything, until we got to my favorite vegetarian restaurant. I actually eat meat, but I love this place because they make the best pancakes, and they have real maple syrup.

Once we ordered the food, we sat quietly for a minute until Lillian broke the silence.

"B... I wanted to tell you something..."

"Wait, before you do, I want to tell you something."

She looked at me suspiciously. "Are you going to apologize to me?"

"Maybe... Why? Were you going to apologize to me first?"

We cracked up. Turned out we were both planning to say sorry to each other.

"I know I'm self-centered and narcissistic," Lillian began,

"but I don't do it with malice, I swear. I love you, and I love hanging out with you. Not because I consider you my side-kick, but because you are smart, and funny, and way more courageous than I am."

"Shit, Lil — you're gonna make me cry."

"Oh, shut up! Go ahead, now! It's your turn!"

"I'm . . . very, very sorry. I'm a loudmouth, and I speak before I think. I didn't mean to hurt you with the things I said the other day. I was just afraid that you could be right . . . and, sure enough, you were . . ."

"What?" she screamed.

"I'm not going to tell you all the details of the last forty-eight hours, but I promise that I will, as soon as I feel a little stronger. What I want you to know is that I'm not working with Madame anymore."

Lillian took a deep breath of relief.

"Well, one thing I can tell you," Lillian said, "is that you got a sparkle when you started your part-time job, but it's turned into a less flashy, more solid glow now."

"Gee . . . thanks," I said, knowing that she was somehow right.

"Do they sell wine here? We still have to toast your promotion!"

We got a couple of glasses of sulfite-free wine and toasted to my success.

"So what are you going to do now that you have Bonnie by the balls?" Lillian asked.

"I don't know," I said, looking away, embarrassed. Lillian thought that I was promoted because of the UK Charms slo-gan. She didn't know anything about the bathroom record-ings, and how I'd blackmailed Bonnie. It's true, I deserved that promotion, but I wasn't proud of the way I got it, and

that was a sign — a sign that there was a pea under my tower
of mattresses. The next morning I would have to go back
to work and — though I had a better title and a window
office — I would still be working for Bonnie, and I wouldn't
be any better than she was.

Film Forum, an art-house theater in my neighborhood,
was playing a restored version of *Juliet of the Spirits,* another
Fellini movie. I dragged Lil to watch it with me, and though
she fell asleep halfway into it, I loved every frame of it. Obviously, the movie made me think of Simon, but — I don't
know why — I wasn't hurting so bad anymore.

I went home after the movie and found a couple of messages on my answering machine from headhunters who'd
heard about my promotion and wanted to congratulate me
and ask me if I was interested in offers from other agencies.
How the hell did they figure this out and get my home number so fast? I immediately thought that Mary Pringle had
been spreading the good news in the advertising world. I
love that woman.

I figured I would check with the headhunters on Monday
and, in the meantime, sat down by my computer and wrote
a letter that I'd been thinking about the whole night. After
printing the letter, I went to sleep. I woke up the next morning feeling as if I had taken a huge weight off my shoulders.

I had decided to start from scratch.

CHAPTER 34

I arrived half an hour late to the office, and I walked straight into Bonnie's den. She was alone this time.

"Hey, Bonnie." She looked up at me with her Medusa eyes for a split second before I added, "Have a nice life!" I left my resignation letter and the audiotape of her rant against the Chicago Boss on the table, and walked out. I had decided that the wise thing to do was to let go. Getting my title through blackmail would turn me into another Bonnie, and I didn't want to be one. Now that I believed in my talent, it was time to move on and choose my own boss.

The day flew by as I made a few phone calls to the head-hunters, and worked on some details of the UK Charms campaign, but I made a point of keeping the news of my departure to myself, secretly enjoying my newfound freedom.

That afternoon, I went to the gym, with renewed enthusiasm. I changed my clothes and stepped on the treadmill, but before I could start walking, I looked through the windows into the dance studio across the street. When I saw the girls warming up for the ballet class, something dawned on me.

Why couldn't I cross the street? Why couldn't I get into that ballet class and flaunt my extra pounds in front of whoever was there? Madame's words resonated in my head: *What other people think of you is none of your business.*

Before I knew it, I'd grabbed my bag, left the gym, and crossed the street to the dance studio. If I wasn't embarrassed about having my feet sniffed by a British royal, or having my body massaged with chocolate by a *Playgirl* centerfold, I think I could stand the pressure of being the only fat girl in the ballet class, even if the floorboards collapsed under my feet. I could take it. I could take it all.

I paid for the class at the front desk and walked down the corridor toward the ballet studio. That's when I noticed that across the hallway from the ballet class there was a loud salsa class in progress. Two of the male students were hanging out outside.

"Looks like a fun class. Why are you outside?" I asked.

"There's not enough girls to dance with. Do you want to join us?"

"I'm not much of a salsa dancer."

"*¿De dónde eres?*" one of them asked in Spanish

"I'm Cuban," I replied.

"Oh, come on!" said the other one. "All Cubans dance salsa! Step in!"

I gave a quick glance at the ballet class, and then I gave another one to the salsa class. Ballet is about being with a mirror, salsa is about being with a partner. I was sick and tired of mirrors, and sick and tired of dancing by myself.

Fuck ballet! I told myself.

"Where do I have to sign?" I asked them as I entered their class.

The salsa teacher was a fabulous lady called Caridad. Interestingly enough, she had been the prima ballerina of the Cuban National Ballet, but in spite of her classical training she preferred to teach salsa. According to her, the world needed more fun and less discipline. And fun we had.

She started with an old-fashioned rumba called "Yayabo," the kind of song that in a split second will make you join a conga line. Later, she played these great old songs by Rubén Blades and Willie Colón, some classic Johnny Pacheco, and to top it off "Besitos Pa' Ti" by none other than La Lupe.

Needless to say, I danced my ass off. The joy of dancing with a partner has no comparison. I would say that it's as good as sex, but I suspect that it's actually better. When you coordinate your moves to those of your counterpart, you feel in total harmony with the universe. I could swear that you develop some type of telepathy that allows you to guess what the next move is going to be. Every turn and twirl becomes an adventure and a confirmation that the magic is happening.

"You have to come dancing with us," one of the guys told me after the class. "Every Tuesday we go to a Dominican club on the Lower East Side to dance merengue. Can you make it?"

I exchanged numbers with all of them and promised that I would join them. It's so funny: when you feel strong and happy, everybody wants to hang out with you, but when you allow yourself to feel miserable and lonely nobody will touch you with a ten-foot pole.

As I was strolling toward the subway, with a renewed sense of joy, I walked past the homeless guy who insults me every time I walk by. I braced myself, getting ready for the

usual "Hey, fat ass, give me a dollar," but I guess my detrac-
tor had been abducted and probed by aliens, because as I
walked by he yelled something very different:

"Nice ass, bitch."

Okay, I didn't appreciate the "bitch" part — nor do I want
to encourage that type of language — but he did make me
smile, so — finally — I gave him a dollar.

"Thanks for the dollar; how about your number?"

I must have changed a lot, because, even though this guy
was a filthy drunk, I ended up laughing like a silly geisha,
accepting the second compliment with a blush, and walking
away with a huge smile on my face. As I placed my wallet
back into my bag, I noticed that my red cell phone — which
I forgot to return to Madame — had a flashing light.

I opened it and found a text message:

PLEASE LET ME TALK 2 U. PLEASE. SIMON

I would say that my heart skipped a beat, but it actually
stopped completely for about five minutes, as I read the message over and over. I held the phone against my chest and felt
confused and relieved at the same time. I hopped on the subway on my way downtown, trying to organize my thoughts.

Part of me felt ashamed, and resentful; part of me never
wanted to see Simon again. But another part of me —
clearly — was moved by his persistence.

Maybe he wanted to apologize, shake hands, and send me
home with an "I'm sorry for the misunderstanding, I didn't
mean to insult you." That would be nice, right? Wrong. That
would be horrible. Why? Because, even if he acknowledged
that it was inappropriate for him to pay me after that Friday
night, from my perspective, I'd made love to the man I was

falling in love with, but from his perspective, he'd had sex with a prostitute.

There was also the possibility that he wanted to make peace with me so he could hire me again. After all, the guy couldn't sleep without me. But if he tried to book me again, he would destroy my heart beyond repair.

Maybe the right thing was to close the door on the whole thing before it got even worse.

Maybe I should just ignore this message and move on — just like I did with Bonnie, I told myself. After all, this is a guy who paid me to sit sixteen and a half inches away from a pillow. Maybe he had other crazy fetishes, maybe this was just the tip of the iceberg.

But what if he feels about me the same way I feel about him? I asked myself. *How the hell could I know what he feels if I never talk to him again?*

As I was sitting in the subway car, tormented by these and other thoughts, I decided to clear my mind by listening to more of my *despecho* songs in my iPod. Coincidentally, the iPod started playing an old Mexican song by Linda Rondstadt that I hadn't heard in many years. It's called *"Pena de los Amores."*

In the middle of the madness of the crowded wagon, that old Mexican song got through to me, loud and clear, and every verse hit painfully close to home.

> *How sad, those words that were not spoken,*
> *and those that were pronounced but got lost . . .*
> *How sad, those kisses that were not given,*
> *and those lips that were secretly expecting them . . .*
> *How sad, those lovers that parted,*
> *without even giving each other a good-bye kiss*

Should I leave Simon without giving him a goodbye kiss? Without telling him that he had been important to me? That, even if it wasn't meant to be, he wasn't just one more guy who went through my life. That he meant something special to me.

As I asked myself these questions, the old guy sitting next to me fell asleep on my shoulder. I laughed to myself. *Here we go again. It seems like I was born with the gift of putting people to sleep in the subway.*

But then I noticed the strangest thing. Across the aisle from me, there was another girl my size, and a skinny woman next to her who had also fallen asleep on her shoulder. Then I noticed that, down the aisle, there was a big guy who had a teenager sleeping on his shoulder, and also a fat lady who had a skinny blonde with a little black dress snoozing by her side.

I rushed through the things in my bag, looking for the measuring tape that I'd started carrying to position myself on Simon's couch, and then I measured the width of one of the empty subway seats.

It was sixteen and a half inches exactly.

CHAPTER 35

When I was in college, I had a photography teacher who was a concentration-camp survivor. One day in class, without any explanation, he started talking about his life in the concentration camp, and he made the most shocking confession I've ever heard: he told us that the day he was liberated from camp he felt sad, he didn't want to leave.

For a child like him, those horrible barracks were home, and he was sad to leave the only home that he knew. Maybe all human beings are the same. We develop feelings for everything, even for our jail cell. We feel trapped in it, we hate it, and yet — even if the door is open — we're afraid to leave.

I know my jail cell very well. It has been a place where I'm a victim, a place where my self-esteem is based on the comments of people who don't like me. A place where everything I see and hear is a confirmation of my worst suspicions about myself.

I wouldn't be surprised if Simon's cell is a place where he's ashamed to reach out for love and warmth.

We could come up with a million theories to explain Simon's obsession with those sixteen and a half inches — a traumatic childhood, a bad heartbreak, an absent mother — but we might never know the truth. So, from this moment on, everything is going to be speculation. Okay?

Cool, so let's speculate:

First and foremost, it's pretty obvious that fat people are more huggable than skinny people. If you don't believe me, go to a toy store, pick up a teddy bear and a Barbie doll, and tell me which one you'd rather snuggle up in bed with. So getting all relaxed, happy, and sleepy next to the heavy ones should not come as a surprise.

Second, let's be honest here, asking for love is embarrassing. Asking for sex might be abrupt, inappropriate, distasteful, but nevertheless acceptable. If a guy walks up to a woman and asks for a quickie, he might get slapped, or he might get lucky. Yet, if he asks for a hug because he feels lonely or depressed, he'll be considered a mega-loser. In our world, asking for closeness or tenderness is embarrassing.

So I wouldn't be surprised if someone new to New York — where not even celebrities get a second look on the street — someone who just came in from a godforsaken town in Arizona — like, let's say Miami-Globe — someone naturally shy and shut down, someone who has a low opinion of himself for stupid things like, I don't know, growing hair on his back — would probably have a hard time connecting with and getting warmth from others.

What would a person in that situation do to grant himself the human touch? Chances are that a guy like him would try to borrow that affection. It's very likely that this person would put himself in a place where the human contact happens by accident, a place where warmth is provided — and no questions are asked. It's very possible that a guy like him would end up in a place like — let's say — a crowded subway car. It's very possible that this guy would sit next to someone who spills over her seat. Someone who'll touch you because she can't help it, because that's the way she was built: she was built for touch. She was built for tenderness. She was built for love.

Maybe Simon — like so many others — discovered the warmth of fat people in the subway, and he started using it to sleep and relax. That's why he took his *Sleeping Beauties* photos. Later — when he got money, and success — he was still in need of human touch, so he hired women like me, who could give him a little bit of that peace that he had found in the trains.

I got off the subway feeling overwhelmed by these thoughts, but as I turned the corner of the Salmonella Deli to get to my apartment, everything stopped. I found a big surprise waiting outside my building: Alberto was there, standing outside his limo.

"Hey, Alberto!" I smiled. "What's going on?"

"Madame asked me to bring you something," he said as he opened the back door of the limo. And that's when Simon stepped out of the car, holding a single red rose.

"Oh, shit," I said, taking two steps back that almost put me in the path of a killer taxi rushing down the street.

"Would you talk to me, please?" Simon said with puppy eyes.

I stood there for a second, looking at Simon, and then at Alberto, who smiled and stepped back into the car, either to give us privacy or to keep me from yelling at him for bringing Simon to my doorstep. But I wasn't in the mood to yell, and — for once — I was unable to talk.

"Please," begged Simon.

How could I say no? When a man of few words like him wants to talk, it's wise to listen, even if it's just to hear him say goodbye. I didn't want to be like one of those sad lovers that parted without even giving each other a final kiss.

We walked into my building in complete silence, climbed the three flights of stairs, entered my apartment, and sat on my couch — but no measurements were taken this time. I could tell that he was scared, but he dared grabbing my hand and spoke.

"I need to explain..."

"Yep, you need to." I smiled.

"B, I didn't want to insult you. I just...I'm such an idiot..."

He paused, and his eyes welled up with tears.

"I don't know...I...I just couldn't believe that someone like you could care about someone like me."

I couldn't say a word. In one sentence, he'd described the way *I* felt about *him*.

"I wouldn't blame you if you never want to see me again, but I just didn't want you to leave thinking that I was *that* kind of guy."

I took a deep breath. "And I didn't want you to think that I was *that* kind of girl," I answered.

We looked into each other's eyes and smiled.

"Could we start from scratch?" he asked.

I nodded, and he extended his hand in a formal handshake: "Hi, my name is Simon," he said, and smiled.

I accepted his hand and replied, "Nice to meet you. My name is Beauty."

CHAPTER 36

According to my friend Gaston, nothing compares to the sensation of being naked in public. I wouldn't call him a nudist, but he is definitely the kind of guy who would only go to the beach if he could walk around in the buff.

He says that the only thing more exciting than being naked in front of other people is getting up naked and walking up to other naked people at the beach to talk about the weather, the stock market, anything but the fact that they're all nude. He says that that's his biggest thrill.

I'm not sure if I can top off Gaston's adventures, but I can tell you that seeing pictures of yourself naked on the walls of a gallery is not chopped liver either. And seeing them sell like hotcakes is pretty exciting too.

The pictures that Simon took of me were exhibited at an art gallery in Chelsea. Everybody and his mother was there: the artsy people, the fashion people, and more press than at a celebrity divorce trial.

Simon is not much of a talker, but I know that it was an

important night for him. After all these years taking fashion shots of gorgeous models, he was taking a risk, but he felt that he was back on the track of his subway pictures: following his intuition and breaking new ground. I've heard that art is "making the invisible visible." If that is true, that's what he did with my beauty. He made it visible to me and to everybody else.

There were a lot of old and new friends at the gallery: Lillian, Mary Pringle, Myrna, Lorre, the "copettes" — Carol and Elaine. I even asked Madame to invite my former customers too. Every single one of them had helped to pave the road to this significant moment, so I wanted everyone there.

The only person I didn't invite was Bonnie. I didn't hate her anymore, but if she couldn't feel happy for me — and, guaranteed, she won't — what's the point of having her around? I wish her the best. May she find it far away from me.

It's been six months since I met Simon, and things had changed a lot for me, and for almost everyone around me. Lillian got engaged to Aureliano, a short and cute guy from Ecuador who doesn't look at all like the type of man that she's been after all these years. He was a teacher, so he has no BMW convertible, and no house in the Hamptons, but I'd never seen Lillian so happy.

Myrna started her own comfort-providing service for Plus Size Mamas. She showed up in a Mercedes with her husband, who looks a lot like Eddie Murphy. I understand that they're picking a lot of former customers from Madame.

Lord Arnfield looked like he had aged about a million years in the last six months. He's so cute! I tried to explain to him that I wasn't a working girl anymore, but he kept following me around, looking at my feet, and salivating.

Guido came with his wife. She straightened all the pictures on the walls, and that kept her busy while Guido was trying to hit on Elaine and Carol.

Elaine and Carol were living together now. Either Carol was a lesbian and she didn't know it, or Elaine talked her into it. The truth is that Elaine could talk a fire hydrant into turning lesbian. Five more minutes with her and who knows where I would be now. Good for her—I wish I had that power.

Richard Weber had a gorgeous girlfriend who agonized the whole night, while he talked and flirted with every woman in the room. She chased him around like a mother after a two-year-old. She has no idea what she's gotten herself into.

Ludwig Rauscher—the Nazi officer—showed up too, and he bought three of my photographs. Turned out that, after all, I *was* fat enough. The only one who didn't come was Mr. Akhtar—he's too shy for this kind of event—but he made my black lace cocktail dress, and I looked spectacular in it.

"Honey! You look gorgeous in these pictures, but, again, when don't you?" Madame told me, giving me a hug. She came to the opening on her way to the airport.

"I'm going back to Russia. People in New York don't know how to have fun anymore. This is becoming a communist state."

I gave her a deep hug, knowing I was going to miss her like crazy. People come into your life for a good reason, and then they leave your life for a good reason too. I feel like I earned my Ph.D. in life with her. Thanks to Madame, I now have an inner voice with a Russian accent that talks me out of all my self-deprecating moods. It always tells me, "There are no victims, only volunteers." Wise words.

Naturally, Simon was there. My pictures gave him a push

ALBERTO FERRERAS

in the right direction, but it's not like he doesn't need to work in fashion anymore. He pays a big mortgage for that studio in Tribeca. Whenever he's ready to live a more modest life, he might send fashion to hell, move to an old factory in Brooklyn, and take only photographs that make him happy. He's not ready yet, but it'll happen when it needs to happen. Every artist in history has worked for somebody: from the Catholic church to some big corporation that needs artwork for the lobby of an office building. He knows it and he's at peace with that. I do have to say that he has stopped torturing himself, looks happier, and sleeps like a baby. Not bad for starters.

And what about me? Well, I'm doing great. After I left my agency, it merged with a bigger one. Bonnie was laid off, because the new agency had another Bonnie on staff and — fortunately — there's only room for one in every corporation. These types of snakes don't like to share the same cage. The Chicago Boss left the agency with a truckload of money, and opened a creative boutique that specializes in Latino advertising — 'cause everybody says that it's where the future of the business is. Determined to "choose my boss," I called him up and met him for a job interview, and he was thrilled to discover that I was Cuban. He brought me in as his creative director, and Mary Pringle as his executive assistant. Now I get to speak Spanish every day, I have co-workers who play merengue out loud all day long, and though it has its ups and downs, like every other job, I find every day a challenge and an adventure.

Some of the people at the party noticed that I was sporting a brand-new engagement ring. Yep, I was — and it has a big-ass diamond. Simon gave it to me. I'm not crazy about diamonds, but I had to accept it to keep Simon from suffering a serious heartbreak.

He wanted to get married right away, and though I've spent the last twenty-eight years of my life waiting for that proposal, I had to decline. I need to get to know him better, and I want him to get to know me better. I'm not in a hurry, because I don't feel like I'm "investing time" in him. I'm living in the moment, and being in the moment for me means enjoying his company, and taking time to decide if the chemistry is right. Just like I do when we try a new perfume. So far, all I see in him rocks my world, and all he sees in me rocks his. So it will happen when it happens, not out of loneliness, not out of desperation, not out of fear of being alone: simply out of love. What a concept, huh?

In the meantime, I'm glad to inform you that I haven't lost one pound. My body is changing, though, and that is the biggest mystery on earth: I love my legs, I love my ass, I love my boobs. I walk around feeling that everything fits and falls nicely into place—my clothes feel good on me, and my face glows when I look in the mirror. I don't know what the hell I'm doing other than taking ballet and salsa classes, but, whatever I'm doing, I'm doing it for love—because I love myself—not because I'm punishing myself for being fat. Every time I hear a moron in the gym saying, "No pain, no gain," I want to slap him. Every second of your life is "gain" if you just open your eyes, appreciate what you have, and are grateful for it.

Do you want to feel beautiful? Here's my advice: learn to see yourself through the eyes of people who love you.

Trust me, I know about these things. After all, my name is Beauty.

ACKNOWLEDGMENTS

To Myrna Duarte, Olga Anderson, Trina Bardusco, Diana Ristow, Juline Koken, Vienna Wilson, Carol Goldstein, Richard Segalman, Ayesha Ibrahim, Inmaculada Heredia, Albino Ferreras, Olga Merediz, Mariauxy Castillo, Helena Bethencourt, Helena Ibarra, Fanny Diaz, Kathy Sontag, Simon Mammon, Patrick Lynch, Mosé, Cisco, Nyna Kennedy, Chris Denniston, Daniel Merlo, Jose Luis Alonso, Caridad Martinez, John Reginald Sullivan, Evelyn Ayllon, Wilfredo Cisneros, Raul Flores, Kipton Davis, Debby Afraimi, Tatiana Acosta, Mister Mark, Lorre Powell, Craig Houser, Juan Herrera, Gerik Cionsky, Lawrence Grecco, Marcelo Lesson Lloyd Des Brisay, Gastón Alonso, Antonio Tijerino, Ray McKigney, Leyla Ahuile, and Millie Ferreira for their support and inspiration.

To Enrique Chediak, Kara Baker, Adrienne Avila, Maud Nadler, Fernando Ramirez, Beth de Guzman, Franzine LeFrak, Andrea Montejo, Tareth Mitch, Terry Zaroff-Evans, and The Fabulous Selina McLemore for their trust, support, and invaluable feedback.

To Rob Oliver and my Healing Singing friends, for helping me find my voice.

To Mike, Deb, Sterling and Dahlia Walter, and all my friends at 'SNice for putting up with me, and giving me a home and an office.

To Albino Ferreras Rodriguez—for teaching me to love books and foreign languages—and Teodora Garza—for her love and support, and for letting me grow to be the tree that God wants me to be.

To Yolanda Ferreras—my second mom—and Sara, Albino Nicolas, Asier, Borja Ignacio, Daniel, and Matías, for all the things they have taught me.

To my friends at Ty's, Mary's Off Jane, the Sweetheart bench, and Celebrate Touch, for reasons that will remain a mystery.

And, most of all, to my Saturday-morning friends. You know who you are, and in case I never told you, you saved my life. Thank you.

READING GROUP GUIDE

1. We live in a society that is increasingly obsessed with plastic surgery and the search for the perfect body. Because of this, B is surprised to discover that some men like overweight women exclusively. Do you think these men represent something positive, because they are celebrating women in different forms? Or is this just another way to objectify women? Is exclusively liking overweight women any different from exclusively liking thin women? Is it ever okay to judge someone on physical traits? Have you ever been judged in this way?

2. B talks about how, in ancient Greece, people saw life as a struggle to balance reason and passion. Do you think it is always a good idea to live by such a rule? Give an example from the book in which you think B balanced reason and passion well, and an example of when you think she didn't. Can you think of particular moments in your life when you have allowed either one to take over?

3. When B changes her attitude, she feels that her physique changes as well. Have you ever had that sensation? Can you mention specific moments when being secure and in a positive state of mind made you feel more attractive?

4. Being the daughter of immigrants, B often talks about the life in Cuba that she never lived, and how she feels that both cultures have shaped her. Are you in touch with your family's roots? Can you identify what impact your roots have had in your life? If not, do you know people who could relate to B's feelings because of their own family background? How do you think they'd react to B's story?

5. When B meets Simon, she doesn't find him attractive at all, but little by little, as she gets to know him better, she finds him irresistible. When do you first notice the shift in her feelings for Simon? Do you think if B had met Simon earlier in the story she would have felt the same way about him? Why, or why not? Have you ever found yourself in a situation where your feelings for someone changed after you got to know him or her? What do you think makes for a more passionate relationship: one that builds slowly, like Simon and B's, or one that starts with love at first sight?

6. B has a hard time relating to the unwritten rules of corporate America. Do you relate to her perception of life in a big company? If you were in her situation, how would you have handled working for a boss like Bonnie?

7. While listening to the song "Pena de los Amores," B decides that she cannot ignore Simon; she needs to see him at least once again, so that no words are left unspoken. Can you

relate to this experience? Did you ever walk away from a relationship without getting or giving closure? How did it feel?

8. One of Madame's pieces of advice is "What other people think of you is none of your business." Do you agree with this idea? What would be the impact of that principle if you applied it to your daily life? Would you be able to ignore other people's opinions of you? Would you be able to keep your opinions to yourself? Is this always a good idea? What are some examples of situations, in the book and in real life, when following Madame's advice would be helpful, or harmful?

GUÍA PARA GRUPOS DE LECTURA

1. Vivimos en una sociedad que está cada vez más y más obsesionada con la cirujía plástica y la búsqueda del cuerpo perfecto. A causa de ésto, B se sorprende al descubrir que a algunos hombres sólo les gustan las gorditas. ¿Cree usted que la actitud de estos hombres es positiva porque celebra la diversidad de la figura femenina? ¿O cree usted que ésta es simplemente otra manera de ver a la mujer como un objeto? ¿Hay alguna diferencia entre los que sólo aprecian a las gorditas y los que sólo aprecian a las flacas? ¿Cree usted que hay momentos en la vida en los que es justo juzgar a una persona por su apariencia física? ¿Se ha sentido usted alguna vez juzgado de esta manera?

2. B dice que en la antigua Grecia, la gente pensaba que el mayor reto de nuestras vidas es mantener el balance entre la razón y la pasión. ¿Cree usted que ésta es una manera útil de enfrentar la vida? ¿Podría dar un ejemplo del libro en cual usted cree que B logra equilibrar las dos, y un ejem-

plo en cual usted cree que ella no lo logró? ¿Puede recordar momentos de su propia vida en los que usted permitió que la razón o la pasión lo dominaran?

3. Cuando B cambia su actitud, ella siente que su físico cambia también. ¿Ha tenido usted esta sensación? ¿Puede mencionar momentos en los que usted se sintió más atractivo (a) porque se sentía seguro de sí mismo?

4. Siendo hija de inmigrantes, B habla a menudo de la vida en Cuba que ella nunca vivió, y de cómo ambas culturas la han formado. ¿Conoce usted las raices de su familia? ¿Puede identificar el impacto que estas raices han tenido en su vida? Si ese no es el caso, ¿conoce usted a alguien que pueda identificarse con esos sentimientos de B que son consecuencia del origen de su familia? ¿Comó cree usted que esta persona reaccionaría al leer esta novela?

5. Cuando B conoce a Simon, no le parece que es guapo, pero poco a poco, al conocerlo mejor, lo encuentra irresistible. ¿Cuándo notó usted por primera vez el cambio en los sentimientos de B hacia Simon? ¿Cree usted que si B hubiera conocido a Simon más temprano en la historia hubiera sido capaz de desarrollar los mismos sentimientos hacia él? Explique por qué sí o por qué no. ¿Ha estado usted alguna vez en una situación en la que sus sentimientos hacia alguien cambiaron después de conocer mejor a esa persona? ¿Qué tipo de relación es más apasionada: la que crece lentamente como la de Simon y B, o la que empieza con amor a primera vista?

6. B tiene problemas en asimilar las reglas implícitas de la América corporativa. ¿Está usted de acuerdo con la percep-

ción de B acerca de la experiencia de trabajar en una gran empresa? Si usted estuviera en la misma situación de B, ¿comó haría para trabajar con una jefa como Bonnie?

7. Cuando B escucha la canción "Pena de los Amores," decide que no puede ignorar a Simon; necesita verlo por lo menos una vez más para cerrar ese capítulo de su vida. ¿Puede usted identificarse con esta experiencia? ¿Ha tenido usted alguna vez una relación en la que no tuvo la oportunidad de cerrar ese capítulo? ¿Comó fue esa experiencia?

8. Uno de los consejos de Madame es, "Lo que otras personas opinan de ti, no es tu problema." ¿Está Ud. de acuerdo con ese precepto? ¿Cual sería el impacto de esta regla si usted la aplicara a su vida diaria? ¿Podría usted ignorar las opiniones de los demás hacia su persona? ¿Podría usted guardar sus opiniones sobre los demás para sí mismo? ¿Es ésta una manera positiva de vivir la vida? Enumere ejemplos del libro y de la vida real en los que seguir el consejo de Madame sería o no sería útil.

ABOUT THE AUTHOR

Alberto Ferreras is a New York City–based writer, filmmaker, and performance artist. He has directed and produced the critically acclaimed *Habla* series for HBO, and his independent film work has been presented all over the world, including the prestigious Berlin Film Festival. As a performance artist he is known for playing "Doctor Truth," a character who makes himself available in public spaces to answer any question with complete honesty.

B as in Beauty is his first novel.